ENDURING FREEDOM

JAWAD ARASH and **TRENT REEDY**

ALGONQUIN 2021

Published by
Algonquin Young Readers
an imprint of Algonquin Books of Chapel Hill
Post Office Box 2225
Chapel Hill, North Carolina 27515-2225

a division of
Workman Publishing
225 Varick Street
New York, New York 10014

The authors gratefully acknowledge Katherine Paterson for her
permission to quote from *Bridge to Terabithia*.

LIBRARY OF CONGRESS CATALOGING-IN-PUBLICATION DATA
Names: Arash, Jawad, author. | Reedy, Trent, author.
Title: Enduring freedom / Jawad Arash and Trent Reedy.
Description: Chapel Hill, North Carolina : Algonquin Young Readers,
2021. | Audience: Ages 12 and up. | Audience: Grades 7–9. | Summary:
"In this dual-narrative tale, a teenage American army private and an
Afghan boy living under the horrors of the Taliban, caught on separate
sides of the world during the tumultuous times leading up to and
following 9/11, come to discover how much more they have in common
than they ever could have imagined"—Provided by publisher.
Identifiers: LCCN 2020048422 | ISBN 9781643750408 (hardcover) |
ISBN 9781643751634 (ebook)
Subjects: LCSH: Afghan War, 2001—Juvenile fiction. | CYAC:
Afghan War, 2001—Fiction. | Friendship—Fiction. | Soldiers—Fiction.
| Taliban—Fiction. | Muslims—Fiction. | September 11 Terrorist
Attacks, 2001—Fiction. | Operation Enduring Freedom, 2001—Fiction. |
Afghanistan—Fiction.
Classification: LCC PZ7.1.A723 End 2021 | DDC [Fic]—dc23
LC record available at https://lccn.loc.gov/2020048422

10 9 8 7 6 5 4 3 2 1
First Edition

*To the memory and honor of Haji
Mohammad Munir Khan (1936–2020),
beloved and respected grandfather,*

*Ayesha Siddiq (1960–2015),
cherished aunt and caretaker,*

*and all those who served in Operation
Enduring Freedom (2001–2014)
in Afghanistan,*

this book is respectfully dedicated.

KABUL, AFGHANISTAN
September 10, 2001

Nothing in the world was so comforting or wonderful as the Afghan family. Never was that clearer to Baheer than at mealtimes, especially on one of the last warm nights in September when the entire family could eat outside together. Well, they wouldn't quite all eat together, as there was no dastarkhwān that could be spread wide enough to fit all eighteen of them—twenty if you counted Uncle Kabir's newborn twins—to gather around. The women and girls would sit on the floor of the concrete porch with their meal on the larger cloth, for the women and girls far outnumbered the men in this family. The men and boys would gather around the other dastarkhwān right next to them. Soon the sound of two conversations, the women talking about spices they used in the meal and what they were up to and the men discussing their business, would echo through the back courtyard off the high compound walls that provided them privacy and kept them safe from the outside world.

Baheer's sister Maryam walked past with a big bowl full of salad made of tomatoes and onions. "You could help, you know." She elbowed him. "Don't just stand there smiling and doing nothing." At seventeen, she was only a year older than Baheer, but she sometimes acted as if a decade were between them.

Baheer's father, Uncle Kabir, and Uncle Feraidoon had returned from a hard day producing and selling woven rugs, and they waited over by the pomegranate bush, discussing the day.

Aunt Zarlashta, Baheer's favorite aunt, smiled as she placed dishes of korma, a thick mutton curry, out for the family to eat. Baheer prepared the water pitcher and basin that would be passed around so everyone could wash their hands.

Eventually all the family gathered around plates covered in mountains of rice, salad, and korma. Everybody was ready except for the one person without whom the meal could never start, Baheer's grandfather, Haji Mohammad Munir Khan.

"My dear," Grandmother called into the house. "Will you please put that thing down and come eat?"

Baheer and some of the others looked toward the east wall of the compound nervously. Even though she had not mentioned a radio, everyone was very aware that a talib, a member of the Taliban, lived on the other side of that wall. If he had heard grandmother and somehow guessed what she was talking about, they could all be in a lot of trouble.

"I'll go check on him, Grandmother," Baheer offered, rising from his place and heading into the house. He found Baba Jan, as he often did in the evening, in the main room with the radio perched on his shoulder, the volume low. He nodded at Baheer, stroking his long white beard.

Baheer could barely hear BBC Pashto. "*Da London dai, BBC raadio . . .*"

Baba Jan turned the volume down further.

Baheer's stomach rumbled. "Grandmother wants you to—"

Baba Jan held up a hand for silence. A moment later he shouted, "What!"

"What happened?" Baheer asked.

Grandpa turned the knob to click the radio off. In a daze, he put his hand on Baheer's shoulder as he walked out to join the others.

"Is everything OK?" asked Baheer's father.

"I heard you shout," Grandmother said.

"The Taliban have killed Ahmad Shah Massoud," Baba Jan said.

"The Lion of the Panjshir," Baheer said quietly. That's what many people called the last mujahideen commander holding out against the Taliban. Without him and his forces, the remaining free parts of Afghanistan in the northeast would fall to the Taliban.

The family washed their hands, prayed, and then finally began eating. Baheer picked up a mouthful of rice in his fingers, dropping a few grains as he hadn't done since he was a toddler.

Uncle Feraidoon frowned as he chewed. He glanced at the east wall and spoke quietly, breaking the tense silence. "If the Taliban have finally succeeded in killing Massoud, they will be bolder than ever. We will all need to be more careful to follow their so-called precious rules."

Uncle Kabir pointed at his brother with a piece of naan. "Speaking of Taliban rules, keep your turban on at all times when you go out. Your beard isn't long enough, so you need to keep your head shaved."

Uncle Feraidoon protested. "I don't like shaving my head."

"Oh, Zarlashta, you did such a wonderful job with this korma." Grandmother's smile seemed forced. "Don't you all—"

"The Taliban have tried to kill the Lion for years," Baba Jan said. "They couldn't have succeeded without help. I've heard of their new allies. This Al-Qaeda. Dangerous men. Outsiders."

Uncle Kabir shrugged, wiping a bit of sauce off his beard with the back of his hand. "Ever since I was a teenager there has been one terrible thing or another. The Soviet invasion. The civil war. The terrible—"

Uncle Feraidoon coughed loudly. "Careful."

"The Taliban," Uncle Kabir said quietly. "Fighting never stops, but we push on. More rugs to sell."

Baheer fought the urge to check the east wall. His brother Rahim, sitting next to him, leaned over to bump his shoulder against Baheer, raising his eyebrows as if asking if Baheer could believe all this. Baheer and Rahim didn't always need words to communicate.

"I think tomorrow we might have chicken," Grandmother tried again. "I have an idea to try some new spices."

"That sounds wonderful," Baheer's mother said nervously.

Baheer knew they would not succeed in changing the subject. Even if they did, he felt sure Maryam would ask Baba Jan a question to get them back on the topic of Ahmad Shah Massoud. She loved keeping up with Afghan and world events.

"This situation is different. I can feel it," Baba Jan said.

Baba Jan was the bravest man Baheer had ever known. He had been chief of police many years ago. After the Soviet Union invaded, he was eventually arrested for continuing to follow the ways of Islam. He was sentenced to death, but his friend, a high-ranking military officer in the puppet Afghan government the Soviets had established, convinced the Russians to release him. Baba Jan was unstoppable, but now he tugged his beard, the lines in his face deepening somehow. Baheer hadn't seen him this way in a long time.

"Allah will protect us," Grandmother said.

Baba Jan stared toward the east wall and the talib's compound. "Something very bad will happen soon. Allah have mercy."

"You know Allah's words from the Holy Quran. Trust him." Grandmother sounded soothing.

"I know. Allah says in his book, in chapter 22, verse 65, 'For God is Most Kind and Most Merciful to man.'"

His grandfather was also the wisest man Baheer knew. He read the Holy Quran every day, memorizing many passages. He read histories and poetry. He remembered and sometimes talked about better times in Afghanistan, when the country was so wonderful and peaceful that Westerners would visit on vacation. And he sometimes spoke of the terrible tragedy of the country's wars. There were ruins of a stall in the bazaar a few blocks away that Baba said used to be a bookstore until it was burned down during the civil war among the Mujahideen. No one dared to open the bookstore now in the dark era of the Taliban. Baba Jan sometimes told Maryam, Rahim, Baheer, and his other grandchildren about how he had often stopped by the stall to talk to his friend, who owned the place, and to pick up a new treasure in the form of a book.

Baheer might have understood such enthusiasm for learning back at his school in Pakistan, where his teachers were kind and they cared about student success. Back where the Taliban didn't control everything.

The Taliban had a special department called Promotion of Virtue and Prevention of Vice. Their job was to make sure men kept long beards, tied turbans on their heads, went to mosque at the five different prayer times, and did not sing or listen to music, have televisions, watch movies, dance, fly kites, own pet birds, possess pictures of people or animals, or own forbidden books. They were the Morality Police.

Baheer hated them. Baheer feared them. Whenever he left home—and now even at home, since the Taliban family had moved in on the other side of the wall—Baheer felt like he was a little kid trying to sneak a treat without getting caught. Except the Taliban had so many rules and enforced them so harshly it was hard to escape the constant feeling that at any moment he might face cruel punishment. It was exhausting. It left him feeling physically sick deep in his stomach.

Just a few days ago the Taliban had turned up at school, policing turbans, making sure the boys hadn't shaved, and checking to see that none had long hair. As they'd approached the school on their bikes, Baheer and Rahim checked each other over and nodded. Neither had shaved because their beards hadn't begun to come in. Their grandfather made sure their hair was always cut very short, not because of the Taliban but because that was the way a man's hair should be. With their turbans fixed, they were in good shape.

A few of the other boys hadn't seemed so confident, trying to hide themselves behind other students. But there'd be

7

no escaping the Taliban. All the boys stood in line, waiting to be examined by the talib leader.

"How are you, guy?" the talib said in a low voice. His black kohl-lined eyes gazed down at Baheer as a smile, such as one might display before a delicious meal, spread across his lips. He grabbed Baheer's arm and pulled him closer, the rough fingers of the talib's other hand caressing Baheer's cheek.

"I'm fine." Baheer breathed deeply through his nose and tried to pretend this wasn't happening.

The talib leaned down so his face was right in front of Baheer's. His breath reeked of sharp spices and blew hot across his cheek and neck. "You've been a good boy." With a strange noise—half grunt and half laugh—the talib swatted Baheer's bottom and sent him away, already reaching for Rahim.

When they had cleared the monster, they hurried to class. They never talked about the Taliban inspections afterward, the talib's lustful looks and wandering hands. It wasn't safe to discuss those things in public, and at home Baheer only wanted to forget it, to keep the dark cloud of the Taliban on the other side of the warm walls of his family compound.

When they'd lived in Pakistan, Baheer had loved talking to Baba Jan about everything he'd learned at school, and his grandfather would usually have some insight to add to the day's lessons, either from the Holy Quran, classic Persian poetry, or from one of his many other books. Back then Baba

Jan had often talked about the growing problem of a generation of young people raised on bullets instead of books, and as the post-Soviet civil war dragged on, followed by the Taliban era, he continued to say Afghanistan's many problems grew from a lack of education. "Too many know nothing, and wouldn't know how to think if they did know anything," he'd say. In Pakistan, doing well in school, Baheer had dreamed of returning to Afghanistan, learning all he could, and eventually teaching other young Afghans so that his country could heal.

Then he'd discovered Afghan schools were a Taliban nightmare.

"Hey." Rahim elbowed him. "What's the matter with you? Where did you go?"

Pakistan, Baheer almost said.

"Yes." Baba Jan nodded to Uncle Feraidoon. "If we make sure the windows are blacked out and the sound is very low. You have it?"

He must have been talking about a VHS tape. A very illegal VHS tape. Probably an Indian movie with plenty of dancing and singing.

"Wrapped in a rug in the house," Uncle Feraidoon said quietly.

Maryam gave a little squeal and clapped her hands. She loved movie nights more than anyone else. Baheer couldn't disagree. Uncle Feraidoon had a way of sneaking in the best films. That night, they would watch *Koyla*, a famous Indian movie. When the meal was cleaned up, the family, except for the little kids, crowded into the main room in Baba Jan's house. As the opening music played, Baheer was sent outside. His job was to make sure no flickering light from the illegal television showed through the blackout curtains and to ensure nobody outside the house could hear any of the sound. He even walked the whole east wall that separated their home from the talib's compound, to make sure they were safe.

Only then was he allowed to return. But before he could sit down, a hard pounding rattled the compound's front door. The laughter among the adults froze. Uncle Feraidoon stopped the movie.

"I'll see who it is," Baheer asked. He didn't want to answer the door. Who could be knocking at this time of night? But he didn't want to seem like a baby, afraid of everything, and he was already up.

Uncle Kabir stopped him in the front courtyard. "Stay back. I'll check."

The pounding continued on the street door, until Uncle Kabir opened it a crack.

Two men stood in the street. A man with a black turban and a large belly pulled Uncle Kabir by his collar. "Do you live here?"

"Yes," Uncle Kabir replied.

Baheer stepped back, heart pounding, a sharp cold tingling down through his body. Baba Jan was right. The death of Ahmad Shah Massoud must have emboldened the Taliban. Had they heard the television?

"Drag him," the man in the black turban said to the other one.

The two men grabbed Uncle Kabir by the collar and yanked him toward the street, smashing his face against the steel door frame as they pulled him outside. Uncle Kabir tried to speak, but he was thrown down on the hard dusty street.

Baheer froze for a moment, shaking. *Move! Do something!*

Finally, it was as if he broke free from his chains and ran to the others. "Baba, they took Uncle Kabir!"

"Who took! Why? Where?" Baba Jan asked, getting to his feet. His grandfather quickly rewrapped his turban and put on his glasses while his father and Uncle Feraidoon hurried with their turbans as well.

Baba Jan breathed deeply, hard fury in his eyes, but his voice was calm and firm. Even in his old age, the man was still respected in the neighborhood for fairness and justice.

Baheer wished that he had even half of his grandfather's strength, but his legs were shaking, his heart thundering.

"Let's go," he said to his two sons, breaking Baheer out of his panic.

"Baba Jan, I want to go with you," Baheer said. He felt partially responsible. He was supposed to have been the one to check the door. He should have been able to help his uncle.

"Bachem, it's not a big deal. Stay home and sleep. We'll be back soon," Baba Jan said.

"I'm going," Baheer insisted. As if sleep would be possible with Uncle Kabir taken by the Taliban.

Baba Jan sighed. "OK. But you stay near your father." To Baheer's father, he added, "Sakhi, watch him."

It was dark on the street. Most people in Kabul only had electricity for two or three hours a night, but the Taliban, or those with close connections to them, could sometimes have electricity twenty-four hours a day. Baba Jan led the way to the single light at their talib neighbor's compound.

As they approached, they heard the talib shouting about Islamic law, heard Uncle Kabir calling out in pain. Baheer's grandfather knocked firmly on the door.

A half-bowed man came out. "Who are you?"

"I am the father of the man you brought here," Baba Jan said.

The little man pushed the door open, and Baba Jan led the way inside. Uncle Kabir lay in the dust, his collar torn, his beard a mess, and his hands tied behind his back.

Baba Jan stared at his son, breathing heavy through his nose, his shoulders heaving. "Why have you taken my son?"

One of the taliban stepped up to Baba Jan. "Your men watch our women during the day when I am not here." He pointed to a window that faced their house.

The window was in Uncle Kabir's room. Baheer and Rahim rarely went in there because of the twin baby girls.

The window had been covered with a blanket since the girls were born, to prevent dust and cold air from coming in.

"That window!" Baba Jan said loudly, taking a step closer to the talib. "How would you even know whose window it is? Without thinking, you just grabbed the first man to come to our door? Anyway, it's been blocked for months. Besides that, my son works from early in the morning until night in his shop. He has no boys. So no man was looking out that window!" He was shouting now, his voice booming throughout their compound. "Who told you our men were peeping into your home to look at your women?"

The talib answered, a bit quieter than before. "My women."

"Your women?" Baba Jan laughed.

Baheer's legs shook. He had never seen anyone speak to a talib this way. He remembered his classmates being beaten or severely punished for doing far less.

"What do you mean?" The talib was even angrier now.

Baba Jan's sons moved closer to their father. Baheer stepped behind his own father.

Baba Jan continued as if he hadn't noticed his family's presence, as if he didn't need their support. "Look at your window right there!" He pointed at a very small hatchlike window that faced Baheer's family's compound. "How do I know your women aren't watching my men when you are not here? You come to my home tomorrow morning around eleven! I will show you how easy your women could be looking at us! According to Islam, you should first find the truth of the matter, then if something wrong has been done, you punish the wrongdoer! Not before you know the facts!"

"How dare you accuse my women of doing this?" The talib's voice squeaked a little as he shouted. His forehead wrinkled. "If you were not a white-haired man, I would have you beaten to death and buried right here, and no one would ever know what happened to you."

Baba Jan thumped his chest. "Do it! Do it, if you have the courage! Or come see tomorrow! I am Haji Mohammad Munir Khan! You know where I live!"

The talib said nothing for a long moment, but his eyes darted from Baba Jan to Uncle Kabir, then at the ground.

"OK," he said. "He can go. We'll investigate the matter and talk tomorrow."

Baheer's father and uncle untied Uncle Kabir and helped him to his feet. Baba Jan's fierce gaze remained locked on the talib until his three sons and grandson were heading out of the compound. At last, Baba Jan turned his back on the man and walked out.

"Don't tell the others about what happened here tonight," Baba Jan said outside the door of their own compound. "The women and children will be scared."

"But you invited the man to our compound tomorrow," Baheer said.

Baba Jan shook his head. "He realizes his mistake. And he is a coward. Deep down, most of the Taliban are cowards. He will not come."

"Bale, Haji Agha," said Uncle Kabir. "Tashakor."

"You're welcome." Baba Jan smiled and squeezed Uncle Kabir's shoulder.

"Bale, Baba Jan," Baheer said, a warm feeling rushing in to replace the cold fear that had sent shivers through his body the entire time they were in the talib's compound.

Baheer's father put his arm around him as the men headed into their compound, safe in their private family world behind the security of their high walls. Baheer watched his grandfather, old but firm and sure, laughing as he walked with Grandmother toward their room. He looked up at the cascade of bright stars in the dark Kabul night, and asked Allah to help him find even a small part of Baba Jan's courage and wisdom within himself.

2

KABUL, AFGHANISTAN
September 11, 2001

The next day, Baheer was tired, having had trouble sleeping after the intense events of the night before. From the worrying reports about the death of Ahmad Shah Massoud and Baba Jan's fears about it, to the talib taking Uncle Kabir, Baheer had been plenty wound up, and even though it was a beautiful sunny day with hardly any wind, Baheer still couldn't escape the feeling that something was very wrong.

Or maybe he was only dreading school as he always did. "I hate this," he said, packing his chemistry book.

"What did you say?" his mother asked.

He should not have spoken aloud. His family did not like hearing him complain about school. "Nothing, Mother," he said. "Only this subject is so difficult."

She patted his back. "Ask your father for help. He was a

great student and wanted to become a doctor. If it hadn't been for the Russians . . ." She sighed. "The infidel pigs were kidnapping young kids and forcing them to serve in their army."

"I know the story, Madar Jan," he said. All Afghans knew and shared it. The Russians and their Afghan puppets had ruined everything. They'd arrested Baba Jan multiple times for praying and fasting during Ramadan. Uncle Kabir had wanted to become a police officer like his father. Baheer's father had wanted to be a doctor. Uncle Feraidoon had wanted to finish school and learn how to sew. Baheer used to dream of being a teacher or even of writing for a newspaper, but the Taliban allowed no newspapers, and anyway, few could read. As to teaching, the instructors at his school were so harsh, brutally whipping the hands of their students even just for asking questions, and Baheer could never be part of that. The invasion and brutal war had destroyed over two million Afghan lives and crushed countless dreams.

When Baheer and Rahim finally reached the school, four black Toyota Hilux pickups blocked the entrance, their cargo beds crowded with taliban and their guns. Baheer slowed his bike, gripping the handlebars hard. He'd never seen such a big Taliban presence there before.

"Is this about what happened last night?" Rahim asked.

"It can't be," Baheer said quietly. "If this was about Uncle Kabir and Baba Jan confronting that talib, why wouldn't they just come to the house?" What he'd said made sense, but it did not ease his fear.

"Students!" A voice echoed from a loudspeaker on one of the trucks. "School is closed today. Go home."

The brothers didn't waste any time questioning what was going on but pedaled quickly toward home and freedom. For once, Baheer had no problem with Taliban orders. He thought about what he might do with his spare time. Maybe he and Rahim could play cricket in the back compound. *Or maybe,* Baheer thought with a smile, *I could sneak a book from Baba Jan's study, something better than my school books.*

As they made their way back to the compound, taliban-packed trucks rolled past them, forcing them to pull their bikes off the road three times to get out of the way. Taliban pickups were parked on almost every corner. Maybe they were getting ready to attack those last areas of Afghanistan they hadn't yet managed to conquer because of Ahmad Shah Massoud? Fear of whatever the Taliban were up to warred with his elation over school being canceled.

Back home, Baheer and Rahim hurried to tell Baba Jan what had happened. At first he seemed angry with them, either for interrupting his daily reading time or because he thought they'd skipped school. But after he heard their explanation, he looked off into the distance, stroking his beard. "Yes. Well, go play. Let me think," the old man finally said.

When they'd left Baba Jan's study, the brothers danced all the way to the courtyard. "No school today," Baheer sang, and spun around. "Oh no, no, no!"

Rahim tried to do a flying leap like in the Indian movies. "We are freeeee!" he sang.

"What are you two doing home?" Maryam asked. They told her, laughing and trying to get her to join in their celebration. But Maryam would not dance. "You treat this like a joke," she said. "But you are so blessed to be able to go to school at all. Me? What can I do? Nothing. Try to teach myself from your books. Practice in your notebooks. I'm not stupid, you know. I'd be a great student." She spun around and walked away.

Baheer took a few steps after her, but Rahim held him back. "Let her go. She doesn't understand how lucky she is. Anyway, you know you can't talk to her when she's like this."

Rahim was probably right, but Baheer would have liked a chance to try to explain it to Maryam. School here in Kabul wasn't about learning as much as it was about trying to avoid painful punishment. Maryam wanted to learn. Baheer had been the same way back in Pakistan. Maryam didn't know it, but she was lucky she couldn't go to school. Anyway, it made no sense for her to be mad at him. He had no choice in the matter. The Taliban would never allow girls in school.

Baheer and Rahim spent the morning playing cricket. In the afternoon, they kicked around their old, beat-up soccer ball. The black and white was nearly all worn off, but it was still good to play with. Even Maryam came out and joined them. The day was full of fun and freedom.

The next day schools were closed again. As Baheer and Rahim returned home, their father and uncles were leaving the compound toward their shop.

"No school again?" Father asked.

"Yes. They announced the same thing again like yesterday," Rahim responded before Baheer could even open his mouth.

"OK. Whatever. Come lock the door," Uncle Kabir said. As usual Rahim locked the gate after they left.

The guys began playing soccer once again. Rahim had possession of the ball, showing off, kicking it side to side, foot to foot. "Get ready! Goal!" He kicked it hard, sending it soaring over Baheer, Maryam, and the compound wall, so that it bounced out in the street.

Baheer didn't hesitate for one second. It was foolish to leave something as valuable as a soccer ball out in the street for very long. A lot of kids in the neighborhood would love to have it and wouldn't think twice before taking it. Fortunately, he found the ball quickly.

But as he was walking back, the gates of the talib's compound opened and out thundered a big truck, loaded with old carpets, a few cupboards, and many other household belongings. A group of women in burqas and several children rode in the cab. The talib's mother, wives, and kids, maybe. The vehicle's gears made a horrible grinding sound, its engine roared, and then the truck rolled down the street and around the corner, out of sight.

"Why would they move?" Grandfather said when he heard the news. "They only recently arrived. Something is very wrong."

———◇———

"Haji Agha?" Uncle Kabir called from the front of the compound. It was strange. They'd just left a couple of hours ago. *Why are they back this soon? Is the bazaar closed just like our school?* Baheer thought, late that night after dinner.

Baheer's grandfather waited for his sons to come to him in the study.

"Why have you returned so soon?" Baba Jan must have noticed the worried looks on their faces. "Trouble?"

"I think maybe a lot of it," Father said.

Uncle Feraidoon unrolled a small carpet. "One good thing about working in this business, no one ever questions why we bring so many rugs home." He unrolled the rug and revealed a video cassette.

Baheer smiled. "Oh, what are we going to watch?" With the talib next door gone, they wouldn't have to be quite so careful with the sound.

Uncle Kabir had already returned with the television and VCR. "Our shop neighbor's son keeps a secret satellite dish."

"Very dangerous," Baba Jan said.

By this time, all the adults and the older children had crowded into the study.

"He recorded this a short time ago," said Uncle Feraidoon. "The American channel CNN."

"If the Taliban finds this, they'll murder us all," said Aunt Toba.

"Be sure to keep the sound down," said Aunt Sofia.

"I will," Uncle Kabir promised. "Just rewinding."

When he at last played the tape, Baheer wished he hadn't. As the Americans talked in English, the video showed smoke rolling out of a tall building. A moment later, a plane struck an identical tower in a terrible orange-white fireball. Chunks of the building fell to the enormous city below.

"An American movie?" Aunt Zarlashta asked quietly.

"No," said Baheer's father. "This is real. Today. In New York City."

"Allah, have mercy," said Baheer's mother. "Those poor people."

The video continued showing smoke rising from what Uncle Kabir said was the military headquarters of the United States.

"A bomb?" Baheer asked.

"I have heard it was another plane, hijacked and used as a missile," said Uncle Feraidoon.

Baheer felt a little dizzy. How could this happen? America was one of the most powerful countries in the world. They'd been to space. They had a massive military. And yet this wasn't their military that had been attacked. "How many people live in New York City?" he asked quietly. "How many are in those buildings?" He looked at Baba Jan, who stared at the screen with a kind of intensity that reminded him of when he'd gone to bring Uncle Kabir back from the talib. Baba Jan had been right yesterday. Something dark was coming. *O Allah the most merciful. Please. Please let this not be true. Please help those poor people.*

Aunt Sofia and her oldest daughter, Sapoora, cried. Baheer's mother turned away. Uncle Kabir wiped his eyes. Several gasped as the video showed one of the towers seeming to explode from the top and crash into smoke and ash.

"What kind of godless monster could do something like this?" Baheer's grandmother asked. "This is evil."

They watched the second tower collapse, and since Baheer had studied English in Pakistan, he tried to understand what the Americans were saying, but they spoke too quickly. More words rolled by at the bottom of the screen. He tried to read them, but again, they moved too quickly. He could understand some parts of their phrases and some of their words, though.

"I think . . . Several times they've said the word 'Muslim' and 'Islamic,'" Baheer said. "Often with a word like 'extreme.'"

"What does it mean?" Baba Jan looked at him intensely. "Quiet, all of you, so the boys can try to understand what they're saying!"

The terrible footage repeated, and the Americans continued talking about it. Baheer listened. It was one thing to score ten out of ten on an English quiz, but another to make sense of what these upset people were saying. He kept hearing another word repeated, though, and when he heard it, he caught a look from his grandfather.

"They keep saying something in Arabic. Their accents make it hard to understand."

"'Al-Qaeda,'" Baba Jan said.

Finally, the photo of an Arab man appeared on screen. He looked fiercely into the camera, wearing a tight white turban, a long black beard, and a green and brown camouflage jacket. Baheer read the name, written in English letters. "'Osama bin Laden.'"

"This man," Baba Jan said. "This Saudi maniac. He is responsible." Baba Jan was breathing heavy through his nose again. "The Americans are furious. They're going to blame us for this."

"We had nothing to do with this attack," Aunt Zarlashta said.

"Look at him!" Baba Jan shouted and hurried to put on his white turban. "The Americans won't care that he's not Afghan. These monsters who attacked them claim they are Muslim, so the Americans will think this murder is part of Islam."

Baheer's father spoke up. "The Prophet—"

"Is a mass murderer in their eyes!" Baba Jan shouted. "They will see no difference between me and that man. Would you?" He tugged his beard. "When the Russians

24

ravaged our country, do you think the Mujahideen took pity on a young Russian boy who had just arrived here and not yet committed any crimes? No! They killed every Russian they could, because Russians were killing us. The Americans see people who claim to be Muslim killing them, and they will kill all Muslims!"

"Why would Americans kill us?" Maryam muttered. "Why would these people kill Americans in the first place?"

"Don't worry, Sister," Baheer said. "Nothing is going to happen." They were bold words. Baheer tried hard to believe them. The fear in Maryam's eyes mirrored what Baheer felt inside.

Baheer's grandmother put her hands on her husband's shoulder and spoke quietly to him.

Baba Jan nodded. "Yes. You little ones. Somaya, Roma, and Yusuf? Off with you. Don't worry. Allah will keep us safe. I will keep you safe."

"What do we do?" Uncle Kabir asked when the kids had gone.

"If the Americans do bomb us, they will start here in Kabul, the capital," said Baheer's father.

"Maybe no trouble will come to Afghanistan," said Uncle Feraidoon. "Look around Kabul. What else is left to bomb?"

"We could go to Farah," Uncle Kabir suggested. "Uncle Mohammad Saeed Khan lives there. He could help us. Farah is nowhere. Nobody cares about it. They wouldn't bomb there."

"I am an old man," Baba Jan said, speaking more quietly than before. "I have seen all of this before. The Lion of the Panjshir tried to warn the West. He warned them about these Arabs working with the Taliban, but they would not listen! Now it is too late. The Americans will come, like the Russians came. They will kill us, as the Russians did. They will bomb everything. The schools will be closed, people banned from gathering together or leaving their homes. They will torture our elders and our children just like the harami Russians! Think what the Russians did to us, and after we did *nothing* to them. Imagine how much worse it will be from the Americans who think we have killed their innocent people. I have . . . I have *seen* all this before."

Baheer tightened his muscles to keep from shaking, thinking about what it would be like to suffer the kind of attack Baba Jan feared. He imagined streets of fire, the walls of every compound across the city blown to pieces. He tried to focus on the one light of hope in all this. The Americans were welcome to close the school. He hoped they'd bomb the building and destroy all the books so he wouldn't have to go back to that torturous place ever again.

The horrible tape reached its end.

"Shall we watch it again?" Uncle Feraidoon asked.

"No," Baba Jan said. "We've seen enough. We've all seen far too much."

3

RIVERSIDE, IOWA, UNITED STATES OF AMERICA
September 11, 2001

It was only first period, and one of the World Trade Center towers had collapsed, the other was burning, and Lower Manhattan was full of smoke and fire. Joe Killian held a tight, angry grip on the edge of his desk in Mr. Kane's journalism class, watching the TV in disbelief like everyone else. Several thousand people were dead in the most horrific, surreal day of his life. His senior year of high school, like the whole world, had been completely altered in just a few hours.

The news replayed President Bush's short announcement, made from an elementary school in Florida. *"Today we've had a national tragedy. Two airplanes have crashed into the World Trade Center, in an apparent terrorist attack on our country."* Shocked murmurs came from the people of Booker Elementary School who stood behind him. *"I have spoken to the vice president, to the governor of New York, to the director of the FBI, and have ordered that the full resources of the federal government go to help the victims and their families, and to conduct a full-scale investigation to hunt down and to find those folks who committed this act. Terrorism against our nation will not stand. And now, if you'd join me in a moment of silence."* It was a brief moment before the president continued. *"May God bless the victims, their families, and America. Thank you very much."*

There it was, the president confirming beyond a doubt that the nightmare was a terrorist attack. He talked about hunting these monsters down. Joe couldn't wait for the bombs to start falling on whoever had done this. He wanted to see the tanks roll and the machine guns fire and—"I'm a soldier," he said out loud. He'd actually fired an M240B machine gun at basic training at Fort Leonard Wood, Missouri, that summer. Joe—Private Killian—had enlisted in the Iowa Army National Guard for the college money, so he could pay for his own education instead of having to accept one penny from his father. Besides basic training the summer before senior year and a month of infantry job training the summer after graduation, he was supposed to serve one weekend a month and two weeks every summer.

Plus wars.

I'm a soldier. Now my country is under attack.

"I'm a soldier," he repeated aloud.

Mr. Kane looked at him sadly.

Joe was a real soldier now, and the country was at war.

His National Guard armory could be calling his home right now. He might be shipping out to fight in some country tomorrow. He might be sent to New York to help. He had official responsibilities. His heart hammered in his chest, and his muscles, honed by a summer of hard Army workouts, were tight, tense the way they were before the bayonet course or hand-to-hand combat training. This wasn't training now. This was war. He was a soldier.

"Mr. Kane?" he said. "I need to make a phone call." He swallowed. "To check for orders."

Mr. Kane nodded. "Good luck."

He ran out of the classroom, cursing himself. He should have made this call a lot earlier. What if his unit was already suiting up? What if he was late? In the Army, a soldier must never be late.

In the hall, Joe heard the intercom signal sound, and the principal's voice echoed all over the school. *"Teachers, if you haven't already, you may turn on the news. Students who do not wish to watch the news may be dismissed to the library at any time."* Mr. Tecklen paused. *"Even though Iowa is a long way from New York, I understand that people may be frightened at a time like this. I want to tell you all that I have personally walked the grounds and the school, checking locks and making sure everything is secure. You are safe. I will not let anything happen to you. I swear to God. I will keep you safe. We're going to continue doing the best we can today, supporting one another the way Riverside Roughriders always do."*

Joe nodded. It was a cheesy message. He'd had a hard time relating to all that school spirit stuff since the Army had given him a wider view of the world, but being in the National Guard had also taught him to respect good leadership, and Mr. Tecklen's speech was something of a comfort. Joe had enough to worry about without also being afraid for the school.

A group of freshmen, out of their classroom for whatever reason, were messing around, talking, laughing, and shoving one another like they were little kids on the elementary school playground. How could they be so cheerful on a day like today? Why'd they have to block the whole hall?

I don't have time for this. "At ease! Make way! Make a hole!" Joe shouted the way drill sergeants had done to quickly get through crowded hallways in the barracks. The freshmen jumped clear, and Joe ran on to the main office.

It was chaos. Mrs. Abrams, the school secretary, and Cynthia, one of the education aides, frantically answered phones.

"No," Mrs. Abrams said. "Mrs. Yoder, the building is safe. You can come pick him up if you want to or wait for the bus to bring him home like always. No, I don't have any more infor— You'll have to watch the news like everyone else. I have to go now. I need to clear this line. Goodbye!" She hung up the phone a bit forcefully and put her hands over her eyes. Cynthia squeezed her shoulder. The phone rang again.

Mrs. Abrams sighed, then pressed her lips together and

picked up the phone. "Riverside High School. This is Donna speaking. How may I help you? No, we do not plan to dismiss early. We believe it's safer to keep everyone together. The parents of most of our students are at work, and we don't think the kids should be sent home to be alone." A pause. "Yes, you may come pick her up whenever you like." She hung up a moment later.

Joe pushed to the front of a line of students and stepped up to the counter. "Excuse me. I need to use the phone."

Mrs. Abrams' phone rang again. So did the one Cynthia was manning.

It sounded like they were answering the same call over and over.

When Donna hung up again, Joe spoke up right away. "I need to make a phone call."

Tabitha Blaylin, a white-blond junior who was super into band, entered the office crying. Cynthia came out from behind the desk and hugged her. "You're going to be OK, sweetheart."

"My . . ." Tabitha sobbed. "My uncle works at the Pentagon."

Cynthia patted her back. "Well, I'm sure he's . . . He's probably OK."

Both phones rang again.

"Mrs. Abrams, I need to use the—"

"Joe!" Donna shouted. "I'm busy! If someone calls for you, I'll—"

"I'm National Guard," Joe said. He hoped he had not spoken too dramatically, like the way TV FBI guys showed up on crime scenes, taking over investigations. It was a simple statement of fact. A crazy fact in a crazy new world. "I need to check for orders."

Mrs. Abrams and Cynthia froze, their phones still ringing.

"Joe," Mr. Tecklen said, gesturing toward the door to his private office. "You can use my phone."

It was strange to be offered a seat in the principal's chair, and Joe wondered what it felt like to be Mr. Tecklen right now. Joe shook his head. He had his own responsibilities. He called home, only to get the answering machine. *"You've reached the Killian residence. Please leave a—"* Joe pressed the star button, and a moment later the machine's computer voice came on. *"Please enter the code."* He keyed in the four digits that allowed remote access to the messages.

"Kathy, this is your mother. You're probably at work. Or maybe you're shopping for emergency supplies. Or I guess you could be—" Joe hit the six key to skip the rest of the message from Grandma.

"Don't hang up! You don't want to miss this exciting offer from—" Skip.

"Joe, Krista, this is your dad. Are you watching the news? It's horrible. I just wanted to tell you both that I—" Skip. Definitely skip.

"End of messages," the computer finally said.

That was it? Nothing from his armory? What was he supposed to do now? He'd hoped at least his team leader or his squad leader would have called. Unless something had come by email. But if it had, that was a problem. The school's internet filter didn't allow anyone to check web-based email.

"Everything OK?" Mr. Tecklen said from the other side of the room.

Joe understood what he meant, but it was kind of a stupid question. The CNN website on Mr. Tecklen's desk was plastered with terrible information and photos of fire and smoke. "I need to check my Hotmail account."

Mr. Tecklen pointed to his computer. "I don't have the same lockouts as the rest of the school. Go ahead."

A moment later he'd logged in to his email to find three junk ads. And one email from Sergeant First Class Black. A cold dread sank deep inside him, and his breath was shaky as he opened the message.

To: KillJo01@hotmail.com
From: Anthony.A.Black@us.army.mil
9/11/2001
8:38 a.m.
Subject: TERRORIST ATTACK [Unclassified]

All Delta Company Soldiers:
Several commercial passenger jets have been hijacked and used as weapons in terrorist attacks on U.S. soil. At

this time, there are NO orders for activation of any
of our soldiers. Unless you are reporting terrorist
activity in your area DO NOT CALL THE ARMORY!
Our phone lines must remain open for the Governor
and other authorities. Maintain situational awareness.
Do not travel any further than 60 miles from the armory
without prior authorization. If you did not update your
contact information at our last drill, or if your contact
information has changed since then, notify your first-line
supervisor immediately with the relevant information.
Further instructions will come via your chain of
command.

    Sergeant First Class Black

Joe breathed a sigh and sank lower in the principal's chair, his back squeaking on the leather. He blinked his eyes against the sting that came with the flood of relief. A minute ago his imagination had raged with images of him dodging bomb blasts and firing a machine gun in Saudi Arabia or Iraq or even New York. He'd been almost convinced that high school was over for him, that he'd be finishing his education through combat. In an instant, he'd returned to the reality that he was still a high school student. No war for him. Yet. The release of that tension came with a surge of adrenaline and emotion that was hard to contain and control.

"I have—" He licked his dry lips. "I have no orders. Not going to war."

"Well that sounds like a good thing," Mr. Tecklen said while Joe logged out. "I mean, you're only in high school for crying out loud."

Joe nodded, grateful that last statement was still true. "Thank you, sir, for letting me check in."

"No problem. If you need anything like that again, let me know."

By the time Joe returned to his journalism class in the computer lab, the news was reporting that federal buildings in Washington, DC, had been evacuated. All commercial flights across the country were shut down, and no flights were allowed to enter the country.

"What are we even doing here?" said Bobby Theisen, from his usual seat near the front of the room. "It's not like we're going to do any work today."

Nicole Abbins glanced at him. "Where else should we go? What're we supposed to do?"

"So we just go to our next class in a few minutes, like it's no big deal? Just another class and nothing has changed?"

Joe sat at his desk near the back of the room, thinking about the rows of seats on the hijacked planes, wondering what it must have felt like to be aboard one of them, flying toward destruction. He could imagine the sadness and fear those people must have felt. The more he thought about it, the more he gripped his desk, fury tightening his muscles.

———◇———

Worried there would be no gas available tomorrow due to war in the Middle East, Joe volunteered to fuel up both his car and his mom's old minivan that night after school. The line at the gas station was three blocks long, giving him a needed break from nightmare news once he'd shut off the radio. Every station was all terrorist-attack coverage, all the time.

It was almost dark by the time Joe finally climbed the worn wooden stairs to their small apartment above Mom's friend's insurance office. It was all they could afford after Dad split, but it was kind of cool living right on the town square.

As soon as Joe entered, Mom looked up from some papers she had spread out on the kitchen island countertop. She offered a sad smile in greeting.

"How'd it go?"

"Long line. Gas station owner had to come out to stop one guy from filling up six big gas cans in addition to his truck. Crazy." Joe nodded at Mom's papers. "Still working?"

"Well, the store's closed tonight and tomorrow," Mom said. "Nobody wants to make it a Blockbuster night and rent movies. I thought I'd catch up on my paperwork, try to get corporate to send us more VHS. They're pushing DVDs, but people around here won't give up their VCRs." She sighed. "Trying to make myself feel a little less helpless and useless."

"Is it working?" Joe asked.

Mom shook her head.

"Anything new on the news?"

"No," Mom said. "It's all repeats, and it's all horrible."

The kitchen was open to the living room, and Joe flopped down on the sofa next to his sister, Krista. She said nothing but handed over a bowl of mini pretzels. Joe grabbed a few and crunched down. News coverage of the attacks continued, like scenes from the alien-attack disaster movie *Independence Day* he saw in junior high. They watched as terrified people ran away from the burning, and then collapsing, towers, and as firemen ran in the other direction to help. Every channel on TV, from the regular networks through ESPN, was running the horrible footage. They watched video clips of people hanging out the burning towers, waving clothes, begging for help. Many, knowing no help was coming, chose to jump to their deaths rather than face the fire raging in the building.

"We were supposed to have a volleyball game tonight," Krista said. She let out a weak half laugh. "So . . . stupid to"— her voice grew rough with sadness—"think about that now."

Joe put his arm around his sister's shaking shoulders as she cried. "No," he said after a long moment. "It's not stupid. You've worked hard in volleyball. You're fifteen. Volleyball should be one of your top concerns. Not"—he motioned at the carnage on the screen—"not this."

———◇———

That night, after Mom and Krista had gone to bed and Joe had finally shut off the TV, he didn't even pull out his bed, just sat on the sleeper sofa, holding his pen over a blank page in his notebook. He needed to write about what had happened. But how could anyone write the story of today? He imagined the newspapers the next day. They'd all have big banner headlines in all capitals. He put pen to paper and wrote:

ATTACKED!
~~New York Washington D.C. New York, Washington D.C.,~~
~~Pennsylvania~~ September 11, 2001

America suffered the deadliest terrorist attack in its history today. ~~The total loss of life unknown.~~ Several thousand innocent Americans were ~~killed~~ murdered today as a nation watched in horror.

In response, President Bush has promised the full resources of the federal government would be devoted to helping victims and finding ~~those responsible~~ the sick monsters who ~~committed~~ were responsible for the terrorist acts.

Across the country, people ~~grieve and are furious~~

People are dead, and there's nothing that can be done to change—

No words were enough.

He gave up and tossed his notebook and pen aside.

Joe had spent the summer in Army basic training becoming a soldier and listening to his drill sergeants talk about their time in the Persian Gulf War. America was the most powerful country in the world. Now America, for all her power, had been brought to her knees, nearly helpless, reeling from a massive attack and weeping for the dead. And Joe, watching those firemen rush in to help, hearing about fighter jet patrols protecting DC and about police and soldiers rushing to protect other sites, thought about being a soldier in this new war. He longed for his uniform and his weapon. It was the strangest paradox. Of course he wished this attack had never happened, and he wanted to continue with his normal life, running cross-country, hanging out with his friends, graduation, and then college. But longing for normal life seemed so pointless. Like Krista had said, that kind of thinking seemed stupid at a time like this. They'd murdered thousands and terrorized hundreds of millions, including his mother and little sister. If he had to be a soldier, then he wanted to get into the fight, to hit these terrorist monsters back hard. He wanted to protect his country and make them pay for the evil they'd done.

KABUL, AFGHANISTAN
September 23, 2001

B aba Jan wasted little time before following through on
his promise to keep the family safe. It had only been a
little over a week since the terrible attack on America, and
already he had purchased a house in Farah with help from
his brother who lived there.

When Baheer had first heard the family would be
moving to the small western city on the opposite side of
Afghanistan, he'd been worried. Kabul had its problems,
but it was Afghanistan's most modern city. Would their
new house even have modern toilets, or would they have
to squat over dirt holes, which wasn't uncommon? Baba Jan
had grown up in Farah, and his brother still lived there, but
Baheer had never visited. He hoped it wouldn't be too difficult an adjustment.

Baheer was no stranger to moving. He'd moved with the family before, even across international borders. But this time was different. He was surprised at how much he regretted having to leave some of the people he'd come to know at school. He wouldn't call them friends, exactly. With school discipline being so brutally harsh, there wasn't much of a chance to get to know many of the other boys. But despite having to be constantly looking out for Taliban patrols, he and Rahim did talk to some of them on the bike ride to and from school.

He'd remember Malik, who was always telling the most unfunny jokes. Malik also loved Indian movies and once tried to style his hair like one of those actors. When the Taliban found out, they arrested him. Baheer and Rahim had caught up to Malik on the street a few days later. The Taliban had shaved his head, and they hadn't been too kind about it. Another classmate, Mohammad, who absolutely loved soccer, had his bike smashed up by a talib after he was caught ringing the bell on his handlebars. Music was forbidden. What would become of these guys if the war Baba Jan feared came to pass, if Kabul was bombed to pieces the way Baba Jan dreaded?

"We have to trust Allah," Baba Jan had said when he announced the move. "As he says in the Holy Quran, chapter 3, verse 159, 'Certainly, Allah loves those who put their trust in Him.' So, don't worry. I've taken care of everything."

For two days the family packed their belongings and

prepared to leave. Only Uncle Kabir would remain behind, to finish some business and to guard some larger pieces of furniture that would not fit on the bus for this trip. Everyone else boarded the packed bus just after morning prayers. Soon its engine rumbled to life and they slowly rolled forward. Uncle Kabir waved goodbye out in the street. The bus bumped over cracked pavement as it rounded a corner and Uncle Kabir disappeared from view.

"You all can sleep. Don't worry. It's a long journey," Baba Jan told everyone.

Baheer joined his grandfather near the driver. "May I sit with you? I want to see the way."

It was Baheer's first time aboard such a bus. The interior was red with curtains hanging over the windows. Baba Jan squeezed him close to his side.

It was a tiring journey of three days and two nights. Except for a few paved patches in downtown Kandahar, the uneven roads sent the bus lurching over bumps or slogging through mud. Several times Baheer asked Allah to help them get through. Even the concrete road out of Kandahar was so full of deep cracks that the driver chose parallel dirt roads despite the danger of land mines.

On the third day of the journey, they drove through the open desert. No trees. No houses. Only rocks and sand to the horizon. Baheer was grateful for the presence of his family and even the bus driver. Out there, the loneliness hung heavy and complete.

Finally, Baheer spotted a building. "Baba, what is that hut on the left?"

Baba squinted as he gazed into the distance.

"Oh, that is a mosque for the travelers," Baba Jan said. The family looked out the windows.

"Oh, good," said Aunt Zarlashta. "I need something to remind me of other people."

"Burqas and turbans!" Baba Jan shouted.

Baheer looked back. The women scrambled into their burqas. Maryam struggled with hers. She hadn't had one for very long, and wasn't as practiced putting it on as the other women. Baheer rushed to her side and held the blankety dress upright, helping her get the little cloth mesh window over her eyes. Then he hurried to make sure his turban looked right. Everyone was finally ready as the bus began to slow down.

Ten turban-clad teenage Taliban soldiers, pale and skinny, not even grown enough to have beards, waved at the bus. Their eyes were red, lined with black makeup. Each carried a deadly Kalashnikov rifle. Outside that mosque, the Taliban had built a small hay-topped hut.

Baheer's heart raced, but he tried to reflect the same courage he saw in his grandfather.

The old bus's brakes screeched as it slowed to a halt. Two of the taliban boarded the bus. The first one wore a huge black turban tilted to the side, covering his left ear. The other wore a proper white turban. They looked everyone over, confident and cruel, as if they owned the bus and everyone on it. The women wore their burqas and turned away. The kids stayed near their mothers.

Baheer had always lowered his eyes whenever the Taliban came around, but this time he glanced at them, and despite Baba Jan's warnings, he couldn't help but wonder when an American bomb might end them.

White Turban greeted Baba Jan, most likely because of Grandfather's gray hair and perfect white turban.

Black Turban pointed his rifle at Baheer's father and Uncle Feraidoon. "Off the bus!"

Baheer started to reach out to hold back his father, certain it was terrible if they got off the bus. But his father and Uncle Feraidoon immediately obeyed, not wanting any trouble with all the women around. Baba Jan followed his sons, and before Rahim could stop him, Baheer went along with him.

The two taliban ordered Baheer, Baba Jan, Baheer's father, and Uncle Feraidoon to stand next to the hut. Black Turban shouted at Uncle Feraidoon, whose beard was shorter: "Remove your turban!"

As Uncle removed his turban, a third talib with kohl-painted eyes shouted. "Shave his head!"

Baba Jan caught the talib's hand and stood in front of his son.

Baheer admired his grandfather's courage, but wished in that moment that Baba Jan could be, like Baheer, less brave.

It was one thing to challenge the one talib who lived next door and was obviously in the wrong, but Uncle Feraidoon had broken the Taliban's stupid rule. There were ten taliban. *All those guns. Even one of them could kill us all.*

"What has my son done?" Baba Jan asked.

"Your son's beard and hair doesn't match." A tall man wearing white clothes with a light brown sweater vest came out of the hut. "Haji Saheb, we respect your gray hair, but you have not taught your sons Islamic manners."

"My sons pray five times each day, fast during Ramadan, and read the Holy Quran. They don't cheat, lie, or do any forbidden acts. All my children know Islam," Baba Jan responded.

The talib burst with laughter. "You didn't teach them to keep a proper beard."

Baheer exchanged a worried look with his father. The laughter was almost worse than the guns. Baba Jan was a haji. He had made the Hajj, the holy pilgrimage to Mecca. He was a wise man, respected by all. He could quote more passages from the Holy Quran from memory than anyone. These Taliban fools probably couldn't even read. Now this talib dared to mock his grandfather?

Baheer shook with fury, but remembering the rifles, he took deep breaths to calm down.

The leader pointed at the barber talib.

Baba Jan called upon the leader, "It is by no means against Islamic manners."

Despite Grandfather's plea, Black Turban pulled Uncle Feraidoon down to his knees.

"Sit down!" the leader shouted.

"Never go against the rules of the Amirul Momenin!" Black Turban pressed his rusty straight razor hard, leaving one bleeding bald stripe on Uncle Feraidoon's scalp.

Any pride Baheer had felt for the way his grandfather had stood up to these criminals was quickly overshadowed by his fear for his uncle and cold terror over the way the other taliban aimed their rifles at the rest of them.

After the shaving, the leader shouted, "Get on the bus! Follow our rules."

The rules. The Taliban rules. Every part of his life was governed by these horrible rules. Afghanistan had always been an Islamic country, but up until the last few years, they hadn't been forced to live under the boot of thugs like this.

Baba Jan stood firm, motioning his sons to board and shooting a dry look at the closest talib before he boarded the bus. The driver pretended nothing had happened and drove away.

There was a long silence on the bus. Grandmother brought a clean wet cloth to wash Uncle Feraidoon's bloody scalp. She sighed. "May Allah punish them."

"It's fine, Mother," Uncle Feraidoon said. "It doesn't hurt much. Once I get to Farah, I will shave it all. No big deal."

"Baba," Baheer said. "What was that 'Amirul Momenin' the talib mentioned?"

"That phrase means, 'the leader of the believers.' A real leader of Muslims never tortures people. He preaches with compassion and love. He rules with peace and tranquility, not with cruelty. This is *not* real Islam.

"Allah says, in chapter 3, verse 159, to our Prophet—peace be upon Him—about being a good leader, 'It is out of God's mercy that you have been lenient with them. Had you been rough, hard-hearted, they would surely have scattered away from you. So pardon them, and pray for their forgiveness, and take counsel from them in matters of importance,'" Baba Jan said. "From this verse we learn that a good Muslim leader should be lenient, kind-hearted, and forgiving. Not like these monsters."

"I know, Baba Jan," Baheer said, happy he had been taught this way, hoping Baba Jan would quote more of the old words.

Baba Jan kissed Baheer's forehead. "This is my son."

In addition to the many truths of Islam, Baba Jan also often talked about the former glory of Afghanistan and the Islamic world. *We led the world in mathematics, art, everything. Our poetry was second to none!* he might say. He'd often discuss the need to return to that kind of a society. To Baheer, it all sounded great. Living in a country with no fighting, where everybody was free to improve life for himself and for his family, where each person's rightness with Allah was between the person and Allah, not judged by meaningless signs such as the length of a beard.

Baheer watched his grandfather, the product of a different

and better generation, who always championed education as the best hope for a better society. While at school in Pakistan, Baheer had believed him. *Study hard, boys. You are the future of Afghanistan. Someday it will be up to you to rebuild our country.* But it wasn't up to him or Rahim or anyone good. Baheer looked at Uncle Feraidoon's brutally shaved stripe, the red and brown blood stains on the wet cloth he used to try to clean himself. It was up to the Taliban. Even if the Americans came to destroy the Taliban, even if anything was left standing after the Americans attacked, the schools were still run by teachers who beat their students with hoses or electrical cords for simply asking honest questions. It was hard to find hope in all of this, but Baheer closed his eyes, took a deep breath, and mentally recommitted himself to trusting Allah the way Baba Jan always said they should.

The day was hot despite the approaching winter as the bus turned left and continued into another desert. Baheer first thought the driver was taking a shortcut, but the bus kept going toward nowhere. Finally, in the distance, another clay-made hut came into view. A huge white flag waved above it.

Maryam, who had kept her burqa on her head but had flipped it up in front to make it easy to breathe, stepped closer to Baheer. "That white flag means Taliban, right?"

Baheer nodded. Maryam had hardly left the compound over the last several years, so it made some sense she'd have to ask such an obvious question. "Yes," said Baheer. "But don't worry. We'll be OK."

"Reegee checkpoint. Kind of the main entrance for the city," Baba Jan explained.

The bus crawled by the building. Next to it, the barrel from an old junked tank pointed at the road. Hulks of old Russian tanks, troop carriers, and shreds of their helicopters, whatever people hadn't been able to move or salvage for scrap metal, were almost as common all over Afghanistan as Russian minefields.

The bus crossed the concrete bridge over the wide river, swerving to dodge a hole. A short time later it bumped up onto blacktop.

"Wow!" Baheer said. After the long, rough ride, it felt like the bus was gliding across still water.

Baba Jan laughed. "Yeah, this is the only kilometer of asphalted road in the entire province. Farah's mayor collected money from the shopkeepers on both sides of the road."

Baba Jan directed the driver toward their newly purchased house in the downtown area.

Every residence in Afghanistan was surrounded by high walls, making each street something like a canyon. After a few more turns down crude uneven dirt roads, Baba Jan counted the doors in the walls on one street before he told the driver to stop.

"We're here," said Baba. "The compound needs renovation because I asked our farmer to stay and guard the place from intruders. He kept his animals all over."

"Intruders?" Baheer asked.

"These are bad times. If the land mafia sees an empty compound, they will bribe the Taliban and forge documents showing it is theirs. Last year, my friend returned from Iran to find he'd lost his downtown shop this way. The real documents aren't registered in the books at all. The fake ones are."

"Oh. Thank Allah that you asked someone to stay," Grandmother said.

Baheer looked at the many cracks in the front wall of the compound with more than a little doubt. If people in Farah were working with the Taliban to simply take away other people's homes, how much better than Kabul could this place be?

Baba Jan got off the bus and knocked on the compound door. An old man with a dark brown turban and a brown waistcoat came out of the house and kissed Baba Jan's hand. Baheer was relieved to see the two men speaking pleasantly. The farmer was the first kind person they'd encountered on the long trip. After a moment, he bowed with his hand over his heart, and then left.

The women entered the compound first, followed by everyone else. Uncle Feraidoon led the driver to the guesthouse. The rest of the family gathered in the front courtyard. But instead of exploring the several buildings within the compound walls, they all stared in shock.

Two buildings shaped like the guesthouse were lined up along the back wall. In front of that, a small light brown calf nursed from a spotted cow. Nearly every meter of ground within the compound was filled with loose soil and manure covered with bits of hay.

In addition to the guesthouse and the rooms in the rear of the compound, the property featured a large house with three rooms which, though not ideal, was the cleanest part of their new home. The women and little children went in that building.

Baba must have noticed Grandmother's doubtful expression. "Don't worry. We'll fix it."

In keeping with the customs of good Afghans, the neighbors on the other side of the wall brought chicken, rice, and naan for lunch, so that the family, tired from traveling, wouldn't have to cook. After lunch, the work began, and it continued for over a week. Baheer and Rahim quickly realized they were no longer living in a fancy city like Kabul. Life was going to be very different in Farah. First they had to dig paths through the manure just to get from one building to another. Then they unloaded the bus, temporarily storing their belongings in the guesthouse. After that, they shoveled out three truckloads of manure before hauling in gravel, needed because the ground inside the compound was below street level. Baba Jan had a modern-style toilet installed, and many walls had to be resealed and plastered. The whole family worked on dozens of tasks every day, from just after the morning prayer until late at night. It was exhausting, but Baheer also liked seeing the compound slowly begin to shape up into a fine, livable home.

In early October, Baba Jan went back to Kabul to help Uncle Kabir move the rest of their belongings. The work continued through the next week, all of it by hand, as the family put finishing touches on their new home.

After Baba Jan returned with Uncle Kabir from Kabul, the family was invited to a banquet outside Farah, at the compound of Baba Jan's elder brother, Mohammad Saeed Khan.

Everyone spent extra time cleaning up, making themselves as presentable as they could. Baheer wore his freshest, whitest perahan tunban, and both Rahim and Maryam laughed at the way he tried to avoid touching anything for fear of getting dirty.

"Make fun of me if you want," Baheer said. "But we've never met this part of our family. I won't be the one to make them think we're slobs. Tonight is important."

"They're family, Baheer," Maryam said. "This isn't some Taliban inspection."

Her joke flattened the mood a little, but nothing could take the energy out of a night like this one. Last year, Uncle Feraidoon had sneaked an American movie dubbed over in Pashto. The film was about a rich American family who lived in a big house. To celebrate a holiday they called Christmas, the family decided to take a trip to Paris, France. But they left one of the young boys home all alone. This would have never happened in Afghanistan. Afghan parents loved their children too much to abandon them and leave the country. To Afghans, family was everything.

One of Baba Jan's nephews arrived with a tractor pulling a trailer, to give them a ride. When they arrived, the women and kids entered the compound and were led to one of the houses. Baheer started to follow them, but Baba Jan stopped him and Rahim. "A new beginning in a part of the country that's new for you. Time to start growing up."

Baheer exchanged a smile with his brother as they followed the rest of the men into the guesthouse. No matter how close an extended family was, men and women sat separately. Later, the women might come and say "salaam," but their gathering would consist only of women and small children.

Baba Jan's elder brother waited for them in the guesthouse doorway. Baba Jan kissed his elder brother's hand and so did everyone from their family.

Baheer was surprised the dinner was ready so early. Life was different in Farah. People here ate right after the evening prayer. The dastarkhwān was spread and naan was served with shorwa, a type of stew made of lamb meat.

"It's good to have you all here!" Baba Jan's brother was as loud and bold as Baba Jan. His smile was big and sincere.

"Tashakor!" Baba Jan replied. "How good to be reunited with my brother, to see our families all come together."

The conversation continued, warm and friendly, and Baheer quickly realized that although it was, as Baba Jan had said, time to grow up, that did not mean he was particularly welcome in this conversation. The grandchildren of

Baba Jan's brother smiled at Baheer and Rahim, apparently understanding.

The meal and conversation went on for a very long time. Tea was served and then served again. Finally, there was a sound in the distance like thunder.

Baba Jan's brother paused his story for just a moment, but then shrugged and continued. "Anyway, that's how we've managed to have any kind of success in farming. Next season we hope to—" A loud boom shook the air. Dust and bits of mud-brick fell from the ceiling. Baba Jan and his brother exchanged a serious look. "The roof!" Baba Jan's brother scrambled to his feet and led the men out of the room, up a set of stairs to the flat roof of the high main house.

"Look!" Baheer pointed. In the distance pickup trucks loaded with taliban fishtailed in the dirt, creating great clouds of dust in their wake.

But above the sound of their engines came a deep roar. Baheer felt his heart beating heavier.

"There!" Rahim pointed to the sky.

Baheer looked up, barely able to see the aircraft in the moonlight. But there it was, somewhat unreal, like a ghost, with its long fuselage, swept-back wings, and four big engines. It was the first time he'd seen the American presence in Afghanistan. A second later there was a flash like lightning in the distance, then the loud, hard boom as the American bomb exploded. It hit one of the Taliban's trucks, and in a second the truck was reduced to dust, fire, and smoke.

It was hard to tell in the semidarkness, but there must have been six taliban in that truck. Now they were gone. Baheer breathed heavily through his nose, clenching his fists and watching the fire in the distance. *How do you like it? Think you're so tough picking on my uncle, picking on kids at school? Now there's a bully bigger than you! Finally someone tells you to STOP!*

"They're bombing the Taliban!" Rahim shouted.

"Never cheer for a foreign invasion. Some celebrated the Russians, too," Baba Jan said.

"The Americans must be better," Baheer whispered. He couldn't openly disagree with his grandfather. He wondered if they should take cover, but even some of the women had come to the roof to see what was happening. He couldn't run away now.

The line of Taliban trucks fleeing Farah fired back with their rifles and, from the checkpoint outside of town, there was covering fire from the only Oerlikon heavy machine gun they had. It was a useless effort. They were powerless.

Baheer smiled. The silly far-off dream of the end of the Taliban's power might at last have been coming true. *Thank you, Allah the most powerful, for this miracle.* A Taliban truck crashed into a big rock as its frantic driver tried to speed away. The monsters in back were thrown everywhere.

Baheer pressed his lips together, fighting to hold back tears. Tears of joy? Of relief? He didn't know.

"Munir Khan?" Baba Jan's brother said to him. "I don't

think it's a good idea for you and your family to go home tonight. Please be our guests at least until morning."

Farther off, the Taliban machine gun fired again as the enormous American bomber made another pass.

Baheer felt Baba Jan's firm hand on his shoulder. "Come. Let us go to bed. This could continue for another two decades."

5

FARAH, AFGHANISTAN
December 1, 2001

The merciless war of American revenge that Baba Jan had feared hadn't arrived. Instead Baba Jan heard on the radio—a radio they no longer had to hide—that the Taliban fell quickly, with some holdouts fighting around Kandahar and Bagram. More and more American and British military forces poured into the country, but apart from a few aircraft flying overhead, they hadn't seen any of that. One evening in Farah, men lined up at a barber shop to have their beards shaved off, something they hadn't been allowed to do during the Taliban era. Music played, and it was a happy time, both around Afghanistan and in Baheer's family's compound.

Early one morning after the compound renovations were complete, Baba Jan called Baheer and Rahim to his study in the guesthouse building. Baba Jan sat on a narrow mattress called a toshak, leaning back on a pillow. He was reading *Monajat-e-Khwaja Abdullah Ansari*, a centuries-old book of poetic dialogues with Allah. The rest of his library had been proudly arranged on the shelves behind him.

Uncle Kabir had questioned whether it was wise to keep books in the guesthouse, but Baba Jan had responded, "The Taliban have fled. There's no one to punish me for my books. Let our guests see them. This may encourage them to read as well."

Now Baheer and Rahim waited for Baba Jan to tell them why he'd called for them, but he was so intensely immersed in his text that he didn't seem to notice they were there. While they waited, Baheer marveled at Baba Jan's library. Thick history books. Hardcover treatises on Islamic philosophy. A few gleaming, masterfully decorated volumes by the ancient master poets. Most important, and never far from use, was Baba Jan's beloved Holy Quran. When Baheer was in Pakistan, he'd thought he might read these books, wondering if anyone besides his grandfather could read them all. But Baheer hadn't touched a book since he and Rahim had been released from the prison of their Kabul school.

Baba Jan stroked his beard as he turned another page. Was he ever going to talk to them?

"Assalamu Alaikum," Baheer finally said.

"Ah. Walaikum Salam. You kids are here," Baba Jan responded. "Come sit next to me." As the two of them took their seats, he leaned forward, turned a few pages, and began to recite the poem, rolling his index finger over the lines.

"'O Allah. Bestow wisdom upon us to not stumble over Your path and confer Vision not to tumble in Darkness.'"

Baheer thought of the long drive from Kabul to Farah, a trip spanning most of his country. He remembered the sands blowing past the high mountains that had stood there since Allah created the world, and thought that the same poet who wrote those lines may have gazed upon those same mountains. For centuries, millions of people had read his poetry. Hearing these ancient words here in this new place helped Baheer feel more at home, connecting this strange city to his country and history.

Baba Jan smiled. "See the beauty of this verse. Every time you pray to Allah, make sure you ask for wisdom and vision."

"And Allah will give these things to us?" Baheer asked.

"Through education, reading, books." Baba Jan pointed at his shelves. "Speaking of books." From behind his pillow, he produced two brown leather schoolbags, placing them on the floor in front of the brothers. One of the bags was Baheer's. He'd tried to leave it back in Kabul, hoping to never see it again. Baheer's hands ached with the memory of the blows his chemistry teacher had given him simply because he'd asked questions. This was it. With the work on the house complete, Baba Jan would send him to school.

"Your uncle Kabir found these books and your bags after we left Kabul. You must have forgotten them," Baba Jan said.

O Allah. Please help me get out of this.

Baba Jan took the Holy Quran from the shelf behind him, kissed it, and turned toward the end. He began to read, reciting each verse first in Arabic then in Pashto.

"'Read, in the name of your Lord who created you. Created all man from a cloth of blood. Read, and your Lord is the most Bountiful. Who teaches you the use of the Pen. And taught man things he did not know.'" He closed the book. "These were the first words of revelation to the Holy Prophet Mohammad—peace be upon Him. The significance of knowledge, wisdom, reading, and education are proven in our scripture." Baba Jan waved the Holy Quran. "And in our literature."

Baheer and Rahim kept their heads down. Despite the respect and belief Baheer had in Allah and Baba Jan's words, dizziness rocked him. He couldn't go back to school. *The Taliban might be gone, but the cruel teachers remain.*

Baba Jan pulled a chemistry textbook from Baheer's bag and a small garden shovel from behind his pillow, placing the book and shovel side by side before him. "I cannot force you to study. The choice is yours. The book or the shovel?"

The sight of the book made Baheer's decision easy, but he worried Baba Jan had a preference and might be mad if he chose wrong. Finally, he reached out to the shovel and pulled it toward him.

"We'll both work," Rahim responded.

Baheer smiled at his brother. He couldn't imagine what he would do if Rahim had chosen school, leaving Baheer behind.

Baba Jan stared at them over his reading glasses. "You have made your choice." He recited a line by Rahman Baba, a Pashto poet. "'Without hardships you won't have rest . . .'" He was quiet for a long moment. "The farm outside the city is overgrown with weeds and shrubs. We must water and take care of the vineyard and the wheat crop. That means digging kilometers of irrigation ditches. You'll start right away."

Baheer smiled. That was so easy. No more school! Fixing up the compound had been difficult at first, but it was kind of fun with Baheer, Rahim, their father, their uncles, grand-father, and even little cousin Yusuf all laboring together. He could have danced, but he sensed his grandfather wasn't entirely happy with his choice.

Baba Jan ordered them to get ready, so they went to change clothes in their room.

"Should I let my father and uncles know we'll be going soon?" Baheer asked.

Baba Jan stared at him silently for a moment. "Your father and uncles have enough to do getting the rug business established here in Farah. You and Rahim will work the farm by yourselves."

Something in the man's tone sent an edge of worry through Baheer. One look at Rahim told him his brother had noticed it, too. "Bale, Baba Jan," Baheer said as he and Rahim hurried from their grandfather's study.

"Why are you so happy?" Maryam asked after they'd put on work clothes.

"We're free!" Baheer said. "No more school."

"At least you're allowed the chance to go to school!" Maryam cried. "And you just throw it all away? You'll regret this decision."

"Let's go," said Rahim. "Forget this bookworm."

Minutes later, Baheer and Rahim walked their bikes next to Baba Jan on the calm, peaceful street. Palm trees waved in the breeze, blessedly free of dust. Swallows sang brightly in the branches.

Two blocks from home, vegetable carts crowded the square. A burqa-covered woman inspected the cabbage and spinach. She was unescorted with no male relative, impossible during the Taliban time. *And she's causing no problems! Why were the Taliban so ridiculously strict?*

"All these vegetables come from nearby farms," Baba said. "You'll sell ours here after harvest."

"Bale, Baba," Baheer responded.

Past the market, a group of boys wearing backpacks passed on the other side of the street, none of them wearing turbans. One of the boys laughed, pushing another, who shouted playfully and swung his bag at his friend. How could they be happy going to school?

"No turbans," Baheer whispered.

"The Taliban really are gone." Rahim smiled.

Music and high-pitched singing echoed from where a large crowd of people gathered outside a shop. A man sold ice cream out of a stall, and a TV on the counter showed *Khuda Gawah*, an Indian movie filmed in Kabul during the early nineties, when Afghanistan knew a little peace.

Baheer and Rahim smiled at each other as the people in the film danced their way down a popular bazaar in Kabul. Baheer laughed as a boy near the shop danced like the actors.

"They should have a blanket over that shop to muffle the sound," Baheer joked.

"Harami Taliban," said Rahim.

"Don't joke about the Taliban, boys," Baba Jan said quietly. "Your uncle's head still bears scars from their razor. They hurt a lot of people."

They turned onto the asphalt street of the bazaar. People swarmed the shops. On both sides of the street, men sold dry fruit, sweets, cakes, flowers, and jewelry. They kept walking, leaving the pavement and buildings and heading toward the open, barren land outside town, passing a deep, dry creek. Baheer spotted an enormous compound, its tall mud walls stretching on unbelievably far.

"That's our farm." Baba Jan laughed. "I have quite a bit of land here."

Inside the compound, Baba Jan took them to a tool storage room. Feeble light shone in through one small hole in the middle of the dome ceiling and a window screened by thick, dust-covered, yellowed plastic.

"Get two wheelbarrows, two shovels, two sickles, and one pickax," Baba Jan called in after them.

The boys stumbled in the shadows until they brought out the necessary items. Baba Jan locked the room and they went to work.

First, they ran the water pump to irrigate the vineyard. After clearing the trenches that carried water from the well, making sure the water flowed properly, they went to cut grass for the family cow.

The boys had never cut grass before. Baheer swung the sickle low like a cricket bat, but only knocked a few blades of grass in the air.

Baba Jan laughed, and although he meant it kindly, it made Baheer feel clumsy and stupid. He wanted to be good at this. He needed to be good at this. If he failed here on the farm, he might be sent back to school. More than that, he was sixteen, far from being a little kid. He needed to be good at *something*.

"Not like that." Baba Jan took the sickle from Baheer. "Hold the handle firm and with your other hand grab the grass. Pull the sickle toward you close to the ground. It will cut. See? Like this."

Rahim grabbed the other sickle and began smoothly cutting big bundles of grass.

"Be careful. It seems easy, but if you go too fast, you may

cut your finger," Baba Jan warned. "Once you fill one sack, we'll take it on the wheelbarrow when we go for lunch."

The cutting wasn't easy. Baheer couldn't cut as quickly as his brother, and once he nearly sliced his thumb.

An hour later, they heaved a large sack of grass onto the wheelbarrow and parked it under the shade of the berry tree as Baba Jan had instructed. But there was no time to relax. One of the irrigation trenches in the vineyard had collapsed, and water had flooded everywhere. Baheer and Rahim hurried with shovels, and as they tromped through the mud, Baheer wondered for a moment if perhaps he'd made the wrong choice. But the trenches wouldn't collapse every day. This was just bad luck.

Baba Jan pointed at a row of shrubberies by the compound's center wall. There must have been hundreds of the twisted, stubborn things. "All those bushes must be dug out."

Baheer stared at the plants. He shivered as a cool wind blew over his soaked body. *OK. Maybe work on the farm will be harder than I thought. But I'll get used to it. Insha Allah.*

Every day, they watered the vineyard, cut a sack of grass, and dug up more bushes. Sometimes Baba Jan would demonstrate how to better do a task or encourage them to keep working, but mostly he sat in a chair near the well, reading *The Interpretation of Quran* by Khwaja Abdullah Ansari.

After a week, Baheer had many bruises. His hands swelled. "Man, this hurts."

Rahim sliced some grass. "At least we're free, out in the sun and fresh air, working like men."

This did not feel like freedom anymore. Baheer had chosen the shovel to avoid the pain of the teacher's whip. Now instead of temporary pain from lashes on his hands, Baheer's whole body ached. All the time. He looked at Baba Jan, who glanced up over his book with a frown. "You're right," Baheer said and returned to cutting.

Through the winter and into the spring, the brothers spent most of their time on the farm. They were never given the chance to have fun or explore the bazaar except when they went there to sell some of the family's extra produce. Baba Jan allowed no free time at home. After the morning prayer, he'd send them on their bikes down that same muddy route past the dried creek.

One morning on the way to the farm, Baheer noticed a girl wearing a black shawl, carrying a bundle of books, standing on the upper edge of the creek right before him. He saw girls heading to school every day around here, unthinkable only months ago, but this girl was different. As he looked up at her, she unveiled her face and smiled. Baheer nearly crashed his bike into a rock. What was she doing? Never in his life had a girl outside his family been so forward with him. Baheer quickly turned his face away and pedaled harder, thinking about the girl the whole way to the farm.

By the end of March, Baheer and Rahim had settled in to the tough, monotonous fieldwork. Baba Jan no longer accompanied them to the farm. They knew what to do. They were like donkeys, functioning automatically, unthinkingly, ceaselessly.

There has to be more to life than this. Baheer rubbed his sore shoulder as he moved quietly through the moonlit front courtyard late one night after everyone else had gone to sleep. He couldn't just eat, sleep, and work.

Knowing the metal door to his grandfather's guest room squeaked loudly, Baheer lifted the door a little as he opened it, taking pressure off the bad hinge. Moonlight spilled into the room, but the books remained in shadow. *O Allah, the most merciful. Please help me pick the right book.* Something to bring a little meaning and brightness to his days. He pulled a volume from the far end of the top shelf, having no idea what he'd taken.

Baheer opened the small hardcover and held it close to his face. He breathed in the warm scent of old paper and deep wisdom. The scent of hope. *Insha Allah.*

The next morning Baheer discovered that by luck or by the will of Allah, the book he'd found was Ferdowsi's *Shahnama*, the epic poetry of Persian kings. He had heard Baba Jan speak of or quote from Ferdowsi countless times growing up, so he knew he'd found something good. He only hoped his grandfather didn't discover it missing before he could read and return it.

The farm work continued, but now the days were brightened a little. He even found himself working faster to finish tasks and steal more time to read. During their traditional rest period after lunch and prayer, Baheer would read from *Shahnama*. On one hot afternoon, he looked at the book in his hands.

This. This was what learning was meant to be. It was different from school. Reading Ferdowsi's *Shahnama*, which was about Rostam, a warrior, and his son, made him think of the Citadel that loomed over the bazaar in Farah. Like that fortress, these words were ancient, a thousand years older than the copy of the book he held in his hands. These words had spoken to people long before the Taliban sought to destroy them, before the Soviets tried to destroy Afghanistan. They were older by far than the Americans who had come to his country now. Unlike all of the empires and ages of history, these words had lasted.

Ferdowsi spoke to him from across the centuries, and although Baheer wasn't sure what all these couplets meant, he could feel in his bones, just as surely as he could feel Afghanistan's winds, that they were important.

"Get up and listen to this . . ." Baheer said to Rahim.

"Who cares? Let me sleep," Rahim mumbled, eyes closed.

"Listen. Ferdowsi says, 'Capable is he who is wise / Happiness from wisdom will arise.'"

"You talk too much. I don't care about any kind of wisdom," Rahim replied.

"How can you not care?" Baheer asked. "Don't you see? This poetry was among the best in the whole world back in ancient Persian times. It's an example of the greatness we can achieve. No wonder the Taliban wanted to destroy books like this. They wanted to hold us all back to their own pathetic illiterate standard."

"That poetry can't pull all these rogue shrubs from this field for us," Rahim said. "It's useless. Maybe the Taliban had a point in banning it. Now let me rest."

Baheer looked at his brother. How had they become so different in so short a time?

"One day you will know the value of wisdom," Baheer said.

Farm work continued through the summer. There was always more to do, and although Baheer's body became more adapted to the work, his spirit became less so. His reading brought him comfort, but it made him long for more and wish that shoveling, planting, and cutting weren't so often in his way.

On many days, either coming from or going to the farm, Baheer would see the girl who had looked at him before. At first, Baheer ignored her, even when she followed him from a distance or looked right at him. One day she even waved at him, holding up her books as if to show them off. Each time he saw her, his heart beat faster, though whether that was out of fear of getting caught being too familiar with a girl outside of his family or because of her smooth skin, dark eyes, and kind smile, he couldn't say. But he knew she was always clean, and carrying many books, and he was often dirty, his one book always hidden away until he was sure nobody but Rahim would see. Compared to Baheer, the Mystery Girl was a scholar. *She must think I'm just a poor ignorant peasant.* The idea bothered him more than it ever had before.

Baheer could tell no one about the Mystery Girl, not even Rahim. His brother had become a different person lately. He was content in their new lives as farmers. Finally, at the beginning of September, Baheer realized he was not. *Something must change.*

Walking home after a long hot day on the farm, Baheer summoned his courage.

"Rahim, school starts in one week. Let's ask Baba Jan to get us admission."

His brother curled his lip in disgust. "Man, I don't care. You want? Go ask him." Rahim marched on ahead of him.

Baheer thought about the prospect of school late into the night. Even if the teachers in Farah schools turned out to be as bad as those in Kabul, they couldn't be worse than the farm work. And besides, the people he'd seen going to the school didn't appear to be dreading it.

Careful not to wake Rahim, he went outside to sit up on the roof. He remembered what Maryam had told him when he'd chosen work over school. *You will regret it.* He looked out across Farah and thought of the poem he'd read in Sa'di's *Gulistan*:

The clouds, the winds, the water, the sun, and the
    Heavens are all at work
So, you do not forget their hardships for you, while
    earning from your work.

He could do something different with his life, something better. It was a new Afghanistan, but Baheer would never be a part of the progress while he was trapped within the confines of the farm-compound walls. He had to try. Tomorrow, he would ask Baba Jan if he could choose the book. He smiled, relaxed, and eventually went back to his room to sleep.

The next day, during breakfast, Baba Jan said, "Eat quickly and go to the farm to prepare the land for this year's wheat crop."

Rahim responded, "Bale, Baba Jan."

"What are you waiting for, Baheer?" Baba Jan looked at him. Although Baheer was done eating, he kept staring at his empty teacup. He couldn't find a way to phrase his request.

"Hey! Are you alive or not?" Baba Jan said.

"I want to go to school," Baheer said quietly.

"What? Come again?"

It was Baheer's worst fear. His grandfather wasn't happy. "I want to resume school."

"Why?" Baba Jan asked. "Because the farm work is too hard for you? You want to run and hide in the school? You were not raised to be a weakling."

"No, Baba Jan," Baheer said quickly. "It was like you said, last year when you asked us to choose." Baheer closed his eyes, trying to remember. "'Read in the name of the Lord who created you. Allah teaches us things we do not know.'"

Baba Jan watched him silently for a long time. "It has been tough for your father and uncles to establish good business here in Farah. We cannot afford to neglect the farm, and—"

"I will work before or after school," Baheer said quickly, instantly regretting interrupting his grandfather.

"What about you?" Baba Jan asked Rahim.

He responded, "I also want to go. I wanted to tell you, but Baheer said it first."

Baheer was surprised, wondering what had changed Rahim's mind.

"OK. I will ask your father to take you today for admission." Baba Jan spoke with a kind of sigh. "But I expect you both to keep up with the farm, and there will be serious trouble if you come back to me asking to leave school. A real man commits himself fully to every endeavor."

Baheer went out to the courtyard and thanked Allah for this new chance. He felt like his destiny was calling to him.

"Why haven't you gone to the farm?" Maryam asked when she saw Baheer still in his room after breakfast.

"Baba Jan's agreed to let Rahim and me go to school."

Baheer smiled when Maryam danced in joy.

"Wonderful! This is the best news, my brothers." Maryam hugged them both.

The joy and excitement were tempered over dinner that night.

Uncle Kabir brought up their recent losses in the rug business. "I don't know what the matter is. Maybe we're choosing the wrong patterns or colors. Maybe people in Farah don't like good rugs as much as they do in Kabul."

Uncle Feraidoon ran his hands down over his face. "It's worse than that, Haji Agha," he said to Baba Jan. "We have to increase the wages almost fifty percent if we want to keep our workers producing."

"Why?" Baba Jan asked.

"It's all because a few Iranian rug dealers have come and destroyed everything. Our workers shear the wool from their huge herds of sheep. Until now, they would use them in our rugs. Now, this new dealer has asked our workers to sell their original wool to them for a very good price. Then, these Iranians gave them synthetic, low-quality wool for almost free to weave rugs for them. When I talked to my workers, they said that the Iranian designs are much easier, allowing for a twelve-meter square rug in a week." Uncle Kabir said.

"How long does it take them for our designs?" Baba Jan said.

"It takes a month," Uncle Kabir said. "And the workers just asked me to raise their wages by fifty percent.

Impossible! From the other side, the harami Pakistan government has increased the import tax on the rugs we sell there. We can't make a profit there either. And, unfortunately, shipping through Pakistan is the only way to get our rugs to the American market, where the real money is."

Baba Jan looked meaningfully at Baheer. He worried his grandfather might change his mind about Baheer and Rahim going to school. Would they have to help Uncle Kabir with the rugs or help his father get his carpentry shop up and running? Was Baheer being selfish?

His grandfather drew in a deep breath through his nose, the way he often did before making an important pronouncement.

Here it comes. No school. No chance.

"These are tough times for us," Baba Jan said. "But we have faced tough times before. We are true Afghans. We are indomitable. We will work hard and keep our faith in Allah. In the end we will prosper."

As Baba Jan spoke the men seated there for dinner sat up a little straighter. A look of hope returned to their faces. His grandfather could inspire people like that, and Baheer was more determined than ever to succeed on the farm and especially in the classroom.

IOWA CITY, IOWA, UNITED STATES OF AMERICA
January 30, 2003

Nevertheless *morale is running high throughout the unit."*

A smiling Army major in a pressed desert-combat uniform stood next to a tan Humvee before an expanse of dry Afghan desert, answering NBC reporter Phil Jameson. *"Our soldiers approach every situation with a firm 'mission first' mentality, and if the mission requires our deployment to be extended for a few more months, or even years, we are prepared to do our duty in support of that mission, and in support of peace and freedom."*

"What is this crap?" Joe said aloud to the TV. His roommate was out at a party, so Joe had the dorm room all to himself. He was supposed to be reading an essay for his rhetoric class, but the first semester had been so easy it was hard to take the class too seriously. Still, he hadn't made the dean's list by being lazy. If he was going to succeed second semester, he had to study. He needed the best grades possible to impress the editors at the *Daily Iowan*, the University of Iowa newspaper.

"*Thank you so much for your time, Major,*" Jameson said.

"That's it?" How could he study with this garbage on TV? He could turn it off, but as a journalism major, Joe wanted—needed—to pay attention to news coverage. If this could even be called news. An Army transportation unit in Afghanistan was all set to return home after its deployment. The soldiers had their bags packed and loaded, ready for the freedom bird to take them back to America. Then they were told they had to stay for another six months. And all Phil Jameson had done to get the story was contact an Army public affairs officer. All the PAO would ever do was regurgitate official Army propaganda.

Joe's infantry company had been subjected to a PowerPoint lecture from the battalion PAO at November's drill. It was all about Operational Security, or OPSEC, how they weren't supposed to reveal sensitive information about troop movements, even in training. And they were not supposed to talk to reporters, but had to refer all questions to the PAO, who would deliver the official position.

But the official position he'd just seen was total garbage. There was no way those soldiers were fine with their extension. He hadn't been in the Army National Guard for long. He'd only finished his month of infantry training at Fort

Benning, Georgia, this last summer, the summer after he'd graduated high school. But he'd been serving long enough to know extending deployment like that would cause serious problems. Oh, the men would follow orders, but morale would not be high.

Joe shut off the TV. It was a little over a year since the 9/11 terrorist attacks, and too much of the country had settled for bland noninformation like this. For the most part, America rolled on as if nothing had happened. They were already debating whether or not to launch the next war. Now here was this Army unit with an extended tour, serving two deployments back-to-back. Other units had deployed, come home, and deployed again.

And Joe's infantry company had gone nowhere. The officers were planning on the normal two weeks of annual training at Fort McCoy, Wisconsin, this June.

I'm just stuck. The war against the terrorists and their Taliban friends was heating up in Afghanistan. He wanted to be there, reporting on it, telling the real truth about the war. The war would be over before he had a chance to fight or write about it.

The phone on the wall rang. Joe happily ditched his book and rose from his chair. Lindsey, a beautiful girl with curly red hair from his chemistry class, had said she might call. It was still early. Maybe they could meet for coffee or go get something to eat. Joe lifted the handset off the receiver after the third ring.

"Hello," he said with a little swagger in his voice.

"Private Killian?" A rough voice. Definitely not Lindsey. It was a man from the Guard. But weekend drill wasn't until the middle of February.

"Yes."

"This is Sergeant Hodgins." A pause. "Stampede."

Joe put his hand against the wall. Cool solid plaster, a crack that ran like lightning beneath his hand. *Stupid thing to notice. Get yourself together.*

"Stampede" was a code word used to notify a soldier that he was being activated for war. Joe knew this moment might come, had even hoped for it, but the possibility had always seemed so remote. He suddenly felt like he was in one of those drunk-driving-accident videos shown before prom every year, with the kid saying, "I thought it couldn't happen to me."

Joe licked his lips. Grateful for the long cord on this old phone, he crossed the room to grab a pen and paper. "I understand."

"Prepare to copy."

"Ready." Joe's hand shook.

"This is your activation call." Sergeant Hodgins spoke firmly. "Elements from your infantry company have been selected for federal active duty. During February drill we will conduct mobilization prep and soldier common-task training. We should have our official federal orders some-time in late February and we will report to the armory for zero seven hundred formation on February 15 for two weeks, in lieu of annual training, for more mobilization prep."

So, they'd moved the two weeks of annual summer training to February.

Sergeant Hodgins continued. "Eventually we'll deploy to Fort Hood, Texas, for additional training, until proceeding to Afghanistan for a year or more. How copy?"

Joe nodded, like an idiot, then spoke up. "That's a good copy."

"Any questions?" Sergeant Hodgins asked.

"Neg—" Joe swallowed. "Negative, Sergeant."

Sergeant Hodgins sighed. "Prepare yourself. Get your finances in order. Your chain of command will be in touch with further instructions. Sergeant Hodgins, out."

Joe stood in his quiet room. Loud bass thumped from a passing car outside. A girl down the hall laughed and shouted about the Hawkeyes. Joe knew, even then, that those things were already relegated to his past. The phone call had broken his existence into two distinct lives. He was no longer simply Joe Killian, but Joe Killian before the call, and Joe Killian after.

Joe was eighteen. He'd only been driving for two years. He hadn't had the opportunity to vote in a presidential election yet. He didn't feel like a kid, but only eight months ago, he'd been in high school. Now he was going to war.

How do I prepare for this? How does anyone?

Where would he even start? He'd have to tell some people he was leaving, his professors for one thing.

And he'd have to tell his family. How would Krista deal with this? Growing up, they'd fought like crazy, but lately they'd become closer. She could be annoying, but she was more a friend now than a sister. Sometimes she even came to him for advice about high school stuff or about looking ahead to college. After Dad split, Joe tried to look out for her. How could he do that from the other side of the planet?

His mother hadn't been super excited about him enlisting. Would she freak out now, wishing she made more money so he wouldn't have felt compelled to enlist to pay for his education? Would she wish she'd refused to sign the parental permission forms for his early enlistment? If he didn't make it home, would she blame herself?

No. Get yourself together, man. Be a soldier. Forget the feelings and execute the mission.

But a guy going to war could no more avoid thinking about the possibility of death than someone buying lottery tickets could avoid thinking about riches. What was war besides people trying to kill one another? People would be trying their best to kill him.

He might have to kill another human being. He hadn't been to church in a while. Faith had been hard after his family split apart. But he hadn't forgotten "Thou shalt not kill." Even if the enemy deserved the bullet, he still had a mother, a family. He was still a person. How did God keep score during war?

———◇———

"Joe, what are you doing home?" Mom looked at him, wide-eyed. He'd come back to the apartment for a few weekends his first semester, but he'd never brought back all his belongings. It took about two seconds for Mom to take in all the boxes and duffel bags in the crowded living room and know something was different. "When did you get here?"

Joe only had two classes that Friday, and after talking to his instructors about the situation he was excused from both. "Krista here?"

"Basketball practice." Mom stepped into the kitchen and dropped her keys on the counter.

"Right," Joe said. It would have been better if Krista could have been here, too, so he could break the news to both of them at the same time. But even now he was reluctant to tell his mother what he knew he had to tell her. "I got back at about two. Walked around the square for a while."

"Walked around the square? But it's freezing out there. What's wrong?"

"Wasn't too bad." He'd been walking around this town where he'd always lived, remembering driving with his friends when he'd first had a license, kissing Beth Finley by the fountain in the square the summer after eighth grade. Except for half a year twelve miles to the north at college in Iowa City, his whole life was right here in this town. Now the Army would be shipping him to the other side of the planet.

"Joseph Paul Killian," Mom said. "Talk to me."

"My unit's been called up," Joe said. "Afghanistan."

Mom was silent for a long moment. Finally, she asked, "How long will you be gone?"

He shrugged. "About a year."

"OK," she breathed, nodding. "OK. We knew this was coming." She drew in a shaky breath, her eyes beginning to well up.

"Hey." Joe rose from the couch and joined his mother in the kitchen. If she started to break down, he was going to lose it, too. *You're a soldier, Joe. Act like one.* He swallowed and blinked. "Hey, it's fine. I'll be fine."

"No. I'm not going to be one of those hysterical mothers." She wiped her eyes. "I promised myself I wouldn't do this."

Joe put his arms around her. She hugged him back. They weren't usually a huggy family.

"It's just hard to think my boy is going—" Mom stopped herself and backed away from him. She closed her eyes and took a deep breath. "I'm here to help you in any way I can. You just focus on getting back here safely."

"I will," Joe said. "I promise."

———◇———

Through the next two weeks, Krista and Mom helped him prepare. Krista insisted on making sure he had music. She couldn't afford one of these new iPods that could store a thousand songs, but she bought him a smaller, less expensive MP3 player. He'd be taking about two hundred songs to the war. Mom had been more practical, emailing him an article from the *Des Moines Register*'s online edition about how

Iowa colleges and universities were adjusting their policies to help their deploying students. She'd also connected him to her attorney, the same lawyer who had handled her interest in the divorce, so that he could prepare a will.

"Mom, I don't need a will. I don't own anything," Joe protested. "Anyway, I'm going to make it back fine, so all of this is just a waste of time."

"You have a car, your books, a bunch of CDs, and the Army will pay you while you're over there," Mom said. "You need to decide who will get it all. Only a fool goes to war without planning for the possibility that the worst may happen."

Joe looked at her in awe as they climbed the few steps to the entrance of the lawyer's office. This wonderful woman, who had worked so hard all her life, especially since Dad left. Apart from the initial threat of tears when he'd first told her about his activation, she hadn't wavered, but had remained a focused source of help and encouragement. In the difficult year ahead Joe would model his determination upon her, and even if he fell short of his goal, mustering only a fraction of her strength, he'd be doing pretty great.

Someone must have told Dad about the deployment, because he called. Joe wished he'd checked Caller ID before picking up. He found himself stuck in the last conversation he was interested in having. "I hear they're sending you overseas," Dad said. He kept talking, but Joe's thoughts wandered. *You're the one who decided you'd changed, that you no longer loved Mom, and that it was time to move out. Dating that woman—what's her name? Crystal?—after only six months?* They'd had a house, a family, and everything, and Dad had ruined it all. ". . . I'm proud of you. Keep your head down over there, OK? I'd like to see you before you go. Take you to lunch or—"

"I'm really busy getting ready to ship out," Joe cut in. That was a lie. He had time for lunch. He didn't want to lie when he could die in a war. *Best to be clear in case I don't make it home.* It was a time for truth. "I don't want to talk to you. You wanted out of the family. You're out."

"Your mother and I got divorced, but I didn't—"

"It's too late to play happy family now. I'll be fine. Goodbye."

"Son, I just wish—"

Joe jabbed the OFF button and put the phone back on its charger. One more step of war preparation done.

———◇———

Mobilization prep in Iowa had been a tedious affair, standing in lines for hours waiting to clear dental, legal, and records.

And they were forced to study the *Soldier's Manual of Common Tasks, Skill Level 1,* constantly. Finish chow early? *Study your soldier manual!* Quickly clean up after morning physical training? *Study your soldier manual!*

Joe hated it. The book included instructions for nearly every combat situation a soldier might encounter, up to and including "React to Nuclear Attack."

Conditions: You are in a tactical situation or an area where nuclear weapons have been (or may have been) used. May have been used? Joe laughed. How was there ever uncertainty about whether or not nuclear weapons had been used? Wouldn't the fact that everything had been blown up be a clue?

You are given load-bearing equipment (LBE), a piece of cloth or protective mask, a brush or a broom, shielding material, FM3-11.3, and one of the following situations:
1. You see a brilliant flash of light . . .

"Be the last thing you ever see," Joe muttered as he read.

Performance Steps:
1. React to a nuclear attack without warning.
   a. Close your eyes immediately.
   b. Drop to the ground in a prone position, facing the blast.
   c. Keep your head and face down and your helmet on.
   d. Stay down until the blast wave passes and debris stops falling.
   e. Cover your mouth with a cloth or similar item to protect against inhaling dust particles.
   f. Notify your first line supervisor of nuclear attack.

Joe threw the manual at the wall and pressed his fists to his temples. He couldn't handle the stupidity. The Army was actually telling him that, in the immediate aftermath of a nuclear blast, he should turn to his team leader Sergeant Paulsen and say, "Excuse me, Sergeant. Sorry to bother you, but I believe that blindingly bright flash and ear-splitting roar of explosion, that massively destructive shockwave, was the result of a nuclear attack. Just FYI. I'll go back to studying my Common Tasks manual now."

It was so dumb he wanted to punch something. Every moment of this mindless training felt years long. And the clock didn't start on his deployment until he reached Afghanistan.

———◇———

Finally, after two weeks, every soldier had been given all the examinations he needed, answered all the common soldier task questions that could be asked, and had packed and repacked and repacked and repacked his gear.

Nothing remained but the goodbyes.

The farewell ceremony at the armory was open to family, friends, and pretty much anyone else. The company stood at attention, enduring a speech from the Iowa City mayor until they were finally released.

Joe weaved his way through the crowd of wives and children saying goodbye to soldier husbands or fathers. Local news cameras pounced on any crying children or emotional soldiers. Joe avoided them.

"Is that what you want to do?" Joe's mother asked, nodding toward the TV reporters.

"I'm hoping to write for newspapers or magazines. Maybe books." Joe shrugged. "Gotta get back from war first."

It was impossible to say goodbye to a lifetime of love with a half-hour reception.

Mom must have felt the awkwardness, too. "I don't know what . . . I guess, be careful."

Joe laughed, grateful to his mom for her strength. "You're pretty cool, Mom."

Mom looked away a moment. "Well, you're a cool kid."

"Sometimes." Krista hugged him. "Write to us? Tell us what war is like?"

"Oh, gosh. Not for me," Mom said. "Just tell me it's all great. Boring even."

"I'll tell you the truth," Joe said. *Maybe not the* whole *truth.* She would worry enough.

"Still writing?" Mr. Kane's lanky form snaked through the crowd, his ever-present satchel on his hip. He smiled warmly and offered a handshake.

"Mr. Kane!" Joe shook the man's bony hand. "It's great to see you."

"I won't bother you too much. I know the last thing you want is to lose precious time with your family talking to your old high school teacher. Only I . . ." He adjusted his glasses, quiet for a long moment. "You remember during your senior year, right before 9/11? You were writing a story about a fight between two students . . ." He shrugged. "Can't remember their names. Doesn't matter."

"I remember the superintendent wouldn't allow you to print my story."

Mr. Kane slapped his bag. "That's the one. What I couldn't tell you, back then, is that I admired how writing the unbiased truth of that fight, the truth as best your sources could tell it, was important to you. America needs those kinds of writers, Joe. Not these cable news people spouting propaganda for one party or another, but real journalists who work to tell the truth."

"I'm not really a journalist," Joe said. "I didn't even get to finish my first year of college."

"But you *will* be a great journalist," said Mr. Kane. "You can be a great writer if you choose to be, and the thing is, whether you realize it or not, whether it feels like it or not, you're about to step into history. You are about to participate in events that will be recorded in one way or another in our history books."

"I don't know about that," Joe said.

"I do," said Mr. Kane. He flipped up the flap on his satchel. "Here. Didn't have time to wrap it."

He handed Joe a worn hardcover book. *Brave Men* by Ernie Pyle.

"Thanks, Mr. Kane," Joe said.

His old teacher tapped the cover with a big grin. "Ernie Pyle, a columnist and probably the most famous World War II correspondent. Now there was a man who turned writing the truth about war into an art form." His face fell serious.

"You be careful over there. But also, take a lot of notes. You have a camera?"

"About half a dozen disposable ones. I'll just mail them home to get them developed."

Mr. Kane nodded. "Good man. Do your best to record this experience. It will make it so much easier to write about someday."

"I will," Joe promised. "I'll write the truth about this war."

"I know you will." He shook Joe's hand again and patted him on the shoulder. "Goodbye for now, Joe. And good luck. Come see us in Riverside on the other side of all this."

"I will," Joe said again.

Mr. Kane took a deep breath and gave a half salute before turning away.

"Your attention, please," the company commander, Captain Higgins, said over a loudspeaker. *"I must ask friends and families to depart. In fifteen minutes all Delta Company soldiers will be aboard the bus to conduct movement to Fort Hood, Texas, to begin training for our deployment. Thank you for supporting your soldier, but it's time to leave."*

"This is it." Joe hugged Krista and then Mom. "See you in a year." He waved and then headed toward the bus out front. He didn't look back. Goodbyes were harder the longer they lasted.

Their bags were already loaded in the luggage compartment of the charter bus. Joe boarded and flopped down next to PFC Zimmerman from the other team in his squad.

"Hey, man. You ready for this?"

"I guess," Zimmerman said.

As First Sergeant Dalton took a head count, Joe pulled his pen and blue notebook from his BDU, battle dress uniform, cargo pocket.

March 1, 2003

A somber crowd gathered on a cold gray early afternoon to say goodbye to friends and family at the Delta Company Army National Guard armory in Iowa City. About forty soldiers saluted and boarded a bus bound to link up with the rest of the task force, soldiers from other infantry and support companies, before conducting movement to Fort Hood, Texas, and thence to Afghanistan, where they will fight to make America and the world safe from terrorism.

Aboard the bus, the mood among soldiers ranged from jocular to optimistic, but all were strong and determined, ready to face the

In the seat next to Joe, PFC Zimmerman sniffed and wiped his eyes. His cheeks were red, and Joe saw him struggle to decide whether to turn away from the guys and look out the window, or turn away from the crowd outside and toward the guys. Eventually he looked down at his lap.

Joe put his pen and notebook away. He wouldn't write about this anymore today. And like the rest of the guys, he did the best he could for Z by pretending he hadn't noticed his tears.

FORT HOOD, TEXAS, UNITED STATES OF AMERICA
March 4, 2003

Mornings in the Army come early, and a week after arriving at Fort Hood, D Company was up, showered, shaved, and back from the dining facility by 0630, ready for another day of training. Specialist Quinn, a huge machine gunner from the other four-man fireteam in Joe's nine-man squad, performed a functions check on his M240B machine gun, a belt of blank ammunition draped over his shoulders. "When I'm getting up. Before I can even make it up." He sang a messed-up version of an old song. Badly. He slammed the weapon's feed-tray cover down hard. "I'll say a prayer for youuuuuuu."

Corporal MacDonald was the most senior soldier in Joe's fireteam besides the team leader, Sergeant Paulsen. Mac sighed, slinging his rifle and cramming two thirty-round magazines full of blanks into his ammo pouch. "I say a little prayer for my discharge papers," he continued. Mac was about twenty-five and in the last year of his enlistment contract. He followed orders and did his duty, but in his heart, he was done with the Guard.

Joe was in the first of four squads in First Platoon, and they were heading out for squad-level dismounted infantry drills. React to ambush. React to indirect fire. Assault a fixed position. They'd been living in old barracks from the Vietnam era, two-story open-bay buildings rumored to have been condemned and scheduled for demolition until they were suddenly needed for troops training to go to war after 9/11. The latrines were rusty and dusty. Many of the mattresses on the bunks bore strange stains. Water leaked through the flat roof on rainy days. The different companies of the battalion occupied over a dozen of these buildings in addition to smaller one-story barracks for officers and senior enlisted. Almost a thousand soldiers and literally tons of gear had arrived in North Fort Hood.

Out in the field behind the barracks, First Squad's squad leader, Staff Sergeant Cavanaugh, wanted to "get in a little hip-pocket training" before Staff Sergeant Connors, the official training noncommissioned officer (NCO) that Fort Hood had assigned to train Joe's platoon, showed up to start the real drill.

"Man, we've been over this stuff a million times," Mac said quietly. "Six years in the Guard practicing this crap, and now we work on this every spare second Sergeant Cavanaugh can fit in."

"Maybe it will help us when we get over there," said PFC Baccam.

Baccam was a cool guy and a solid soldier, and Joe admired his optimism. But like Corporal MacDonald, he wished their squad leader would give them a break. Why did they have to train more than other squads? The rest of the platoon wasn't due on the field for another half hour. He would have liked a little time to read Ernie Pyle's *Brave Men* or to write news stories of his own. Instead they were practicing the same drills for the millionth time. Even if he wrote his best material possible, nobody would be interested in reading solely about repetitive basic combat drills.

"Now, I know we have practiced this before, but I want to make darn sure we know it and can do it in our sleep," said Sergeant Cavanaugh.

"We do this *instead* of sleeping," Mac whispered.

If Cavanaugh heard, he made no indication. "Right. Now, I want a squad column formation, Bravo Team up front. Keep it snappy."

Joe's team leader, Sergeant Paulsen, moved to point and held out his right arm. "Corporal MacDonald, then PFC Killian, in a line back and to my right. PFC Baccam, take that SAW back to my left."

"Roger, Sergeant!" Baccam shouted before running to his position with the M249 squad automatic weapon light machine gun.

Everyone in the squad was in formation before the rest of

the instructions were finished. The squad column formation stacked the fireteams, making a sort of diamond around the squad leader.

"Right," said Sergeant Cavanaugh. "Now spread out. Keep your intervals. Let's move." They walked along the open field. In the distance, the backup bell sounded from over by the dining facility, or DFAC, where a garbage truck collected the refuse from the dumpsters.

Joe carried his M16, trying hard to imagine himself in Afghanistan, in the middle of the war. He wanted this training to count as if his life depended on it, and for all he knew, it did.

"Contact! Three o'clock!" Sergeant Cavanaugh shouted. "Get online!" Everyone in the squad rushed to their new positions in a line formation, both wedges turning to the right and straightening out to face the direction from which the imaginary attack was coming. They threw themselves down on the cold, wet ground. Sergeant Cavanaugh called out again. "Bravo Team! Suppressive fire! Alpha Team! Bound up!"

"Bang!Bang!Bang!" Joe yelled with the rest of B Team. They had to save their blank rounds for the day's official training, so like little kids, they were supposed to make gun noises.

Mac went all in on this, shouting out a weird "Uh-huh-huh-huh-huh! Pew! Pew! Blammo! Ka-POW!"

"Move it, Shockley!" A-Team leader Sergeant Hart yelled. Specialist Shockley was a big guy, and not in the muscular way like Specialist Quinn.

After a few seconds A Team dropped to the ground and B Team was ordered to bound forward, Cavanaugh moving with them, while A Team laid down suppressive fire. Joe sprang to his feet and sprinted forward with his M16. "I'm up!He sees me!I'm down!" He and his fireteam threw themselves back to the ground. Joe slid down in a patch of mud, smearing his knees, elbows, belly, and chest. *Oh man. I just washed this uniform.* He didn't mind getting dirty. That was part of the Army and especially part of the infantry. But now he'd lose even more of his limited free time to laundry.

First Squad continued, providing cover fire and bounding until Sergeant Cavanaugh called out Limit of Advance. "LOA! LOA! Gather round." He looked the squad over. "Right. That was good. Just remember when you're bounding, move ahead fast, but don't stay up long. You don't want to give the enemy time to aim at you. So 'I'm up. He sees me. I'm down.' Now, we have a few minutes before the rest of the platoon gets out here. Let's run it again."

———◦———

A few days later, Joe sat in one of Fort Hood's auditoriums as the lights dimmed and Staff Sergeant Connors switched on the screen to start the PowerPoint. "Good morning. This next block of instruction will concern Improvised Explosive Devices, or IEDs." The slide advanced to a photo of a destroyed Humvee, shredded wide open in the front like a blown-up firecracker. Sergeant Connors began to read from the next slide in the same slow monotone he used on all his PowerPoints. "Some of these slides, I will read for you. Others you can read for yourself."

Joe, and probably everybody else, was done reading the slide long before Connors finished.

Joe rubbed his hand over his face. *It's the same dumb PowerPoint that we saw last week.*

"Explosive compounds such as claylike C4 or gun powder can be reshaped so that they may be placed into many different containers. Such as . . ." Connors advanced to a picture slide for each item. "A Pepsi can. A Coke can. A beer can. Or even a can of chew."

Joe jabbed himself in the leg with his pen to stay awake.

———◇———

As the weeks went by, Joe adapted to Army life. Except on the toilet, he was never alone, always surrounded by hundreds of other soldiers. Living, working, eating, and even sleeping close to these men, Joe soon let go of the rhythms of college and learned to measure life not in midterm exams and semesters, but in marches and ranges for rifles and machine guns. He especially grew accustomed to, if not comfortable with, Sergeant Paulsen, PFC Baccam, and Corporal MacDonald, the guys in his own fireteam.

One morning First Squad gathered near a pole barn outside of which was parked a Humvee, its back in open configuration like a pickup, with benches along either side.

"I wonder what this is supposed to be about," PFC Baccam said to Joe. "Maybe some driving training."

Joe spotted a pile of sand and some shovels about twenty yards away. "I don't know. Doesn't look good though."

"Man, none of this is ever good," Mac said.

Staff Sergeant Connors climbed out of the Humvee and smiled.

"Just got worse," said Sergeant Paulsen.

"Oh goodie," said Z. "Here comes Captain CONUS."

Someone in the company had been talking to Connors and learned the man had never deployed. He hadn't even been stationed some place like Germany, never left the continental United States, hence CONUS.

"Morning men!" said Captain CONUS. "Ready for some more high-speed training?"

"*Huuuuuaaaaaaah!*" Corporal MacDonald shouted the stupid old enthusiastic cry that was only used in Army basic training and nowhere else.

The guys laughed. CONUS didn't seem to understand Mac was making fun of him.

"Roger that! Kudos on that enthusiasm, trooper. Now as you may remember from my IED PowerPoint presentation, we are having lots of problems with IEDs over there." CONUS slapped the side of the Humvee. "Now we can armor these to withstand bullets and some blasts. But where we're having trouble is the underside. If an explosion goes off under the vehicle, it blasts up through the interior." CONUS paused for a moment to let that sink in. Then he smiled and nodded. "But don't worry. In this block of instruction I'll show you how to better protect yourself from IED blasts from below by hardening your vehicle." A quick pause. "'Hardening? What's that?' Is that what you're asking?"

"That's just exactly what I was about to ask!" Mac said.

Sergeant Paulsen bit his lip to hold back a smile as he elbowed Mac.

"Now what you're gonna wanna do when you're over there in Iraq—"

"Afghanistan," said PFC Zimmerman.

"Oh, right," said CONUS. "But when you get there, what you're gonna wanna do is fill up sandbags, see? Now not too full because you want them somewhat flexible. OK? Three to six inches thick. Then, you're gonna wanna place those sandbags on the floor of your Humvee. That will provide an extra layer of protection from any IED blasts."

Joe looked from the Humvee to the pile of sand. This didn't make sense. Humvees were already a cramped ride. How would they all fit if they took off up to half a foot of room from the floor?

"This country has flown to the moon," Corporal MacDonald said quietly.

"Say again?" Captain CONUS asked.

"This country has sent men flying all the way to the moon," Mac started.

"If you believe that really happened," PFC Zimmerman said quietly with a smirk.

Mac ignored him. "We have the best military in the world.

And that's the plan? Sandbags?" Mac pressed the side of his rifle barrel against his forehead. "Sandbags! They couldn't, I don't know, build a Humvee with a tougher bottom, or weld some extra steel down there? So now, we have to stand here and listen to you . . . people . . . tell us that we're all going to die from IEDs blowing up our trucks—"

CONUS held up a hand. "Well, now hold on there. You're not going to die because as soon as you get to Iraq, you're gonna wanna get some sandbags and—"

"Afghanistan!" Mac shouted. "They are actually two different places! This is the stupidest thing I have ever heard. The absolute best America's most gifted minds could come up with is filling the bottom of our vehicle with dirt."

"Well, now," said CONUS. "Actually, what you'll use is sand, and you're gonna wanna—"

"I can't handle it!" Mac shouted.

"Hey, take it easy, Corporal MacDonald," Sergeant Paulsen said. "We'll figure this out."

Alpha Team's leader, Sergeant Hart, joined in. "Excuse me, Sergeant Connors, but if we line the bottom of our Humvee with sand, and a bomb goes off underneath it, won't that just basically make the whole thing a giant sand Claymore mine?"

"Well, now, kudos to you, Sergeant Hart, for thinking of that. See, the idea is that these sandbags will become very firmly packed by everybody walking on them. That will make a kind of wall. So it won't be quite, you know, loose sand. Now, let's all try this out. I have some sandbags here in the vehicle, and a pile of sand and shovels over there. Let's practice hardening this Humvee."

Joe shook his head. There was no way anyone needed to practice shoveling sand into bags. Corporal MacDonald complained too much and was easily upset, but he was right about this sandbag Humvee situation. Joe wanted to throw up. This was the stupidest, scariest thing he'd learned in the Army so far.

———◇———

"What is this supposed to teach us?" Mac asked, several days later. Joe's squad was riding in the back of a Humvee configured like a pickup with sandbags lining the floor. His team sat on the passenger-side bench pointing their rifles out from the vehicle's right. Alpha Team covered the other side. Sergeant Cavanaugh drove. They'd been doing a lot of training in Humvees and five-ton trucks through the last few weeks. Right now they were conducting a simulated patrol during which they would be evaluated on how well they identified and reacted to IED threats.

"We could do this in a video game," Mac said.

Joe didn't mind this training as much. At least they could sit down instead of marching.

"Come on, guys," said Baccam. "This training might save our lives."

PFC Zimmerman craned his neck to look over the Humvee's cab. "What's that? In the tree up there?"

"Oh you gotta be kidding me," Mac said.

Up ahead, at eye level, a Coke can hung from blue inert det cord.

"Hey, Sergeant Cavanaugh," Joe called down into the open-backed cab. "I think maybe that's supposed to be the IED."

The Humvee stopped. Three more halted behind them.

"We need to move," said Sergeant Paulsen. "If this were a real IED in Afghanistan, the enemy would probably have an ambush ready for us."

"I'd call it in on the radio, if this rig had a radio," said Sergeant Cavanaugh.

"Sergeant Cavanaugh?" Specialist Shockley spoke up. "If I may suggest. This IED is hanging there, which means it has to be command-detonated by a trigger man. If we sent one highly motivated individual, such as myself, out into the woods to find and neutralize the trigger man, the IED would be rendered useless, and we could drive through, no problem."

Joe looked at Specialist Shockley. Was he serious? This was just a training exercise.

"That's the dumbest idea I've heard yet," Mac said.

"I can do it!" Shockley insisted. "I have the military knowledge and experience."

"Knowledge and ex— This is all pretend," Mac said. "Don't you get that? There's no trigger man to neutralize because this isn't a war and that's not an IED, but a pop can tied to a branch."

"Some of us are taking this seriously, Mac," said Shockley. "You know, because our lives depend on it."

"Even if this were real, sending you out into the woods by yourself would be the stupidest plan. You'd be shot and killed. Four or five of us would have to carry your fat body back to the vehicle, and we'd all be shot in the process."

"I wouldn't get shot, because I have superior field-craft and infiltration skills."

Corporal MacDonald laughed and was about to reply when Sergeant Hart interrupted. "What if we just go around it?"

"Whatever we do, we need to get out of the kill zone," said Sergeant Paulsen.

"We're going around." Sergeant Cavanaugh cranked the wheel and hit the gas.

"Weapons up," Joe said, pulling his M16 back inside the Humvee as tree branches swept the side of the vehicle. The convoy followed their improvised bypass and returned to the dirt road, driving on. Finally the route bent around a corner to a more open area where the tree line pulled back about fifty yards.

Joe spotted him first. A white guy, with his BDUs turned inside out and a towel wrapped around his head, was rushing out from the woods. "Allah Ackbar!" He ran down the hill with a plastic AK-47. "Abu jabba doodaaa woodaa!"

"This is really pathetic," said Baccam.

Sergeant Paulsen shook his head in disgust at the terrible terrorist impersonation. "Go ahead and shoot off all your blanks." He raised his rifle and pulled the trigger.

"They're blanks," Mac protested. "It's not like we have to aim. It'll just mean we have to clean our weapons forever."

"First Sergeant will make you shoot 'em all off anyway," Joe pointed out. He and Baccam had tried to keep their weapons clean on the last training exercise by not firing their blanks. When they'd attempted to return their sixty blank rounds to the armory NCO, First Sergeant Dalton yelled at them and forced them to fire off every blank they had.

In seconds, Joe's magazine was empty, that warm whiff of gunpowder rising from the ejector port.

"Well," Mac said when the fake shooting was done. "That was pointless."

———◇———

"This is crap," Specialist Shockley said, for the fourth time. Or was it the four hundredth? First Squad was returning from a shooting range in the back of a five-ton truck, on the first warm sunny day in a long time. "I mean, if this is the kind of support we can expect from our leadership, we are all going to die over there."

Joe sighed deeply, adjusted his position, and put his chin on his chest, trying to sleep. Save for the regular rumbling of the truck's engine, it was a nice, quiet day, perfect for a quick snooze. His eyes began to droop for a moment.

"Those were my magazines!" Shockley started up again. Joe jerked awake. Shockley continued, "I cut the five-fifty cord and taped the loops on the magazines myself. I specifically asked if I would get my magazines back, and First Sergeant Dalton said 'Sure.'"

Joe spoke before thinking. "Please stop!" His tone was a little harsh. Technically, Specialist Shockley outranked Joe, who was still a private first class, but in the National Guard, rank didn't really count for much until a soldier made sergeant. "Nobody is going to die because of your stupid magazines, Specialist! They don't matter."

When Shockley was surprised, he'd do this thing where his chin would double up, his mouth would fall open, and his eyes would go wide.

"Why would you even buy your own ammo magazines anyway?"

"I didn't buy them," Shockley said.

Joe frowned. "They were just regular magazines that aren't even secured items?"

"They were mine!" Shockley said. "I taped on loops of five-fifty cord."

Mac was laughing now. Sergeant Hart smiled and sat up.

"Are the magazines listed on your official inventory of gear?" Joe asked. "Do you even have a hand receipt from supply for those magazines? Do you know the serial numbers for those magazines?"

"No, but you see, I—"

More of the squad was laughing now. Joe was relieved they were finally coming to their senses and not taking Shockley's crap anymore.

"I didn't write the serial number down, but anyone could see the five-fifty cord that I—"

Joe imagined himself as a hard-hitting TV journalist. "So last night you obeyed orders and forked over two ammo clips like we *all* did, so they could be loaded before we shot today. After shooting, we all got two magazines back. Just tape on new loops if it bothers you that much."

"No," Shockley cut in. "Not if they're just going to be stolen again, and—"

"Or *don't* tape on stupid loops," said Joe. "Either way, shut up about the stupid magazines! Nobody cares!"

"Boom!" Mac shouted. "PFC Killer comes alive! I like it! Better watch out, Shockley."

Specialist Shockley squinted his eyes and pressed his lips together. For the rest of the ride back to the barracks Joe could finally enjoy some rare peace and relative quiet.

———◇———

By mid-May, the monotony of their training started breaking up. Rumors of impending travel to Afghanistan began to fly. One day, their entire task force, several entire infantry companies, shed their green BDUs and donned the much lighter tan tones of the Desert Camouflage Uniforms.

"This is finally starting to feel real," Mac said to Joe and Baccam. "The official uniform of war."

"I'm just glad for these new tan boots that we don't have to polish," Joe said.

All soldiers were ordered to ship everything home that

they didn't plan to take with them, and all incoming mail would now be stopped until they were issued a new mailing address in Afghanistan.

One day they lined up to draw their weapons from the armory. "Guard this M16 with your life, Private," said the armory NCO. "From now until the end of your deployment, it will be with you, a part of you, at all times."

This was a holy commandment, a rule that must have been written down somewhere in the Army regs, but which was so strictly enforced that it didn't need to be written down. In the Army, no matter what else happened, a soldier never ever lost control of or misplaced his weapon. He would sleep next to it, take it to chow, take it to the latrine. Maybe when he took a shower, he could ask a trusted fellow soldier to keep watch over it. But outside of that, this M16 was to be with him, under his control, at every moment.

By the third week in May, their training burdens lightened. There were no more firing ranges, no more patrols through the woods. Finally Joe and his fellow soldiers had some extra time to themselves. Even Sergeant Cavanaugh couldn't fill every second of every day with redundant training. Joe used most of his free time for reading, devouring the Ernie Pyle book Mr. Kane had given him. Ernie Pyle wrote story after story of soldiers enduring impossible hardships and horrors. The accounts were never gory. They didn't have to be. The details about all the debris washed up on the beaches after the D-Day invasion were enough to give the reader at least some understanding of the horrific scale of the death on that day. Reading the war accounts made him nervous.

Afghanistan is nothing like World War II, he told himself. *And they'd send Special Forces or a big active duty unit into the most dangerous places.* And yet, Joe was uncertain how he felt about that. He didn't want to go to war, but he knew his country had been attacked and it was his duty to fight. If he had to fight, he might as well face the worst of it and make a real difference destroying this Muslim terrorist army.

But even when he thought this way, his heart beat heavy and he had to wipe his clammy hands on his uniform. The night before, during the end-of-day squad briefing, they'd been told they would leave for Afghanistan very soon but, for security reasons, would not be informed of the exact day or time.

Then, at last, the day came when there was nothing left for his company to do but go to war. Everything had been packed up and shipped out. They were all transported to Fort Hood's airfield, M16 rifles or M249 squad automatic weapons in hand, and there before them waited a massive charter jet.

Finally, months of training are over. Three of the longest months in history.

Joe stood in line with his squad, waiting to board the jet. Corporal MacDonald in front of him. Baccam behind him.

"This must be the most unusual flight in America today, hundreds of people carrying knives and guns boarding a civilian passenger jet with no security screening," Mac said.

Shockley huffed. "I don't think the Army is too worried, Corporal. It's not like one of us soldiers are going to hijack the plane."

"I know that, Shockley," Mac fired back. "Take it easy. I wasn't trying to point out a security risk, just noting the weirdness of it all."

Joe pulled one of his half dozen disposable cameras from his cargo pocket. He didn't want to waste all the film here in the States, but this was a big moment. "Baccam, stand here next to me. Hold your M16 up all tough-guy style." Joe put his arm around his friend and, with his rifle slung, held the camera up with his other hand.

"You're going to take a picture of yourself?" Baccam asked. "Hope it looks OK when you finally get it developed."

"Smile, Baccam!" Joe said. "We're going to war!"

Many hours later, after a stop to refuel in Bangor, Maine, their jet was back in the air, leaving America, heading to war.

MAY 27, 2003
Over New Brunswick, Canada.

Several hundred Iowa Army National Guard soldiers departed the United States this evening on their way to Afghanistan in support of Operation Enduring Freedom. Over the past three months, the soldiers have trained nearly constantly, sharpening their shooting skills, practicing reactions to various enemy threats, and learning about the tactics of the ruthless, cowardly Muslim terrorists they will soon have to fight.

Joe put his pen down for a moment. There was more to write, much more, but he couldn't figure out how to express the way he was feeling, at least in the context of the morale of the hundreds of other soldiers on the plane with him, most of whom were asleep by now. For so long, he'd wanted to be an objective journalist, reporting the facts, telling the unbiased truth. The who, what, when, where, and why of the story of his unit was easy to tell, and yet, the summary of it felt completely inadequate.

He yawned and settled lower in his seat, trying to remember something he'd read near the end of Ernie Pyle's *Brave Men*. It was something about how the soldiers had been gone for a long time and how so much had happened to them. How they'd done things people back home could not know or understand. How the soldiers would be changed.

Will I change? Joe wondered. Had he already changed since he'd been activated for duty, beyond turning nineteen and realizing that Army training often left a lot to be desired? *And if I survive my time in this war, how do I get back into real life?*

The view from the window had turned completely to the dark water of the North Atlantic. *Goodbye, America. I hope I'll see you again.*

8

FARAH, AFGHANISTAN
May 27, 2003

W hen do you do your homework?" Baheer asked his brother in their bedroom before school.

"My classmate does it for me." Rahim shrugged and left the room.

Rahim had been acting strangely for months. School wasn't easy. Some of his teachers were very strict. But none of them beat the students, and there were no Taliban to harass them. For Baheer, time spent studying or at school was a welcome break from farm work. Rahim didn't see it that way. Why did he bother with school at all, if he refused to try?

Out in the main room of their house, Baheer's father shook his head as he looked over papers, probably the latest figures from the rug business. Mother held out a small plate with a piece of naan.

"Here," she said quietly. "You'll feel better if you eat something. The business will work out. Insha Allah."

Baheer's stomach rumbled as he looked at the bread. Breakfast had been small. Dinner the night before hadn't been much bigger.

Father waved the food away. "No, no. For the kids." His father seemed to notice Baheer then. "Off to school?" Baheer nodded. Father forced a smile. "Good. Study hard. But hurry back after. Your grandfather has a lot for you to do on the farm. We're all counting on the next harvest."

"Of course, Father," Baheer said.

As usual, Maryam met Baheer in the front courtyard as he picked up his bike, so she could close and lock the compound door behind him. She smiled, eyeing his schoolbag. "Will you please remember to write down more of the questions your teachers ask you so I can go over it all when you get home?"

Baheer smiled. "I always do."

She bumped her shoulder against him. "Last week you left out a lot of what was discussed."

Baheer laughed. "I'm doing my best. It's hard to keep up."

Maryam let out a long breath. "I just wish I could go with you."

"I know." Baheer patted her arm and walked his bike out to the street. She closed and locked the door behind him. Rahim must have ridden on ahead, for he was nowhere in sight. Just as Baheer was about to hop on and pedal off, an enormous truck roared around the corner onto his street and rolled up to the compound next door. It was hauling gravel and sacks of cement. When no one was looking, Baheer sneaked in with a large group of workers who had gathered around the compound door. He was nervous about trespassing, but no one had lived in this compound since his family had moved to the neighborhood.

Who is moving in now?

Inside, a dozen workers spread a pile of river rock to blanket the muddy compound floor. Beyond a tree at the far end of the compound, workers shoveled wheelbarrow loads of manure out of the back stables. Other men stacked sacks of cement. One group was building a concrete platform a little over a meter high by the front wall near the main gate.

Baheer wanted to explore more, but one of the workers shouted, "Boro, kid!"

Baheer hurried out, hopped on his bike, and headed down the road.

At school, Rahim was already playing soccer with his classmates. The bell rang, and the students gathered in front of the principal's office, lining up in order from the best student to the worst.

Baheer watched Faisal, the current genius leading his class, from his own place in the middle of the line. *That will be me someday.*

A middle-aged man in Western-style clothes came in through the main gate, heading toward the office.

From behind him, Omar asked, "Who's that?"

"No idea," Baheer answered.

A low rumble of barely contained laughter rose up from the students.

"You can see the outline of his butt in those American-style pants." Omar laughed and lifted his own tunic, pulling his loose pants tight over his own butt, shaking it at Baheer.

"So what?" Baheer said. "I wore pants and shirts when I went to school in Pakistan. Everyone did."

"It looks ridiculous." Omar chuckled.

Baheer's cheeks burned hot. When he'd first started school here, everyone had assumed he was an unlearned illiterate dirt farmer from one of the remote tribes. It had taken a lot of work, patience, and studying to make his way to the middle of the line and to gain the respect of the other boys. Now, he shut his mouth before they mocked him simply because he'd once dressed like people outside of Farah, Afghanistan.

The headmaster emerged onto the concrete platform outside his office, and the students settled down. The man dabbed his sweaty forehead with a handkerchief.

"Qari Esmat! Come up here and recite some verses from the Holy Quran to begin our day," he said. Esmat was in eighth grade and was often chosen as the Qari, the reciter of scripture, because his voice was soothing.

After prayers and the national anthem, the principal came forward. "Students! Today we have our deputy director

Saheb from the education department with us here. Afghanistan has changed a lot recently. Girls are going to school today. Many of you study English. Two years ago, we had only one or two institutions. Now we have many. It's a new Afghanistan."

Why is he giving this lecture now? Baheer glanced at Omar, who shrugged.

"Our country has changed so we must also change," the headmaster continued. "Now, our deputy director wants to speak to you. Welcome him."

The official nodded. "President Hamid Karzai has ordered all employees of government offices to wear pants of any color along with a shirt. This rule also applies to public schools and universities." He pointed at his pants and shirt as he talked.

After the announcement, the students were sent to their classes.

"Let's ask our parents for the clothes," Faisal said. "We can wear them starting tomorrow."

"They can't force us to change. I'll never put my butt on display," Omar replied. "It's a dumb Western rule. Just because the Americans are in our country."

Baheer couldn't keep quiet. Even if this idea came from the Americans, they'd forced the Taliban into hiding. How bad could they be? But this had nothing to do with the Americans anyway. "The dress code isn't a Western or Eastern idea. In Pakistan, all Afghans and Pakistanis wore a uniform unique to their school. Here, we're allowed to wear whatever color or style we like."

"Baheer is right," Faisal confirmed.

"You Pakistani lentil eater!" Omar shouted. Everyone laughed.

Baheer's cheeks flared hot. This ridiculous hostility toward anything a few people considered non-Afghan was part of the dangerously backward thinking that drove the Taliban. Baheer hoped school was to be the key for a new Afghanistan, so it hurt to see this ignorance in his classroom. He would have said more about it, but the teacher would be in the room any moment. "I didn't expect this from you, Omar." Omar didn't seem to hear him.

The next morning Baheer was careful to delay his departure for school so that Rahim would leave without him. As soon as his brother was out of sight, he pedaled quickly on his bike to reach the spot under the twisted tree by the irrigation ditch. If he timed it just right, Baheer would see his Mystery Girl, and she would see him in his fancy Western-style school uniform. He dismounted to walk his bike and hold on to the moment as long as he could. Although both he and Mystery Girl would be in terrible trouble if anyone found out about them, he was amazed at how much he looked forward to seeing her. That morning she hadn't covered her beautiful face. He felt the sweetest ache deep in his chest at the sight of her bright smile, and he remembered Maulana Balkhi's poem: "Disclosing your blushing, rosy face / Its ecstasy enlivens a stone."

He replied with a quick smile of his own, and, after he passed her, he risked looking back. If anyone saw him do this, they'd know at once this wasn't an innocent interaction.

Mystery Girl raised her eyebrows, pointing at his bag. His cheeks flared hot. They were practically talking now! He couldn't believe it.

He held his palms up like an open book to indicate that he was going to school and had books to read. She showed her books as well.

Baheer climbed onto his bike again and rode off, his heart pounding. He didn't look back, but he couldn't stop smiling. When he'd first encountered Mystery Girl, he'd been dressed in work clothes, looking like an illiterate village peasant. Now he was a solid middle-of-the-line student, with his eye on the top position. If he ever did lead the line, how could he let her know?

He wanted to know more about her, but he would never dream of dishonoring her in any way. He'd like to know her name, though. Was that so terrible? Who was she? Where did she live? How had she managed to get permission to go to school? And maybe the answers to these questions would allow him to help Maryam get an education, too.

———◇———

After school at the farm, as Baheer changed into work clothes, he wondered if he could trust his brother enough to tell him about Mystery Girl. Rahim could be helpful in the future—he could be a lookout when Baheer passed her on the road—but how could he even *begin* such a serious discussion? They all went to school. Maybe he could start there. "School here is better than in Kabul."

Rahim didn't look up from the big tuft of grass he was cutting. "At least here they don't beat us."

Baheer rested his sickle by his side. "Thanks be to Allah, the Americans sent the Taliban running. Everything's so different now. A new Afghanistan, you know?"

"Cut, man. It's getting dark," Rahim said.

"I just mean," Baheer said, picking up his sickle again, "a year ago, who would have thought we'd have new uniforms for school, and that there would be so many girls going to school too?"

Rahim finally looked up, a scowl on his sweaty face. "The uniforms are terrible. The stupid pants are so tight. It's just the Americans trying to make us be like them." He grasped another handful of grass and smoothly whipped the sharp scythe into position. "And what's the point of all these girls in school? They say education is supposed to help us do better in life, but I don't see how reading dumb old poems or learning about stuff that happened a hundred years ago is going to help us cut more grass or fix the family rug business. If school won't help us, it's double useless for girls."

Baheer forced a little laugh. "You sound like a talib."

"No!" He spat on the ground. "But maybe with the no-girls-in-school rule, they had at least one thing right."

Baheer stared at his brother. "That's not funny," he said.

117

"Especially with the rumors that Taliban cells are moving back into Farah."

Any hope Baheer had harbored for his brother's help with Mystery Girl died with this one little statement of sympathy for the Taliban.

———◇———

"You hear, boys?" Baba Jan said later that night. "Tomorrow after morning prayer, go to the farm. Water the vineyard. Then cut double the amount of grass because I'm buying another cow. Finally, water the grass because the land was quite dry yesterday. You're not doing your work."

"Another cow?" Baheer said.

"One cow's not enough," Baba Jan said.

"We have midterm exams soon." Baheer tried his best to avoid sounding disrespectful, but if he did well on these exams, especially in his English class, where he was already one of the best students, he had a real chance to move himself to the front of the line.

"Work. Then study," Baba Jan said casually as he left the room, as if exams didn't matter.

Baheer looked at Rahim and Maryam. "He wanted us to go to school. Now he's torturing us," he said quietly.

"Maybe you haven't noticed, but the family is struggling," Rahim said. "Relax about the stupid exams. No amount of studying ever provided food for the family."

"Shut up," Maryam shouted at Rahim, surprising him. Even though she was two years older than Rahim, it was still uncommon for girls to yell at boys like that. "You should be more serious about your studies. At least you get to go to school!"

Rahim frowned darkly. "Who are you telling me what to do?"

"Stop it, Rahim. She's right," Baheer said.

Maryam broke into tears and left the room.

"What's the matter with you?" Baheer said to Rahim, going after Maryam. He caught up to her before she entered her room. "Forget Rahim. Something's wrong with him lately."

Maryam tried to stop crying. "It's fine, Brother," she said, and went into her room.

Baheer went up to the roof of the guesthouse and sat on a folding chair. Looking up, he saw billions of stars shining in Farah's pitch-black night sky. A brighter star glittered in the east. He watched it shine and whispered to himself, "I hate the farm. That's not the kind of work Allah intends for me."

Maybe Rahim had a point. It was hard to see how studying would lead to more money, and the family business was struggling. But the farm wasn't bringing in much money either.

Baheer loved his teachers, his books, and learning. He put his face in his palms, his thick, rough calluses scratching his cheeks. He whispered, both in prayer and as a promise to himself, "I no longer fear the farm. It will not break me." He looked again to the stars and smiled as he stood. There had to be a way to make school work. *Nothing will stop me from learning.*

9

KANDAHAR, AFGHANISTAN
May 29, 2003

You step off the trail, you die!" An Air Force technical sergeant who looked like he'd spent over half of his time on his deployment lifting weights in the base gym was briefing Joe's platoon about Kandahar Air Force Base. "The Russians left millions of land mines buried all over Afghanistan. We ain't cleared 'em all yet."

He went on talking about base regulations and chow hall hours. Joe struggled to stay awake. The flight had been eternal. From Texas to Maine to Germany to Turkey to former Soviet territory Kyrgyzstan, there'd been so many sunrises and sunsets that nobody knew what day it was. Finally, after waiting half a day among the Soviet ruins in Kyrgyzstan, they were sorted into groups to board military planes on their way into Afghanistan, their new home for the next year.

Apart from Army training in Georgia and Texas, Joe had barely been out of Iowa. Now in one trip he'd been in four different countries. It was all so strange and different. He felt like an astronaut landing on another planet. What should he do? How should he act?

"Wake up, soldiers!" the Air Force guy shouted. Joe sat up straight and took in a sharp breath, blinking away sleep. The tech sergeant continued, "Since you gonna be here at Kandahar Air Base on a temporary basis, we got you set up in temporary housing, in the tents on the other side of the runway. Now remember we got problems with snakes, rodents, and camel spiders. Check your boots before putting them on to make sure nothing's crawling round inside."

Joe looked to Baccam in the seat next to him like, *Is this for real?* Being stuck in a war with the threat of IEDs and the Taliban was bad enough without having to worry about being bitten just putting on his boots.

"Sounds awesome," Baccam whispered.

The sky was beginning to brighten by the time they were released from the briefing and led to the small tent city where their whole infantry task force had assembled. Joe rubbed his hands over his face. He needed a shave. After so much traveling and with no chance to clean up, he was way out of Army shaving regs. But then, so was everyone else.

"Up all night," Baccam said. "But I'm not that tired. I hope the Army lets us adjust to local time."

Joe could see more of the base now, a mix of tents, wood

buildings, concrete structures, and tan mud-brick ruins full of bullet holes. On the flight line, the control tower looked a little more modern and permanent. Dry sand and powdery dust was everywhere, interrupted by a handful of palm trees. Definitely not Iowa. How could people live in this dried-out wasteland? Joe flopped down on a dusty green cot next to a concrete bunker that had been fortified with sandbags. Baccam yawned, put his SAW down on its bipod, and took a seat next to him.

"The sun will be up soon," Baccam said. "Might as well stay awake for our first dawn in Afghanistan."

Joe didn't say anything. He was glad Baccam was here with him. Joe had only been training on one-weekend-per-month drills with Delta Company for about a year. He'd never been to the two-week annual training with them. And a lot of them had served together for years, spent a lot of time laughing over old jokes Joe didn't understand. Some of them, like Shockley or the arrogant former active-duty Third Squad leader Staff Sergeant Lucas, drove Joe crazy. But Baccam was cool and, like Joe, relatively new to the unit.

"Or maybe you already fell asleep?" Baccam asked him.

Joe laughed a little. "No, I'm awake. Just thinking. This isn't what I expected war would be like."

Baccam looked at his watch. "Take it easy, Killer. We've only been in-country for about an hour and fifteen minutes. What'd you expect? That they'd drop us right into a firefight when we got here?"

Joe flicked a frayed bit of his weapon's shoulder strap with his thumb. "No. Just that the perimeter is so far off we can't even see it. You don't even get the sense we're in any danger."

Baccam leaned back and rested his head against the sandbags stacked behind him. "Every war has its rear area. My dad said the big American bases in Vietnam were totally different than the hot zones out in the bush."

"You're Vietnamese?" Joe asked.

"No, I'm American," Baccam answered.

Joe's cheeks went hot. "Oh, dude, I'm sorry. I didn't mean—"

Baccam elbowed him and laughed. "I know what you meant. My family is Tai Dam, an ethnic minority from Southeast Asia living in Laos, Thailand, and Vietnam. My family and I came to Iowa from Vietnam in 1980, but I don't remember that."

"Well, I'm glad you came," Joe said.

Baccam smiled. "To Iowa or to Afghanistan?"

"Both." Joe sighed. "Look at this place. Nothing but dust and scrub brush everywhere." He pointed to a white building with little towers, the tops of which were painted blue. "A mosque, I guess? All shot up with bullet holes."

"Yeah, I hear Kandahar was kind of the last stand for the Taliban."

"My point," said Joe, "is you figure an American Air Force base housing multimillion-dollar aircraft has to be one of the best, most developed places in Afghanistan. If that's true. If this is the best of Afghanistan, this country must really be a dump."

"I don't know, man," Baccam said, frowning. "I bet soldiers said the same thing thirty years ago about Vietnam."

"That was different," Joe said. He didn't elaborate. From what Joe had read, Vietnam was a complicated situation. Afghanistan was simple. These people had contributed to the deaths of thousands of innocent American civilians and had to pay for it.

The smell of smoke drifted over them, and the crunch of boots on gravel betrayed the approach of Corporal MacDonald, holding a cheap cigar. "We're supposed to be one year, boots on the ground. Three hundred sixty-five days to go."

Joe winced at the thought of that kind of eternity here. He was about to tell Mac not to count down the days, but he'd learned that in the Army telling the guys you didn't like something was a definite way to make sure they never stopped doing it.

"Aw, come on, Corporal Mac." Baccam laughed. "You're gonna re-up. Five thousand dollar reenlistment bonus? Tax-free?"

Joe noticed Mac's rifle, a thirty-round magazine in the well. Mac caught his eye and blew out a long plume of smoke. "Helmets, rucksacks, and armored vests are waiting for us in the tent. You gotta get yours, put it by your rack. Then you're supposed to check in with Sergeant Cavanaugh and draw seven fully loaded magazines. One in the rifle, three in each of your ammo pouches on your armor vest."

"Live rounds?" Joe asked.

Mac flicked ash in his general direction. "No, paintball rounds. Yes, live rounds! What d'ya think this is, a church summer camp picnic?"

Joe stood and shot Baccam a look. "Well, let's go get some bullets."

Baccam got up and slapped Joe on the shoulder. "Starting to feel more and more like a war all the time."

—◇—

A couple of weeks later Delta Company took their turn in a big half-moon-shaped tent. Joe sat with his squad, sweating in the heat at 0900. They were finally going to learn about their mission.

An Army captain conducted the briefing. "Afghanistan has been plagued by years of war. In 1979 the Soviet Union invaded, killing many innocent Afghans and deploying millions of land mines, making farming and transportation impossible in some areas. After the Soviets were expelled ten years later, a civil war followed, as different Afghan warlords struggled for power. The civil war was ended in the mid-nineties by the Taliban, a brutal militia that practices an extreme form of Islam.

"The Taliban passed a series of oppressive decrees. Punishment for violating any of their laws could be extreme.

In Afghanistan's capital city of Kabul, they would force crowds into an old soccer stadium to watch them stone people, including women, to death for stuff like being accused of adultery. It took us two weeks to wash all the blood from the ground in that stadium."

"These people are barbarians," Joe whispered.

The captain continued. "Eventually the Taliban allied themselves with Al-Qaeda, the terrorists responsible for the attacks on America on September 11."

Joe wiped his sweaty brow, eager to hear about his chance to hit these terrorists back. He was infantry, after all, and a solid shot with his M16 and half a dozen other weapons.

The captain continued. "You'll help to establish and provide force protection for Provincial Reconstruction Teams, or PRTs. You'll protect Civil Affairs, or CA, soldiers whose job it is to meet with Afghans to assess how we can help them rebuild their transportation, communication, and educational infrastructure. You'll work closely with the Afghans. The military believes a prosperous, stable Afghanistan can more effectively resist becoming a stronghold for terrorism again."

Joe stared in disbelief. This couldn't be right. Help Afghanistan? That wasn't what he had signed up for. He was infantry! He didn't want to help. This was supposed to be payback time. He wanted to fight.

He looked around to see if the others were outraged. A few mumbled with discontent. This was the Army, though.

Not a democracy. Orders were orders and nothing could be done to change them.

"It's a rewarding mission," said the captain. "I've been honored to be part of it for the last year."

A trickle of sweat ran down into the back of Joe's pants. He was holding his notebook in case he needed to write down anything important, and flipping through the pages, Joe saw all his attempts at reporting on his war experience so far. What could he report on now? Nobody wanted to read about soldiers who sat around on bases trying to help people who would probably stab them all in the back at their first opportunity anyway. He was supposed to be writing stories about intense combat situations, letting readers know the truth about what was happening in this war. Now his whole deployment was meaningless.

———◇———

One morning about two weeks later, still living in a giant red-and-white-striped circus tent on Kandahar base, Joe rolled over and ducked further down inside his sleeping bag, hoping to steal a little more sleep. The A10 "Warthog" ground-attack jets had roared at intervals through the night as they took off and landed on the nearby runway. It had quieted a little toward morning, but then the winds picked up, and the tent fabric flapped and fluttered so loud it sounded like a drum.

"Can't sleep either?" Baccam said quietly from the cot next to Joe's.

Joe pulled the sleeping bag down off his face. Baccam was already sitting up and shaking his boots to dump out any possible hostile intruders. "Chow?" Joe asked.

Baccam shook his head. "Coffee first."

There was free coffee in the chow hall, but by now Joe knew Baccam meant he wanted to buy an expensive "frack-acheemo" or whatever at the Green Beans coffee shop near the post exchange store. It was a waste of money, but then there was nothing else to spend his pay on.

"If we're stuck on a humanitarian mission instead of being in a real war," Joe said to Baccam after they'd shaved, brushed their teeth, and ridden the shuttle bus from the transient tent back to the main section of the base, "let's spend the rest of the year here."

"Good morning, ma'am!" they both shouted, saluting a passing lieutenant colonel.

"I'd get bored," Baccam said. "So would you."

They were on the boardwalk now, passing the Burger King trailer and the ice cream hut before they joined the long coffee line. "You and your fancy coffee," Joe said to Baccam. "I hate you. Worse than the Taliban. The Taliban would never make me wait in a long coffee line when there's already free coffee in the DFAC."

Baccam laughed. "That free coffee is weak, and the Taliban would just kill you."

"Yeah," Joe said. "Put me out of my misery so I didn't have to wait with you in this overpriced coffee line."

After chow, Joe and Baccam stopped by the only other place on the base worth visiting, the Morale Wellness and Recreation building. The MWR was a big concrete structure left by the Soviets. One room had computers where people could sign up for fifteen minutes of slow internet. Another room offered phones. Joe preferred the computers. The phones had a delay both ways, making it almost necessary to say "over" to signal when you were done talking so the other person didn't talk over you. It took some practice.

"I'm gonna call my brother," Baccam said. "He just got a cellular phone and might still be up."

Joe waved him off and went the opposite way down the hall. The largest room in the MWR was the movie theater. Soldiers with portable players could borrow DVDs, too.

But as fun as *Spider-Man* might have been, Joe went to what had become his squad's quiet hideout on the otherwise big, loud airbase. The library.

Two couches on opposite sides of a coffee table dominated the room's center. The walls were lined with wooden bookshelves packed primarily with paperbacks.

Sergeant Paulsen had his boots on the table and sipped coffee from a paper cup while reading a book on the transcontinental railroad. Corporal Mac sat next to him.

Sergeant Hart, the A-Team leader, drank his own coffee on the opposite couch next to PFC Zimmerman. Specialist Quinn sat on a chair in the corner.

"Get this," Hart said. "I overheard someone talking, this

one *high-speed* guy who never shuts up about how he used to be active duty."

Joe listened while he looked over the books. A "high-speed" soldier usually meant a good soldier who didn't mess around, but Hart's sarcasm was obvious.

Hart continued, "He kept saying, 'We gotta show 'em who's boss!' like twenty times."

"Third Squad's Staff Sergeant Lucas." Mac laughed. "'Show 'em who's boss'? OK, tough guy."

Joe ran his finger along the spines of the books. Most were paperback Westerns or romances, but sometimes he could find an interesting biography, history, or novel. You never really knew what you were going to find because if you took out a book at Fort Hood, you could keep it or leave it at the base library wherever you ended up.

"He's just trying to show off," said Sergeant Hart.

"Worse than that," Sergeant Paulsen said. "These guys and their 'cracking skulls' mentality won't help us. We can't roll through Afghanistan pushing people around, threatening everybody, and treating them like dirt in their own country."

Joe frowned. This was a war, wasn't it? These people, or at least those wrapped up in the dominant philosophy of their country, had killed thousands of Americans. They had attacked America. They couldn't be reasoned with. Joe squeezed the M16 slung at his side.

Mac frowned. "Well, we're infantry, not diplomats."

Paulsen laughed. "I'm not saying we should let our

guard down. The Taliban are dangerous. But most of the people we'll encounter are just . . . normal people, some of them grateful we're fighting the Taliban."

Zimmerman spoke up. "But if we can't tell the Taliban from regular Afghan—"

"Exactly, Z!" Joe said a little louder than he'd intended.

"It's about our own survival," Paulsen said. "If you want to go home alive, we can't target all Afghans."

"Well, obviously, I'm not going to target all of them," Joe said.

"Wouldn't even have enough ammo for that," Specialist Quinn joked. Everybody chuckled.

"If some Afghan guys get up in our face, I'm not going to waste time asking if they're carrying a Taliban ID card," Joe said. *I shouldn't have to explain this. We're Army. We're the infantry.* "It's just crap we're on some kind of peace mission. That's not what I signed up for. We should be out there finding and destroying the Taliban village to village, door to door. Nobody gets in our way."

"How would you feel if a bunch of foreigners were in your neighborhood pushing your friends around?" Sergeant Paulsen asked. "Threatening your family?"

"I'd kill 'em," said Specialist Quinn.

"They're no different," said Paulsen. "You don't have to like or respect them, but if we go around trying to"—he made air quotes with his fingers—"'show 'em who's boss,' we'll push guys to join the Taliban. Or we'll at least cause some Afghans to not tell us about IEDs they've seen the Taliban deploy."

"Exactly," said Sergeant Hart. "We have rifles and machine guns. We can call in a freakin' A10 for close air support. We don't have to act tough. I swear, some of these guys want to get in a firefight, get people killed, just because they want their Combat Infantry Badge or whatever other ribbons and medals. This isn't the Boy Scouts."

Joe wasn't in this for glory or medals, but he didn't understand Hart's contempt for the CIB. They were only given to infantrymen who had actually been in combat. A lifetime award that said, "You were in the real thing."

Big Specialist Shockley burst in, his face red. "S-Sergeant Paulsen. Sergeant Hart." He took a deep breath. "Everybody. First Sergeant wants First and Second Squads down in the transient tent yesterday."

"What's up?" Sergeant Paulsen asked.

Shockley looked serious. "I think we're going outside the wire."

———◇———

"I said, you'd think maybe the Army could have given us a little more notice before ordering us to move to Farah," Joe shouted down into the Humvee through the gun turret to Corporal MacDonald in the back seat. Baccam was driving. Sergeant Paulsen rode shotgun, manning the radio. "I mean, we get up, average day in Kandahar—if that's a real thing—then *blammo*, we're rolling out."

"Oh, young soldier," Corporal Mac yelled up to him. "You got a lot to learn about the Army. Jerking you around is their favorite activity."

Joe stood behind the Mk 19 fully automatic grenade-launching machine gun, with the top half of his body protruding through a hole in the roof of the Humvee. Theirs was the trail vehicle. Alpha Team drove the lead Humvee, with their .50-cal. machine gun covering the three o'clock. Second Squad's two Humvees were ahead of them, covering forward and nine o'clock. Two Toyota Hilux pickups rode with the convoy, one between each squad's lead and trail Humvees.

When they'd first left the base, Joe had been tense, super alert, carefully watching every car, motorcycle, donkey, and pedestrian in Kandahar, his thumbs never far from the butterfly trigger on the back of his gun. But when they'd finally passed the outer villages into the open empty desert, there wasn't much to watch out for.

Joe looked around in the blazing hot sun as the Humvee bumped down the busted-up concrete highway. There was nothing out there. *It's like those photos of the surface of Mars. All rocks and dirt. Not even any proper sand dunes. Afghanistan can't even get a desert right.*

They rode like that for four hours, the bright sun baking him in his armor vest and helmet. The convoy rolled past an occasional tiny village made out of mud-brick walls and houses, off in the dirt beside the broken-up old highway.

Sometimes semis or shorter shipping trucks passed them heading in the other direction, back toward Kandahar.

And then, off in the distance, materializing through the heat-wave distortion off the highway, there was again a vehicle that had followed them three times before. "He's back!" Joe shouted down to the others. "That white Toyota station wagon is coming up fast."

"Roger that," Sergeant Paulsen called. "I'll call it in."

"He's got to be a Taliban scout," said Corporal Mac. "He passed us once before. Maybe he looped back around on a side road, or pulled off behind one of these zillion walls the Afghans love so much, and waited for us to pass."

"Could be an IED trigger man," Baccam said from the driver's seat.

"You have a machine gun," Mac shouted. "Unlock the turret so you can move the gun around. If he comes up close again, aim the thing right at him! If he tries to shoot us, well, you know what to do."

"I'll blast that car to shreds," Joe said.

But this time the white station wagon pulled up to within three car lengths. Joe shouted at them and tried to motion for them to back up. The car stayed right on them, though. Joe was about to start the procedure to chamber a 40-millimeter grenade round, preparing to fire, when the car finally turned off the highway onto a dirt road and vanished among the mud-brick walls of another small village.

An hour later, with no sign of the vehicle stalking them,

Mac shouted up to Joe. "Hey, there's a village up on the right side of the road. Bunch of boys messing around out in front of their wall." Mac handed up a green tennis ball. "Why don't you toss that to them, Killer?"

Joe frowned, glancing over his shoulder at the village they were about to pass. About seven boys in big loose shirts and pants, the same pajamas that all Afghan boys and men seemed to wear, were watching the convoy roll by. "Hey, kids!" Joe shouted. "Catch!"

Joe tossed the tennis ball in their direction.

The boys screamed. They shouted in their language and ran as fast as they could away from the ball.

"No! No! It's OK!" Joe shouted.

The boys sprinted barefoot across the rocky barren ground. Then the ball bounced. Bounced again.

As quickly as they'd run away, the boys reversed direction, their feet skidding in the dust, and they scrambled for the ball.

What had these boys experienced or heard about Americans that had made them so afraid of a tennis ball?

In the distance now, off the side of the road behind the convoy, the kids were already racing around with the ball, laughing and playing. Joe smiled a little. *All that over a tennis ball. Poor kids. What a country.*

The convoy rolled on, eventually leaving the bumpy broken concrete highway for a bumpy dusty dirt road. Since he was in the trail vehicle, Joe was practically showered in a cloud of the gritty Afghan filth. Joe's back ached between his shoulder blades from the weight of his armor vest. He experimented with leaning his back against the upright gun turret hatch cover, trying to take the weight off his shoulders. It only helped a little bit.

Incredibly, the white station wagon found them again, hundreds of miles and several hours later. This time it sped past them quickly, the Afghans inside it watching them, before the car turned off the crude dirt road and vanished into the mountains.

"OK, be alert up there, Killer," Corporal MacDonald called up to him after a long time. "We're approaching Farah. We're almost home."

10

FARAH, AFGHANISTAN
June 24, 2003

Baheer skidded to a halt on his bike on the way home from school.

The road ahead was blocked by about twenty armed soldiers. They stood spread in a circle around two pickups and four big tan trucks with machine guns on top. For an instant, his stomach twisted in fright, thinking the Taliban were here, right outside his family's compound, but then he heard one of them speak: *"Donletdatkeedthrew."*

Was that supposed to be English?

The soldier closest to him, the only one among them with dark skin like Baheer's, held up his hand. *"Stop! Oldit!"* The American flag was on his shoulder, like the one Baheer's geography teacher had shown them.

The Americans. They're actually here. He knew Afghan workers had been hired to build an American base outside of town, but it wasn't close to ready, and it didn't explain what they were doing on his street. Still, better them than the Taliban.

All of them held serious-looking guns. Most were longer, but a couple of soldiers held short, bulky weapons with larger drums for bullets. More machine guns? Why? There'd hardly been any signs of the Taliban since that night they'd run away.

Baheer's legs were shaking. Could the Americans see his fear? Maybe he shouldn't be afraid, but experience around groups of heavily armed men had taught him to be wary. He didn't want them to think he was a coward, though. *Maybe I know enough English to talk to them.*

Before Baheer could figure out what to say, a white Toyota station wagon turned onto the road. The Americans spotted it at once and began shouting. The soldier closest to the car, the fattest one, raised his rifle a little higher, not pointing it at the driver, but making sure it was seen. "Boro!" he shouted. *"CantgitthrooheerHajji."*

Is he saying "Haji"? The Americans spoke very quickly and with a heavy accent. But then Baheer was sure he heard the word again from another soldier who was pointing at the car. *Why do the Americans care if the driver has ever made the Hajj?* Besides, the driver was Omar's older brother, and he was only nineteen. Baheer was sure he'd never made the pilgrimage.

A cold thought sank deep within him. What if Baba Jan was right? What if the Americans were furious with all Muslims after their country was attacked? Could they be here to hunt down everyone who had made the Hajj to Mecca? Baheer shook his head. That was a ridiculous idea.

The large soldier held his rifle handgrip with one hand, and with his free hand made a motion in the air, like he was miming pushing the car away from them. "Boro! Boro! *Eyemnotduckeenjohkeenbahkupbahkup!*"

The other Americans were looking around, holding their weapons tight like they were expecting a fight.

Omar's brother stared at the soldiers, wide-eyed and helpless. He looked to Baheer. Baheer shrugged.

When the large soldier looked like he was going to point his rifle at the car, Omar's brother backed up a little.

"Thasrigh! Motherduck binollowinus fromKandahar," said the soldier.

He had understood "Kandahar." But even though Baheer thought he'd made progress in English class, it hadn't prepared him for understanding these men. Ducks. He was sure he'd heard "duck." And "mother duck." There were no ducks in Farah. But they had also been talking about Kandahar. Something about following maybe? Was that what he was saying? Following from Kandahar?

"My brother says you study English," Omar's brother called out his car window. "Do you know what they're saying?"

"They don't speak clearly," Baheer shouted back. "I think

they're calling you a duck. Perhaps this is an insult? I think they believe you followed them from Kandahar."

Omar's brother scowled. "I've been at my father's shop in the bazaar!"

"I know," Baheer said. "I'm as helpless as you. I can't get home either."

"Ask them how long they'll block the road," said Omar's brother.

Baheer wanted to talk to them, but his English wasn't that good, and these soldiers with their guns didn't look like they wanted to have a conversation. Who did these foreigners think they were, taking over the street and bossing everyone around?

Suddenly, another white Toyota station wagon turned onto the street and pulled to a stop behind Omar's. Baheer's stomach tightened. The Americans were becoming more and more agitated. Maybe he should hop on his bike and ride away from there as fast as he could.

A soldier with a green rope of black beads hanging off his chest left his big tan gun truck, pointing back and forth at both cars, saying, *"Sameduckingar! Same!"* All the Americans laughed. The guy with the prayer beads leaned toward the cars and spoke very loudly and slowly. "Youu wait heeere!" He made a downward motion with his free hand. "Weee"— he made a walking gesture with his fingers—"go inside. Sooon! Under-stand?"

"Yes," Baheer said aloud without thinking.

Beads Soldier perked up. *"DosdisHajispekEnglish?"* He stepped closer to Baheer, who forced himself to stay still. *"Engleesi?"*

"English, yes," Baheer said. "A little bit." He wondered if it was a good idea to talk to these guys.

"Weeee aaaare gooooing in theeeere," the soldier said. He pointed at the big steel gate of the compound next to Baheer's compound. "Sooooon. You. All. Stay. Back."

"It is no problem," Baheer said. But it was a problem. This soldier must have been lying. They were building a base outside of Farah. Why were they entering a residence?

A group of soldiers came out of the compound. One of them shouted "Clear!" and gave a thumbs-up. The large guy responded with a strange word, *"Rocherdat."*

"Chee mega?" Baheer whispered in his own language. *What did he say?*

With a piercing creak, the steel gate opened and, one by one, all the trucks entered the compound. Just before the last truck rolled inside, the darker-skinned soldier waved at him and said, "Salaaaaam!"

Baheer looked around to see if the American was really talking to him, but there was nobody else on the street. Both cars had already hurried toward their homes. Baheer nodded at the soldier and then made his way toward his family's compound.

Once he was inside the walls of his home, Baheer ran toward Baba Jan's house.

On the way, he found Maryam watching their cousins Sapoora and Moniba playing hopscotch.

"Hey. Why are you running?" Moniba asked.

Baheer slowed for a moment, pointing at the west wall. "There are Americans right in the next compound."

"What?" Sapoora almost screamed. She went for her scarf and covered her head and face as she was the oldest of Baheer's cousins. "Cover your head," she said to Moniba and Maryam.

Maryam watched the west wall. "They aren't looking at us. We're fine," Maryam said, although she pulled her scarf on her head anyway.

"We'll all be fine," Baheer said. After the Americans' aggressive ways in the street, he couldn't be sure. But if they intended harm, why had they bothered explaining to Baheer where they were going? If they came here to hurt people, why wait? And surely they hadn't come to hurt little girls. "Keep playing. I must tell Baba Jan."

"Baba!" Baheer shouted seconds later, bursting into the study.

"What's the matter? Calm down," Baba Jan said, rising to his feet. After taking a moment to catch his breath, Baheer relayed the news to his grandfather.

"We wanted to escape the war," Baba Jan said. "Now the war is next door."

Baheer hadn't even thought about the danger—the Taliban attacking with the Americans so close—and of his family being caught in the crossfire.

Baba Jan raised his hands. "O Allah. Please rescue us from this curse. We once lived with a talib next door. We escaped. Now, Americans are here. O Allah, keep us safe as you kept us from the curse of the Taliban. Ameen."

"That's why all that work was done in the compound over there," Baheer said. "To make it ready for the Americans." But why weren't they just moving into their base outside of town? Were they some kind of spies?

From the other side of the wall a mechanical roar started. Probably an electric generator. A moment later a second screaming engine added its noise to the first.

Worst spies in the whole world.

Baheer and his grandfather exchanged a look. "Baba Jan, we have the worst luck with neighbors."

———◇———

The roar of the American generators continued all night. Baheer doubted if anyone in the neighborhood had slept very much. He hadn't.

On the way back from the bazaar the next morning, where he'd picked up a bundle of naan and three Zam Zam sodas as a treat for himself, Rahim, and Maryam, Baheer slowed as he approached the compound next door. The soldier with the beads-rope dangling from the front of his vest stood with his head and shoulders visible over the wall. Baheer frowned, hoping they weren't looking over the wall into his family's compound.

But then he realized this could be his chance to make a

143

difference, to make his English classes come to life by practicing with this American. The foreigner didn't seem to be in a hurry like he had last night. Baba Jan would probably disapprove of him talking to the Americans, but he hadn't told him *not* to. Anyway, the soldier didn't seem dangerous. He seemed preoccupied.

"Hello!" Baheer finally said. The soldier stood up straight, and Baheer could see the rifle slung from his shoulder, his hand on the weapon's grip near the trigger.

Maybe this was a mistake. Maybe he is dangerous.

The American stared at Baheer. He didn't aim his rifle at him, but he didn't relax either.

"Salaaaaam, rafiq," the soldier finally said.

His Persian was bad, but Baheer got it.

The soldier looked up and down the street.

Don't just stand there, Baheer. Say something. Anything. "You are Americans, yes?"

"*Yeswadouuwan?*" he responded.

Baheer didn't understand, but it was clear the American wasn't happy.

The sun was crushingly hot. Baheer held his hands up over his forehead to shield his eyes. "Can you . . . speak slowly more? Please?"

"*Yuuerdatkeedndabieklasnite! Wenweefursgoheer!*"

Baheer shook his head.

The soldier spoke slowly and clearly. "You're that kid on the bike last night. When we first got here."

144

"Yes." Baheer laughed. "I see when you come. Can I ask question?"

The guy sighed. "Sure. I got plenty of time."

"Why are you all talking about ducks?" Baheer had been wondering about this since last night.

"Ducks?"

"Yes," said Baheer. "Many of you say 'duck' and one of you is calling Omar's brother a mother duck. There are no ducks."

The guy burst out laughing. Baheer thought he had made a mistake in his English.

"Is a duck funny?" he asked.

The American looked around as if he didn't want others listening to his conversation. What was the big deal about ducks?

"Thanks, man. I needed that. But we weren't saying 'duck.'" He explained the word and its many meanings, pronouncing it slowly, starting with an *F*. "That's one of our meanest curse words."

"Oh!" Baheer said. "I am understanding now!" Baheer bit his lower lip. This should never ever be spoken of in front of others. These Americans were sick.

"Yadoneversaydattoon American," the soldier said. "Yoomiendupshot."

Baheer couldn't understand him, so he pointed to the soldier's beads. "For to pray? The beads?"

The soldier chuckled. "No. They are pace beads, to keep track of how far I've walked on a patrol."

Baheer had never heard of anything like that, but then he didn't know much about these foreigners. *I don't even know this guy's name.* He asked.

The soldier slapped his name tape on the front of his uniform. "PFC Killian."

"Your name is PFC—"

"My rank is private first class," he said. "My last name is Killian."

"That is your family name?" Baheer wondered why someone would tell only his last name. Baheer didn't even have a family name. Afghans said their first name with their father's name if asked.

"Yes. I'm not telling you my first name."

"Why will you not tell me this?" Baheer stepped into the shadow near the wall, trying to escape the punishing heat.

"Because none of you need to know that information."

Were all the Americans this rude?

"Get away from the wall," Mr. Killian said.

"What?" Baheer asked.

Mr. Killian leaned over to look down at him. "Back away from the wall," he said louder.

"Why are you wanting me to do this?" said Baheer. "It is very hot today. I want to be in the shade."

"Yeah, I know it's hot! I'm stuck out here in the sun, too. In this heavy armor. I'll survive. So will you. Boro! Boro! Back. Away. From. The. Wall . . . Now!"

These Americans were so arrogant and ignorant. Normal people would never act this way.

He searched his mind for the right English words to explain this. "This is not good" was all he could think to say. "I am not hurting your wall."

"What's your name?" Mr. Killian asked after a moment.

"My name is Baheer." At least he could answer like a normal person.

"Nice to meet you, Baheer." He reached down behind the wall and produced a small green thing wrapped in plastic. "Have a candy."

He tossed it to the dusty ground. *Did he do that on purpose? Like I'm some kind of animal?*

On the other hand, maybe Killian had tried to throw it to him. Baheer picked it up and smiled. "Thank you. I will enjoy this." There was just one more thing he had to try to talk to the American about, or else what good was Baheer's English? "May I ask? How you say? You Americans have very loud noise. All night. A loud machine. For electricity?"

"Our generators, yeah," Killian said.

"Can you be turning these off at night please?"

Killian shrugged. "Sorry, man. Those generators power our computers and everything. The officers—um, my commanders, say they must stay on. I'm sorry."

"It is no problem," Baheer said, unsurprised, but still disappointed, with his response. "But I must return home."

Killian nodded and wiped the sweat from his face. It was

morning, but already very hot. At least Baheer had the right clothes for the heat. The soldier looked miserable in his tight uniform and heavy vest. Hot, sweaty, tired, and tense, like he was expecting trouble from the Taliban or—*No. Could he possibly be afraid of me? Is that why he told me to back away from the wall? Is this guy scared?* It seemed impossible, but then if Afghanistan had an army and sent Baheer to America, or even to Iran or Pakistan, to fight, he knew he'd be afraid.

Baheer looked at Killian for a long moment. *He's thousands of miles from home, he's miserable, and despite his fellow soldiers and all his weapons, he's worried about an attack at all times.*

Baheer reached into his cloth bundle and produced the plastic bottle of orange Zam Zam soda, so cold that the bottle glistened wet in the bright sun. "You like?" Baheer reached up to hand Killian the Zam Zam.

The soldier frowned for a minute, then looked behind him before leaning way down over the wall and reaching out to take the bottle. He looked it over, inspecting the seal.

"Zam. Zam?" Killian asked.

"It is sweet," Baheer explained. "Bubbles."

"Soda?" Killian asked.

"Yes!" Baheer said. *Had Killian's brain cooked in that helmet?* "It is good for you to drink."

For the first time in their conversation, Killian truly smiled. He twisted off the cap with a hiss. Then he tipped back the bottle and drank. And drank. He moaned a little and drank and pressed the cold bottle to his forehead. "S'good!"

Baheer laughed. "OK. This is good. I must go. Goodbye."

"Hey Baheer!" Killian called. "I say 'thank you.' You say? How do you people say 'thank you'?"

"Ah! I understand!" Baheer smiled. "Thank you. Tashakor."

"Tashakor," Killian said with a terrible accent. "'Thank you' is 'tashakor'?"

"Yes," Baheer said. "Goodbye."

"See ya later, Baheer," Killian said as Baheer walked away. "Tashakor!"

FARAH, AFGHANISTAN
June 26, 2003

The officers called the place the Safe House. The men called it the Unsafe House. Nobody ever accused soldiers of being really original comedians. And there wasn't a lot to laugh about in their current location, except for the tragic joke of their miserable situation and their meaningless deployment.

Not for the first time, Joe surveyed his strange surroundings in disgust. The Unsafe House wasn't a base, but a regular Afghan residential compound. Joe spit on the dusty ground. It was like Luke Skywalker's house on Tatooine in the first *Star Wars* movie, all tan mudstone, but without the cool robots. The rooms even had domed ceilings and roofs.

The whole thing was surrounded by twelve-foot-high, two-foot-thick mudstone walls and was divided in half by another wall. River rock covered the ground on this side of the compound, where the vehicles—the four brand-new armored Humvees and the two little civilian Toyota Hilux pickups—were parked.

A row of converted stable rooms lined the back of the compound, where most of the troops would be staying. Someone had come in before to shovel out the manure, but not all of the stench had left. The floor in their baking hot barracks was roughly finished concrete. The bunks were poorly welded black metal frames with plywood beds and thin foam mattresses covered in fabric printed with colorful swirls and the words WELCOME 2003.

"Yeah, me and 2003 are gonna have a serious talk," Mac had said when they'd moved into their crappy barracks and claimed racks. "Because so far this really sucks."

Baccam had chuckled. Joe only shook his head. "Yeah, and Captain Higgins said we're staying here until the base is complete. Could be months."

"You wanted a real war." The Mighty Quinn had spoken up for a change. "War ain't about staying in a fancy hotel."

Joe didn't know what he hated the worst, the fact that he was a little afraid to argue with Specialist Quinn or that the big guy was right.

In the back corner, beyond the row of trucks, was a rough room for ammo storage. That was kind of impressive. There were ammo cans full of 5.56 rounds for their M16s, 7.62 rounds for their M240B machine guns, and .50-cal. rounds for their big M2 machine guns. Other cans contained chains of 40-millimeter grenade rounds for the Mk 19 grenade-launching machine gun. They had four shoulder-fired AT4 antitank rocket launchers and a half dozen Claymore anti-personnel mines. There were boxes of live M67 fragmentation grenades, M18 smoke grenades, and M14 incendiary grenades.

It was all stacked in the mud-brick cave of a room, unlocked and unguarded. Joe smiled a little as he surveyed it all. Never before had he been allowed such easy access to so much deadly military inventory.

Baccam approached, his boots crunching in the gravel and his rifle hanging from his shoulder. "There you are. What are you doing in here?"

"Just curious, I guess," Joe said. "Look at all this. Why do we need all this firepower for reconstruction?"

Baccam shrugged. "I know you were bummed about our mission, but you gotta remember the Taliban don't care what we're doing here. Doesn't matter if we're trying to kill them or working to help the people. The Taliban hate us. They want us dead."

Joe ran his fingers over the green AT4 tube. "All this ought to make it a lot harder for them to get what they want."

"Yeah, man," Baccam said. "But it's crazy hot and smelly in here." He pointed toward the metal door in the center dividing wall next to the palm tree. "Cook has coffee."

"Hot coffee? In this heat?"

Baccam laughed. "Fine, but he already ran a shopping

mission to the bazaar. There's an ice factory somewhere. Cooler full of cold water in there."

The two of them went to the other half of the compound, the center of which featured a one-story mud-brick house with a big center room and four rooms in the corners: three barracks and a kitchen.

Sergeant Tanner, their cook, waved his hands around a small electric stove like a model showing off a sleek car. "Look at this electric powerhouse! One step up from my daughter's Easy Bake Oven!"

Joe chuckled with the other soldiers hanging around.

"Got your work cut out for you, Cookmaster," Mac said, entering through the back door.

"Where did all this stuff come from?" Joe asked quietly.

First Sergeant Dalton overheard him. "A team of Army intel guys contracted with Afghans to rent this place and turn it into a palace fit for kings!" He slapped the cheap metal table. "Probably charged us two grand for this flimsy thing."

"Well, ya'll better not be counting on chow like in Kandahar." Cookmaster pointed at the small fridge in the main room. "Because *that* thing is our only cold storage. I hope you like MREs and T-rations."

Joe wiped his sweaty brow. How did these people live in houses like this? It was more animal den than house. No, not a den, more like an oven, like the wood-fired oven at his favorite pizza place back in Iowa City. Joe sighed, wondering if he'd ever return there again.

Baccam handed him a bottle of water from the cooler, and Joe pressed it to his face for a moment before drinking, then swatted an annoying fly.

"Hey, PFC Killian," First Sergeant Dalton said.

Joe froze. Generally, it was not good to catch the notice of the first sergeant. He took his role as the highest-ranking enlisted man in the company very seriously. He was notorious for dropping soldiers for many push-ups because of minor infractions.

Joe stood straight with both hands behind the small of his back. "Yes, First Sergeant."

First Sergeant Dalton chuckled. "At ease there, Private. This isn't a parade review." The man sipped coffee from a paper cup. "I heard you talked to one of the local nationals while on guard duty the other day."

"Sorry, First Sergeant," Joe said. "It won't happen again." Would he be dropped for push-ups in this heat?

"It's OK to talk to them. Just be sure you don't get complacent. Maintain situational awareness."

"Yes, First Sergeant."

The first sergeant leaned forward, his elbows on the table. "He gave you a pop? Was it factory sealed?"

"Yes, First Sergeant. It was sealed."

"Good," said First Sergeant Dalton. "We need to be careful about accepting food or drink from local nationals. Stuff could be poisoned."

"Understood, First Sergeant." Joe spoke like he agreed

with him because he was not *allowed* to disagree with him. But he thought back to that soda, and how good and sweet it had tasted in that terrible heat. Joe didn't trust these people, but he was pretty sure Baheer hadn't been trying to poison him. Surely maintaining situational awareness didn't mean situational delusion. There were plenty of real threats to watch out for without imagining fake ones.

That night, after a meal consisting of a small square of imitation-meat lasagna and a scoop of corn, Joe's squad sat in a bit of shade on the concrete front porch.

"I'll give you guys the notes for tonight," Sergeant Cavanaugh said. "The commander says under no circumstances should anyone go outside this compound without permission. OK? The Afghan who sold us ice said the Taliban contacted him, said they plan to try to kill us sometime this week."

Mac flipped pages in his own pocket notebook. "Excuse me, Sergeant Cavanaugh. Can we send a message back through the ice man? This week's not going to work for me. I'm afraid I'm booked solid sweating here in cesspit base. Won't be able to see them anytime in the next three weeks."

Cavanaugh, who was always super serious, cracked a smile and pretended to write something down. "I . . . will . . . pass that message along. Master Sergeant Dinsler put out a strict standing order reminding everybody to wash their hands with soap and water after the latrine and before eating anything. He'll be setting up hand-wash stations soon.

Until then, use bottled water." He stuffed his notebook back in his pocket. "Right. OK. Now I know it's hot, but we all must sleep. We're due to relieve Second Squad on guard duty in a few hours, and that will start our three hours on, three hours off rotation. Try to get as much rest as you can because tomorrow, our squad will have its first mission, escorting our engineer to the PRT base to see how construction is coming along. Questions?"

Mac raised his hand. "When do I get my discharge papers?"

Cavanaugh snorted. "They're working on them right now, no doubt."

Joe laughed at Mac's old joke. *What would it be like to go to war at the end of my enlistment contract like Mac instead of at the beginning of my Army Guard time the way it is now?* It was probably best to get the deployment over with right away. Then, with the war over, he'd be able to ride out his six-year enlistment without having to worry about shipping out again, probably getting promoted faster due to war experience. *If you could call a reconstruction mission "war."*

Minutes later First Squad settled into their dark mud-brick cave barracks and hit the rack. Joe rested on his sweaty back, his head on his rolled-up uniform top, the pathetic foam mattress doing next to nothing to keep him off the plywood slab.

In addition to an extra notebook and a few pens, Joe had packed one other indulgence, a tiny battery-operated reading lamp. By that bit of light he tried once again to write.

June 26, 2003

Farah, Afghanistan
Soldiers of first and second squads of first platoon of
Delta Company of the second battalion, 199th infantry
regiment Iowa Army National Guard have taken the first
step in establishing a lasting American military presence in
the western Afghanistan province of Farah. In an effort to
help revitalize the local Afghan economy, the U.S. Army
has hired Afghan engineers and laborers to construct a
permanent American base outside the city of Farah. The
challenge is enormous for the men of first and second
squads. Forced to endure primitive conditions in a rented
Afghan residence, they are surrounded ~~on all sides by~~
~~potentially hostile~~ by

Joe couldn't think of what to write. Baheer and his family
lived on the other side of the east wall. His offer of a cold soda
hadn't been hostile, no matter the first sergeant's warning.

by people completely unlike any the soldiers have ever
met before. Their mission is to somehow help the Afghans
overcome centuries of mindless fighting in the hope that
they will afterward no longer help terrorists to murder
innocent Americans. Delta Company's leadership continues
to remind their soldiers to be alert for Taliban or other
enemy forces that might seek to do them harm, and toward

157

that end, the men are well armed. When they at last occupy their permanent base, they'll be well positioned in an armed and fortified outpost. Until then, the soldiers find their greatest protection, their only protection, in one another, as their struggle through deployment has only begun.

"Killer," Corporal MacDonald whispered. "If you don't shut off that light, I'm going to shove it up your nose."

Joe switched off the light and put his notebook and pen aside. He thought of the soldiers of Second Squad keeping watch on those guard platforms, making sure nobody hurt him tonight.

———◇———

Someone shook his shoulder after what felt like an instant. "Private Killian." It was Sergeant Paulsen. "Wake up, Killer. Time for guard duty."

His cheap Casio Illuminator watch told him it was June 27, 0400 hours. He bit his lip and slapped his own face to wake up. Three-hour shifts didn't work. It took about a half hour to get to sleep. Someone woke them a half hour before going on duty so they could get ready. They had round-the-clock intermittent duty punctuated by what were actually only two-hour sleep breaks. Waking and sleeping at odd hours around the clock blurred time and mushed his days together so he never knew what was going on.

There was nothing to do on guard duty but stand there making sure nothing happened. It was incredibly boring. Joe looked up to the clear night sky, gazing with his mouth open. "I'll say this for Afghanistan," he whispered to the billions of bright stars in the heavens. "It has just about the most beautiful night sky I've—" Joe cursed, jumped back, scrambled to pull his rifle to the ready. His heart pounded, muscles tense, ready to kill.

The black cat that had been slinking along the top of the wall arched its back and hissed. From the next guard platform over, down the wall in the direction the cat had come from, Baccam stood hunched over, hands on his knees, laughing so hard Joe worried he'd get them all killed by accidentally waking First Sergeant Dalton, who slept out in the open in the back courtyard near Baccam's position.

"Get out of here!" Joe lunged toward the cat, sending it rocketing down the top of the wall and around the corner toward the neighbor's compound. "Stupid thing."

Sergeant Paulsen was the S-O-G, the Sergeant of the Guard, assigned to moving from post to post, making sure all guards were awake and had everything they needed. He nearly fell down from laughter as he approached Joe. "Way to be alert there, Killer," he said quietly, wiping his eyes. "Nothing's sneaking past your position."

At 0700 Joe's team was relieved. They'd lose sleep time if they ate breakfast—powdered eggs and oatmeal, flies buzzing over all—but there was so little food that nobody dared avoid eating. The only time they ever sometimes skipped a meal was in the blazing midday heat.

"Oh, you guys should have seen Killian last night," Baccam said as soon as he sat down with the group around the table in the main room. He laughed again, telling the story of the stupid cat. "I thought he was gonna crap his pants."

"Speaking of crapping your pants." Z set his cardboard tray of eggs aside and ran out of the room.

"What's his problem?" Shockley asked.

The Mighty Quinn looked up from his meal and grunted. "The Farah Flu."

Shockley frowned. "What's that?"

"The flies crawl around human-waste soup in the latrines. Then they land on the food we're trying to eat." Mac frowned, his hand to his belly. "So if you haven't had the Farah Flu"—he quickly stood up—"you will," he finished as he ran out of the room, also heading for the latrines.

———◇———

Two weeks later, Joe woke with his sweat-crusted brown T-shirt stuck to his back. He sat up in his rack. *Gross. Only 325 days to go.* He peeled the filthy shirt off his grimy body and grabbed his little notebook from under the rolled-up shirt he'd been using as a pillow. He X-ed out one more day on his chart. *325. Almost at the end of the 300s. Almost the upper 200s.* Still an eternity.

He needed sleep to prepare for guard duty, but this heat was making it impossible. At 0900, it was over eighty degrees. Somehow, in the racks all around him, his squad slept. Second Squad was still on guard.

There might not be a wait for the laptop. He could check his email.

He scratched his arm, disappointed to see he'd begun scraping off what he'd thought was a good tan. *Just dirt.* They were allowed one three-minute shower every three days, but on his last few shower days, the well was dry by the time Joe had his chance.

He hadn't been clean in a long time. He pulled on a fresh pair of socks. Showers, clean underwear or T-shirts, clean uniforms, could wait. Socks could not. After three days sweating in the same socks, the flesh between his toes cracked and bled. He was now dressed save for his uniform top, crispy from yesterday's sweat.

He heard a gunshot. No big deal. Guns went off around town a lot.

Another gunshot rang out. Close. Out the glassless window in front of their barracks room, Joe watched Lieutenant Riley tense up next to PFC Underwood on Position One. Underwood slipped into his armor.

Machine gun fire. Close. Again, from right down the street. Lieutenant Riley jumped from the guard platform.

What should I do? Where should I go? Taliban said they'd attack. Here they come!

Growing up, Krista had sometimes watched *Star Trek: The Next Generation.* When the ship was under attack, someone would shout, "Battlestations! Wake up! Battlestations!"

First Squad rolled out of their racks. Absurdly, Joe

finished buttoning his uniform before scrambling into his armor vest and helmet. Then he was out the door, M16 in hand.

Sergeant Paulsen met him in front of the barracks. "Who's ready?"

"Me!" Joe said.

"Can you fire the AT4?" Paulsen was already grabbing the big green shoulder-fired antitank rocket launchers.

"I guess!" Joe said. AT4 warheads were expensive, so soldiers trained by firing 9-millimeter tracer rounds from the enormous weapon. Worthless training. But he'd done it.

"You're with me!" Sergeant Paulsen shouted. "To the roof!"

Joe shoulder-slung an AT4 and sprinted after Paulsen toward the house side of the compound.

More machine gun fire went off somewhere.

"Where are they?" someone shouted.

Joe and Paulsen grabbed the sun-baked steel ladder, heaving it from the ground and slamming it against the side of the house, cursing against the pain in their seared hands. Paulsen was up an instant later, reaching down to grab Joe's AT4.

As Joe climbed, time seemed to stretch out the way it had when, as a kid, he'd realized he was about to fall from a tree or off his skateboard.

This is my last day on Earth. We don't have enough men to defend this position if the Taliban come in force.

Two rungs up the ladder.

I'm gonna die today. We'll fight hard, but it won't be enough.

Four rungs, hands burning.

I'll have to kill human beings. Remember what the Army taught me. Put the front sight-post center of his body, breath control—in, out, in—easy trigger squeeze. Drop them. Don't think, shoot.

Six rungs up.

A chaplain will knock on the door. Mom will see him and cry, knowing her son is dead. She'll have to tell Krista. And Dad. They'll be so sad.

He put his rifle up over the short wall at the edge of the roof.

These savages want to kill me because we want school for their kids, want to make this country a little less like garbage?

A leg over the top.

They want a fight? I'll give them one! I'll kill 'em all! Come on! Let's do this!

"I got this way!" Joe pointed to the back of the compound. He took up a position between the mud-brick roof dome and the wall on the edge.

"I got front!" shouted Sergeant Paulsen.

Each would cover his sector, destroy any enemies, and wouldn't dare turn his back for any reason. All roofs in Farah featured gently sloped domes over each room but were mostly flat, and the Taliban could pop up on any of them.

A quick glance across the motorpool side of their compound and the west wall allowed a partial look into the compound next door. As another burst of machine gun fire went off from somewhere down the street, Baheer hurried across a courtyard between two houses, rushing a girl along. "Baheer, get inside!" Joe shouted. Baheer vanished from view an instant later.

Second Squad's Specialist Dodge was on the guard platform on the west wall. "I got this side! Cover the south, Killer!"

He's right! Do your job! Pay attention!

His rifle ready, stock to cheek, he scanned his sector. He was a good shot. He'd shoot any haji coming up with a weapon. Joe panned his weapon along the rooflines. *Empty. Empty. Empty.*

Movement.

His heart leapt, almost hurt, but it was just an old man with a gray beard walking along his roof.

"Get down!" Joe screamed.

The man didn't need to be told twice. He turned around and vanished in a second.

"Good." Sweat ran down Joe's back. A few more gunshots went off. Still not on them yet as far as he could tell. "Where are they? Come on, you Taliban freaks. I got you."

A boy, maybe ten years old, emerged on a different roof about a block away.

"Get off the roof!" Joe shouted.

The boy smiled and waved.

"No, no, no," Joe said. If the Taliban appeared behind the kid, the boy would be killed in the crossfire. Then CNN or some other network would show up with a camera crew, talking about how terrible American soldiers were. Worse, there'd be a dead kid.

"Get down right now!" Joe shouted again, but still the boy waved.

The kid had to get out of the way immediately. Joe bit his lip, wiped his eyes. "O Jesus, please forgive me." He lifted his M16 and aimed it directly at the ten-year-old boy. "I'm not joking! Get the—"

The boy screamed and scrambled to flee the roof.

"Killian, you good?" Sergeant Paulsen called.

Joe snorted. "Oh, awesome. All clear over here."

The sound of gunfire had vanished. Farah baked in an eerie quiet heat. Joe continued scanning his sector over the top of his rifle, and very slowly, almost against his own will, he relaxed. His breathing and heart rate slowed. His whole attention had been focused on shooting any hostiles that showed up, but now other thoughts wandered in.

"Hey, Killer," Cookmaster said from below. He held up a can of Mountain Dew. "Thirsty?"

Joe was thirsty, now that he thought about it. Cookmaster tossed up the soda, and nothing had ever tasted so good.

Somehow the attack hadn't reached them. He was still alive. Everyone remained at their improvised battlestations for another hour before returning to what passed for normal at the Unsafe House.

FARAH, AFGHANISTAN
July 23, 2003

Through a slow, brutally hot July, the soldiers' empty existence dragged on, reduced to guard duty, attempts at sleep, constant hunger, swatting flies, sweat, filth, and fear. The Farah Flu ripped through everyone's guts.

At a nightly meeting, they'd learned that the near attack on the Unsafe House had been foiled by the local Afghan police, operating on orders from the Farah provincial governor. The police intercepted and stopped two Taliban pickups. There were no survivors.

"I guess it's good news that the local police decided to side with our allies in the new Afghanistan central government," Sergeant Cavanaugh had said.

Although conversation about the incident had died down after a few days, Joe couldn't stop thinking about it. Despite their substantial weapons and ammunition, the Unsafe House would have lived up to its name if the Taliban had come in force. It was not a very defensible position. A few grenades lobbed over the walls from the street, one truck ramming through the steel gate in the front wall. They would have been overrun quickly. *I owe my life to the Farah police.*

He also couldn't stop thinking about that boy on the roof. Why didn't he just get down when Joe told him to? Couldn't he hear the gunfire? Now he probably thought an American soldier had tried to shoot him. Would the boy ever forgive him? *And why should he? I'm a soldier in an occupying army, and I aimed an M16 at him.*

Sergeant Paulsen, PFC Baccam, and Corporal MacDonald all said he'd done the right thing. Even Specialist Shockley had said Joe's actions were consistent with all his military knowledge and experience.

"Whatever, Shockley," Mac had said. "You'd probably have shot the kid."

What Joe didn't tell anyone was that he couldn't get the incident out of his head, even when he slept. Twice, he'd dreamed about that day on the roof. But in both dreams, the boy wouldn't get down. In both dreams, Joe had shot him. It made no sense. It was just a stupid dream. But each time, the kid's chest exploded, and he screamed, and there was so much blood.

During the day, there wasn't much to keep his mind occupied. Guard duty seemed infinite. Sitting or standing on that concrete platform quickly became boring. Position One, by the front street and main gate, was the least boring of the guard posts. Sweating there on a 120-degree afternoon, Joe heard barking. Down the street some boys laughed and threw rocks at Almost Dead, the scruffy old dog that lived on the garbage pile in that section of the street.

"Hey!" Joe shook his rifle, careful not to point it at the boys. "Leave that dog alone! He's officially under the protection of the United States Army!" The boys scattered. Almost Dead sniffed around the trash a little before settling back to sleep.

An hour later, a barefoot boy and girl, perhaps siblings, played on the other side of the street between the ditch and the wall. The boy dragged a shoebox by a piece of yarn, perhaps pretending the box was a truck or train.

The girl, in her ragged dress, followed him. She didn't even have a box, only yarn. These were their only toys.

Joe's parents hadn't always had much. His dad had been laid off when Joe was six, and the family had struggled. Since Dad had left, Mom was challenged with the budget. But whatever the trouble, he and Krista had always had more than a box and yarn.

Their parents should have worked harder. But even as he thought it, he knew that was stupid.

There was a certain comfort in staying mad at these people. The anger would help if the Taliban finally did attack and he needed to shoot them—to kill them.

But Joe knew that unlike his mom and dad in America, these kids' parents didn't have many jobs available. He'd been told about how evil the Taliban had been. They wouldn't have let their mother get a job or even leave the house. Before that, the Soviet Union had devastated this country. Joe had seen their land mines at Kandahar and their abandoned military vehicles on the way to Farah. Whatever problems haji had, at least some of them weren't their fault.

Staying angry and hating these people didn't help that day on the roof. And if he really wanted to get payback on all Afghans, why was he still freaked out thinking about that boy he'd had to aim at?

"You kids like candy?" He waved a couple of Jolly Ranchers around. *What is the Dari word for "gift"? Something like "Baksheesh."*

The boy left his sister by the opposite wall and crossed the street. Joe tossed him the candies. "Enjoy, kid."

The boy ran back. He and his sister examined the gifts, talking it over. They unwrapped them and took cautious licks. A second later they both smiled big.

Joe gave a thumbs-up. "You like?" The kids laughed and vanished through a door behind their wall. "Good luck, poor kids."

A while later near the end of his guard shift, Joe's stomach heaved. He leaned over the wall, wincing, the mud-brick hot on his chest and arms. He gagged a little.

"Are you fine, Killian?"

Joe opened his eyes, dry heaved one more time, and stood up straight. "Hey, Baheer." He shook his head. "What did you say?"

"You do not look OK." Baheer smiled. He was holding another cloth-wrapped bundle and had probably just come back from the bazaar.

"Oh, just the noonday nausea," Joe said. "Couldn't really eat breakfast, and I just couldn't stand another MRE, er, a field ration, for lunch. Especially not in this heat. After a while the hunger changes to a kind of sickness, makes me feel like I'm gonna throw up."

"This is not good," Baheer said. "You should eat."

Joe shrugged. "I'm getting used to it. There'll be another square of imitation-meat lasagna tonight."

Baheer reached into his bundle and pulled out some kind of naan wrap. Squinting in the bright sun, he held the sandwich up toward Joe. "You have this. Feel better."

This guy was too nice. "I can't take your food, man. The Army takes care of me. More or less."

"Please eat it," Baheer said. "It is no problem. These are very little money. Little boys sell them around the bazaar. It is some chicken and beans, good things, inside the naan. It's fresh. You eat this. Why not? I have more." Baheer opened his bundle a little and showed him a few more of the wraps and a bag of dry rice.

First Sergeant Dalton would be mad if Joe accepted food from Baheer. But, then again, First Sergeant Dalton was sitting on his butt in the air-conditioned Tactical Operations Center, the TOC, sipping an ice-cold soda ration, not out here roasting in the sun.

"OK." Joe reached down and grabbed the sandwich. "Thanks, man." He bit into the wrap and closed his eyes. The chicken was flavored with some glorious spice he'd never tasted before, and the beans filled it all out, balanced by the crunch of lettuce or some kind of vegetable, all wrapped up in the warmest, softest naan he'd ever had. "Oh." Joe spoke with his mouth full. "Tashakor. This is the greatest thing, man. Tashakor so much."

"It is good, yes?" Baheer asked.

Joe leaned forward against the wall and devoured the sandwich. "Yes. You have no idea how good real food tastes right now. Tashakor."

When it was gone, Joe grabbed a bottle of water from the cooler and chugged half of it down before wiping his mouth. Baheer just kept watching with a big smile. Joe pulled a Jolly Rancher out of his pocket, hoping it wasn't too melty. The hard candies held up OK in the heat. "All I got to pay you back is candy," he said, tossing it to him more carefully than he had the first time.

Baheer caught the candy. "Tashakor. But you do not need to pay back. Is baksheesh. Is gift."

"Well, sorry, then," said Joe. "Because your gift was a heck of a lot better than mine."

From down the street came the rumble of a jingle truck.

Shorter than a semi, these cargo trucks hauled shipping containers in big open-top compartments behind the cab. The Afghans painted or carved elaborate designs and pictures on the sides of them. Flowers. Arabesque swirls. Even pictures of fighter jets. Hanging from the bottom edge of these trucks, on all sides, was a curtain of jingling chains. The guys sometimes argued over whether these chains were a decoration like the artwork on the trucks, or if they were supposed to help keep the dust down. Regardless, someone had called one of them a "jingle truck" and the name stuck.

Baheer moved out of the way as the jingle truck rolled to a stop in front of their compound, the driver waving to him. Joe pulled a small handheld Motorola radio from his pocket and hit the transmit button. "S-O-G, S-O-G, this is Ernie Pyle, over." On unsecured channels when anyone with a similar model civilian radio could be listening, they were careful to use code names.

"Pyle, this is S-O-G," Sergeant Paulsen radioed back. *"Go ahead, over."*

Joe hit the transmit button. "S-O-G, Ernie Pyle. Got a jingle truck parked out front, over."

"Roger that. I'll let leadership know. S-O-G, out."

"This truck? It is here for you?" Baheer asked.

Joe supposed some of this fell under Operational Security, or OPSEC, but the presence of the truck was no secret. "Yeah, these guys ship in our food and supplies from our bigger bases." First Sergeant Dalton would probably yell at him for mentioning that food sometimes came on these trucks, but where else would they get their supplies? "In a little bit some of my guys will check the truck over for bombs. Check to make sure the shipping container is still sealed and hasn't been tampered with. Then we gotta unload."

Baheer looked from the truck to Joe and back. "So many soldiers. You all must need many trucks."

"Yeah," Joe said. "And most of the time, like today, they show up right when I'm about to come off my guard shift, so instead of sleeping, I'll have to help unload."

Baheer looked at the truck again. "That is bad. I am sorry to hear this." He turned back to Joe and held up his bundle. "I have to go now. May I go back here later to practice my English?"

Joe laughed. Only a month ago, he never would have imagined voluntarily hanging out with an Afghan. But Baheer seemed cool. "Sure. I'm stuck up here a lot, so I'm not going anywhere."

Baheer smiled and nodded, but remained a moment longer. "Killian," he said. "You be OK."

Joe watched him until he vanished inside his own compound next door.

"Here to relieve you, Killer," said Second Squad's Specialist Ingram.

Joe heaved on his armor, the vest's stiff fabric scratching his bare arms. He climbed down from the guard platform, heading back to his rack to drop off his vest and helmet.

His squad knew the drill by now. They said nothing and went out to the front courtyard to deal with the jingle truck.

"Real steaks, you guys!" Cookmaster said. "No fake-meat T-ration lasagna tonight. I bought Afghan potatoes! We're gonna eat like kings!"

"Finally," said Specialist Shockley. "I've never been so hungry in my entire life."

After the Mighty Quinn and Z had gone out and made sure the truck was free of bombs, the driver backed it into the compound. Cookmaster checked the number on the jingle truck's seal. "This is the right one!" He cut the seal and unlatched the steel doors. "Steak, here we—" He opened the door. *"Go-aaaggck!"* His eyes watered. He gagged, face red.

The stench hit the guys like a sick sour-sweet boiled vomit wave. Cookmaster jumped off the truck and dry heaved, spitting into the rocks. "Truck's from Kandahar. The driver never turned the reefer unit on. All our fresh food, including the steaks . . ."

"Wasted," Mac said.

They formed a human chain and unloaded MREs, T-rations, and several pallets of bottled water. The afternoon heat and the rotted meat crushed them.

"Gotta tap out for a minute," PFC Zimmerman said, leaning forward with his hands on his knees. "Too hot. Gonna pass out."

"Hey!" Cookmaster shouted from inside the truck. He

returned to the door, lowering the rag he wore over his mouth and nose. "We got mail!"

Several giant orange mail bags came off the truck, and the unloading went more quickly.

There was nothing better in the world than mail call. Joe had three letters. One was from Mom, which shared mundane news about work, Riverside, and the extended family. There was a letter from Dad, which Joe looked at for a long time. In the past he would have wanted to burn the thing right away. He'd been so angry when Dad moved out, when he'd started dating right after the divorce. But a couple of weeks ago, as he scrambled up that ladder to the roof, machine guns going off right down the street, he'd been sure he was going to die.

It was a lot harder to stay angry. It was as if his energy needed to be devoted to staying alive, so he had less to spare for anger, especially over the past. But he wasn't quite ready to open the envelope from his father. He stuffed it into a pocket in his rucksack.

Krista had sent a padded envelope with a letter.

June 10, 2003

Dear Joe,

I miss you. Hope you're OK and getting through this war the best you can. It must be so hard. We're all thinking about you. Mom acts fine, but I know she worries. Don't worry about her. She'll be OK.

175

I know you don't care about high school or sports
right now, but we've been practicing in a summer
league, looking pretty tough for volleyball this fall.

She was wrong. Joe *did* want to hear about volleyball and
other normal things. Anything but guns and guard duty
and . . . fear.

That's so dumb to write.
    Sorry, brother. I don't know what to say. You're in a
war! Even after you enlisted, I never believed this would
happen.

He thought about that all the time. He was supposed to
be in college, studying to become a journalist. Instead he was
here, sitting on this bunk next to his rifle in the crushing
heat, desperate for letters.

I've enclosed a book. I know you prefer nonfiction, but
this old favorite was at the bookstore. Our teacher read
it to my sixth-grade class. I loved it more than anything.
So I'm sending it to you. I hope you like it.
    Please stay safe. I want to hear all about your tour
(IF you feel comfortable talking about it) when you get
home.
    Love,
    Krista

As he tucked the letter away, Joe missed his sister more than he thought he ever would.

He tipped the envelope upside down and a paperback novel slipped out.

Bridge to Terabithia.

The cover was a painting of a boy and girl beneath a large tree. All that green looked so beautiful, Joe had to wipe his eyes. Here in the Unsafe House, everything was a shade of brown.

The title sounded familiar somehow, though he'd never read the book. It had one of those gold seals on the cover, the . . . John Newbery Medal . . . so somebody thought it was good. Besides these few letters and sporadic emails, this was all he'd had to read for the longest time.

He balled up his uniform top for a pillow. Then, lying on his back, he began to read.

Krista was right. *Bridge to Terabithia* wasn't Joe's usual choice of book, but he absolutely loved it. To hold a book in his hands again, to feel the smooth pages at his fingertips, to smell the paper—that scent of hope and endless possibility—to drift into the blessedly faraway world of the story, leaving everything else behind, was, in that lonely place, like a first precious gasp of air after finally surfacing from a deep, dark lake. It felt like he was coming alive again.

The Army provided enough food and water for him to stay alive, but the book's first pages helped him realize that it was not enough to simply exist. Human beings require more, or they begin to die inside.

And in *Bridge to Terabithia* Joe found so much more. From time to time, he copied into his notebook lines that particularly moved him. "He thought later how peculiar it was that here was probably the biggest thing in his life, and he had shrugged it all off as nothing." He thought about the war, about how he was in the middle of the biggest experience of his life, and how most days he couldn't even comprehend that. He only struggled to stay awake on guard duty, to endure the pain in his back from the weight of his armor, to keep his weapon clean and ready. He hadn't been in Afghanistan very long, but Joe doubted he would return the same person he was. If he returned.

By some miracle, Joe had enough time to read the whole book in one sitting. The Unsafe House, Afghanistan, and the war all faded away as Joe read. And as he turned the last page, he blinked back his tears, certain of three things: Katherine Paterson was one of the greatest writers of all time, her beautiful book had saved him, and he must not let the guys see him crying.

"OK," Joe whispered, when he had finished. As long as kids like Jesse and Leslie, the main characters in the book, could have such meaningful, life-changing friendships, then he could keep going. One more day. Then another.

Sergeant Paulsen came into their room. "You OK, Killer?"

Joe took a deep breath and sat up. "Better than I've been in a long time."

"That's good, because we have a dismounted neighborhood patrol in one hour." He woke everyone and issued orders to be geared up in forty-five minutes. "Drink a lot of water. Gonna be hot walking around in full battle rattle."

"It's times like this," Shockley said, rubbing his eyes, "the leadership should be stabbed in the face."

Normally, Joe would have also been frustrated, but as he downed a bottle of water and checked his ammo pouches to make sure the rounds in his magazines were clean and ready to fire, he wasn't upset. He didn't feel like he was really there, in the war. He couldn't stop thinking about the beauty of the language and of the friendship in that book.

———◇———

Later, his squad walked down the middle of the street in squad column formation. Sergeant Paulsen had point. At equal intervals a couple meters back and to the left and right were PFC Baccam with the SAW and Corporal Mac. Joe kept his spacing, back and to Mac's right.

Staff Sergeant Cavanaugh and Second Lieutenant Riley marched in the middle. Sergeant Hart, Specialist Quinn, PFC Z, and Specialist Shockley formed an opposite arrow covering their six.

Joe was supposed to scan their three o'clock sector for hostiles, people with guns who looked like they were about to shoot. Instead he saw curious or bewildered Afghans watching them marching down the middle of the street. Lieutenant Riley had warned them to stay alert. He even had Z and Mac carrying AT4s, just because, in his words, "We want the locals to know we have firepower."

Joe knew he should be focusing on watching for danger, but his thoughts kept drifting to *Bridge to Terabithia*. The kids in that book were growing up poor, and all around him in Farah were people living in poverty the likes of which he had never seen or imagined.

After a few blocks, they turned the corner and passed an old Soviet tank. *You sick Commie monsters.* What kind of fight had it taken to stop that thing? How many Afghans died kicking out the invaders? Tens of thousands? Millions? And now, if what his leadership said was true, some of the Afghans had risked their lives preventing a Taliban attack on the Unsafe House. Whatever he had once believed, or had forced himself to believe, he now had to admit that these were brave people. The Farah police could have simply allowed the Taliban to carry out their attack. He owed them his life. And he hadn't forgotten Baheer's kindness.

A group of kids playing soccer in the street moved aside and waved. Many of them lacked shoes. One small girl wore only the shabbiest green dress. She looked with amazement at the soldiers and offered a shy smile.

Joe took a deep breath. That little girl, like those kids playing with the yarn and shoebox across the street—all these kids . . . they were not the enemy. They couldn't possibly be, and no amount of anger over 9/11, or similar hatred Joe might manufacture to help him shoot the enemy if the time ever came, could continue to delude him into thinking these people really were the enemy. They were more of a victim of the Taliban and Al-Qaeda than he would ever be.

A line from *Bridge to Terabithia* echoed through Joe's head. "He felt that it was the beginning of a new season in his life, and he chose deliberately to make it so."

He was exhausted, filthy, in pain, and plenty fearful. Each part of every day was a struggle to reach the next part. But that night PFC Joe Killian felt that something new, something better had begun.

13

FARAH, AFGHANISTAN
August 11, 2003

I will not do it!" Baba Jan's voice echoed across the courtyard from his study. Baheer slowed down so quickly he
worried for a moment that the teapot would fall over on the
tray he carried. Baba Jan sometimes liked tea when he was
reading, but from what he had just heard, Baheer suspected
his grandfather would not be very interested today.

"Father, please listen to us," Uncle Kabir said. "We need
to face the truth of our situation. The family finances are in
trouble."

"We may run out of food this winter," Baheer's father
added.

"I am listening to you," Baba Jan said sharply. "Have you
no faith? We have faced greater hardships than these, and
that land has been in our family for generations. Would you

sell your birthright to some lazy slob who will let the land go to waste?"

Baheer froze outside the door to his grandfather's study. *They're arguing with Baba Jan? And they're still alive?* Baba Jan's word was law, and they were challenging him. But could they actually convince Baba Jan to sell the farm? *Then I'd finally be free of that torturous place.*

"The farm is not making enough money," said Uncle Feraidoon. "In fact it may lose money this season."

"The boys will work harder," Baba Jan said. "They will make it profit. I'll be sure of it."

Baheer pressed his lips together. Despite the heat of the morning, he felt a chill. He and Rahim worked incredibly hard on the farm. He didn't understand how they could make the land produce more. Baba Jan was living in the past, holding on to the old family land, trying to live as his family had when he was a boy.

But this was a new Afghanistan. Whatever Baba Jan said about the Americans, however much their generators annoyed everyone all the time, their arrival was a chance for Afghanistan to start again. And when Baheer had seen that truck arrive for the soldiers next door, he'd come up with a plan that might just be the solution to their problems.

But Baba Jan was not in any kind of mood to hear this sort of idea. He distrusted Americans—those infidels, as he called them—even more than Baheer distrusted his teachers back in Kabul. But here at last was a chance, maybe, to put his education, all those English classes to work to help the family.

"The money from the sale would be more than enough to feed us all through winter, with enough left over to fund the business improvements we talked about," Uncle Kabir said.

"I do not want to hear any more talk of selling our land! My grandfather used to say that owning land is the pride of every man. I am not selling my pride," Baba Jan shouted. "Maybe the sale would get us through this winter, but what about after that? Hmm? Have you thought of that? No! With our land we can always at least feed ourselves, but without it . . ."

Baheer smiled as the idea came to him. Baba might listen to his proposal if it meant keeping the farm. His history teacher would call it a compromise, and was always saying that this was something Afghanistan desperately needed.

Allah, please help me. Please cool my grandfather's anger and protect me in what I am about to do. Ameen. Baheer took a deep breath and entered Baba's study with the tea. "I know how we can fix the family's financial challenges and keep the farm."

"You were listening!" Baba Jan thundered, wide-eyed.

"Please forgive me, Baba Jan, but you were all so loud, and I was just now coming with hot tea for you. I could not help but hear."

Baba Jan stroked his beard for a moment, staring at Baheer.

"Leave the tray and go," Baba Jan said.

"But Father, can we hear his proposal?" Baheer's father asked.

Baheer didn't wait, but with a fast silent prayer in his heart, he blurted out, "A boy in my school, Omar. His father is a mechanic, and he is restoring an old truck. I heard the Americans pay two hundred American dollars per trip to Afghan truck drivers." He'd heard this yesterday from Killian, but Baba Jan didn't need to know he'd been talking to the soldier. "They need many deliveries, materials of all kinds, probably even more when their base is complete. If we bought that truck, we could earn money hauling supplies for the Americans." Baheer let out a shaky breath.

Uncle Kabir shook his head. Uncle Feraidoon closed his eyes. Baheer's father put his hand on Baheer's shoulder.

When Baba Jan answered, his voice was even but cold. "You know I do not trust those infidel foreigners. Those harami soldiers think we are dirt. They will cheat us. Or worse." Baba Jan poured himself a cup of tea. "Now all of you listen to me. Have faith. Allah the Most Merciful will protect us. We will overcome these challenges without working with the new invaders and *without* selling our land. That is the end."

The finality was clear in his voice, so Baheer's father and uncles led him out into the courtyard, closing the door behind them. "It was a good try, my son," his father said sadly. "But don't worry. He is at least right when he says we will get through this . . . somehow."

On his way home from school three days later, Baheer was surprised to find ten elders who lived on their street, including Baba Jan, standing in front of their compound. Most gatherings were in the tea shop or outside the mosque, not here in the street.

"Keep your voice down!" said Habib Khan, who lived at the end of the block. "They'll hear you."

"Good!" Haji Dilawar, who lived on the far side of the American compound, shook his fist. "I want them to hear me! This cannot continue. From one side of their faces they say, 'We want to help you,' but then their generators run all day and night." He pointed a shaking finger at Habib Khan. "*You* do not live next door to them! Only Haji Mohammad Munir Khan and I share a compound wall with them. They look over their walls! You know they do! They do not have good Islamic manners as we do. You know how they are with their broken families and the way their women run wild."

All the men nodded. Haji Dilawar continued. "They have none of their own women with them, so they try to watch ours. I tell you they must go!"

Baba Jan nodded. "The walls of their compound outside of town are complete. So what if their buildings inside their walls are unfinished. They are soldiers. They can camp!"

Haji Anwar motioned all the men closer to him. They seemed to notice Baheer approaching right then.

"Go on home," Baba Jan said to Baheer. "This is not—"

"Let him hear," Haji Anwar said. "He is not a little child anymore. My son was fighting the Russians with me when he was younger than Baheer is now."

Baheer's cheeks felt hot. It was an honor for the man to remember his name. Haji Anwar was a legend in the community. In the 1980s he had been a local mujahideen commander, leading his fighters in a vicious battle against the Soviets outside of Farah right where the Americans were building their base now.

Commander Anwar spoke in a quiet, deep voice that made everyone, even Baba Jan, lean in closer and pay attention. "Their beliefs do not matter. They are powerful. The Soviet Union is gone. America remains, even after the country suffered a terrible attack. This is not something to take lightly."

Baheer watched the man speaking so passionately, saw the other local leaders look at him with respect. It didn't make any sense to compare the Americans to the Russians. Killian and his fellow soldiers weren't installing deadly minefields or mowing down Afghans with helicopter gunships. They'd ended Taliban control. And Killian was mostly a kind person. Baheer thought about speaking up, but he dare not interrupt the commander.

"This is not like when we gathered together and persuaded our provincial governor to provide equipment to level the street," the commander continued. "The American soldiers will not move simply because we want them to."

At last there was a pause in the conversation. Baheer spoke quickly before he lost his courage. "Excuse me, Com—"

"Don't call me Commander," said Commander Anwar. "That war is over."

You're a fool, Baheer. Baba Jan will be furious if you insult the men. But it was too late to be silent now. "Has anyone tried to ask the soldiers to move to their base?"

Most of the men laughed. But Baba Jan fixed Baheer with a serious stare. Not necessarily angry, but he was clearly not in the mood to be embarrassed.

"This boy is deewana!" Haji Dilawar boomed. "They have rifles. Machine guns!"

The laughter died down when the commander held up his hand. "We do not share a language, and I've heard the Afghan interpreters they've hired cannot be fully trusted."

"They're being paid to do the filthy infidels' bidding," said Haji Dilawar. "How trustworthy could they be?"

"I know English," Baheer said. He took a deep breath, trying to appear confident. "You can trust me." Haji Dilawar looked like he was about to burst out with an objection. Baheer, legs shaking, quickly continued, "If we all go together to ask the Americans to move, we might convince them. The worst that would happen is they would say no, and then we'll be in the same situation as we are now."

Habib Khan raised his eyebrows and shrugged. Some of the other men nodded. Commander Anwar smiled. "I told you, Haji Munir Khan, he is not a little boy anymore. He is your grandson. The decision is yours. But I say we should do as the boy suggests. Tomorrow."

Baheer opened his mouth to speak again, preparing to explain his connection with Killian, but Baba Jan placed a hand on his shoulder. "Are we agreed?" The men mumbled agreement, although Haji Dilawar did not look very pleased with the decision. "Bale," Baba Jan said. "Then we'll meet here tomorrow morning. This probably won't work, but if there is any chance of stopping the endless roar of those generators, we must try."

The men all shook hands with one another, including Baheer, and then went toward their homes up and down both sides of the street.

Baba Jan stopped Baheer just inside the compound gate. "You spoke well to the men. Confident. Well reasoned. But respectful." Baba Jan stroked his beard for a moment. "Do you think you are ready for this?"

Baheer had been working hard on his English, both in school and in his conversations with Killian. PFC Killian might listen to him, and *he* could persuade his commanders. Baheer smiled nervously. If this worked, Baba Jan and the neighbors would be very pleased.

"I can definitely do it, Baba Jan," Baheer said.

"Be ready. Go relax for a while before going to the farm," Baba said, opening Ferdowsi's poetry book, *Shahnama*.

Baheer could not remember the last time his grandfather had spoken about him so kindly. The man did not hand out

189

praise lightly. The compliments almost made Baheer want to dance across the dusty courtyard.

If it didn't work and the Americans refused to leave, nothing would be gained, but nothing would be lost either. In some ways Baheer felt like his prayers were being answered. Tomorrow morning, there was a chance his education might count for something important in the real world. Thanks be to Allah.

———◇———

The next morning, Baheer dressed in his school attire—gray khaki pants and a sky-blue shirt—and joined Maryam outside. She was helping their little cousins make mud pies. Baheer smiled, and a part of him wished he could stay home and play.

Don't go thinking baby thoughts, he told himself. *You look like a respectable Westerner. You speak their language well enough. You know at least one of the soldiers. Time to toughen up and give this a try.*

"Wow! You look like the boss in that Indian movie," Maryam said.

"It's so neat," Sapoora said.

"Thank you," said Baheer. He went toward Baba Jan's building.

"I thought you didn't have school until this afternoon." Baba Jan smiled. "Why are you wearing that?"

Baheer was about to speak when Grandmother said, "Leave the boy alone."

"I'm just asking." Baba Jan laughed.

"Baba Jan, I think dressing this way will help when we meet the Americans." Baheer's face flared hot. He already felt enough like an imposter without being mocked for his clothes.

"Ah," Baba Jan said. "Well, let's hope you're the expert on the Americans."

After breakfast, the men from the neighborhood arrived.

"You ready to tell those filthy infidels to leave us alone?" Haji Dilawar patted Baheer's shoulder. "We need youngsters like you to stand for our people."

"Tashakor, Haji Saheb." Baheer smiled.

"We're all here," said Commander Anwar. "Let's go. You've talked to these soldiers before?"

Baheer nodded. "Bale, Saheb."

"Then we'll follow Baheer's directions," said Commander Anwar.

Just a little pressure.

In a few minutes, Baba Jan and ten respected Farah men headed toward the American compound. Baheer felt honored to be among them as Baba Jan gently moved him to the front of the group.

"Stay away from the wall," Baheer said. "They don't like us too close."

"I'll walk where I wish," Baba Jan declared.

"You're right," Haji Dilawar said to Baba Jan. "These men need to move, not us."

If that's how they felt, there was no turning back. The group had drawn the attention of the guard near the gate. Baheer waved at the soldier. "Hello, sir," he said, keeping away from the wall.

"You talking t'me?" The guard spoke quickly, but Baheer could still understand him.

"Yes, sir. We'd like to talk to your . . . um . . . manager," Baheer said. He knew "manager" wasn't right, but he couldn't remember the correct word and hoped the soldier would understand.

"We don't have a manager." The soldier laughed. "Maybe you wannatalktoourseeay guy?"

The soldier spoke too quickly, and he mumbled, but whoever the soldier was talking about was probably the man they needed, so Baheer pretended to understand. "Yes, sir. That would be good."

The guard spoke into his radio, probably some kind of Army code. Baheer couldn't understand him. A moment later, he asked Baheer, "Who're you?"

"We are your neighbors." Baheer nodded at the elders behind him.

"Neighborstheysay. Yes. One of them speaks English," the guard said into the radio. "Y'all can come to that small gate."

Baheer motioned for the group to follow him, smiling a little when they did so. "They asked us to come to the small gate," Baheer told them.

A few of the men nodded, as if impressed Baheer had gotten them this far.

The gate opened and a big soldier waved them in.

"Come. One. By. One." The soldier pointed at a short wooden stool. "Talashi."

"You want to search," Baheer said in English, entering the compound, but his words were lost in the chaos.

The house inside the American compound was not unlike some of the houses in Baheer's family compound, if a little smaller, but no one he knew would live like this. It smelled like they had ten cows whose manure had never been cleaned, and they'd built a meter-high wall of sandbags along the edge of the concrete porch. In the narrow lane between the house and the far wall was a deep trench and sandbag bunker.

Soldiers watched the Afghans like they were zoo animals. Two of them smoked cigarettes on the concrete guard platform in the far corner. Three green cots were cluttered with blankets, packs, and other gear by the wall. How many men were squeezed in here?

"Stand here. Hands up. Face the gate," the chubby soldier commanded.

Baheer and his neighbors filed in and stood inside the small area while two soldiers closed the door with a loud clang, locking them all in.

"Sa Waayi?" Baba Jan wrinkled his nose, asking what the man said.

"They must talashi. Follow what I do," Baheer said.

He volunteered to be searched first, standing on the stool with his hands up. The large soldier hit Baheer's heel rather hard. Baheer looked back and shrugged.

"Keep your legs wide open," the guy shouted.

Baheer spread his legs.

The soldier patted Baheer, starting at his ankles, feeling up, up, up between his thighs. He shivered. He recalled the way that harami talib had caressed his face in his old school. Why would they search all the way up there?

The soldier stopped centimeters short of too high. "You're done!"

"Baba, please stand as I did," Baheer said.

In ten minutes, the soldier's hands had wandered over everyone.

"This is no way to treat guests, one's neighbors," Haji Dilawar whispered.

"On the radio, the American president said our nations are friends," whispered another. "This isn't friendly."

"I might do the same if I were running a little base like this," the commander said.

Baheer looked around but couldn't find Killian. *You have to be here. I need your help.*

"They're like animals," Haji Dilawar said. "Why don't they clean?"

"They're savages," Baba Jan said. "This soldier's filthy. He smells like an old goat."

Baheer hoped the Americans couldn't understand them.

"This way." Baheer led the others, following the soldier into the small guest room.

The walls and ceiling of the guest room were stained dark. A few blue plastic chairs and a gold-colored sofa were on one side of the long room. The space was too narrow for a proper comfortable guest room.

"Sit down, please," said the American who had searched them.

Baheer translated.

Baba Jan was reluctant to sit. "The previous owners cooked food or burned trash in here," he said, looking at the dark soot patches marring the sofa. "This will dirty our clothes."

Baheer wanted to shout, *Do you want to talk to the Americans or no?!*

"Let's spread out my shawl, Haji Saheb," one of the neighbors said. Baba Jan agreed and, to Baheer's relief, finally took a seat.

A tough-looking older soldier with a pistol holstered on his right thigh entered the room. The Afghans rose to show respect. Baheer smiled when Killian entered behind him.

"Baheer!" Killian said. "How're you?"

"Fine," Baheer responded.

"Please sit down, gentlemen," the older soldier said. "So, you speak English," he said to Baheer. "Would you translate for me?"

"Yes," Baheer said, nodding eagerly. *Now we're finally getting somewhere.*

The man spoke slowly and clearly, pausing between phrases to let Baheer translate. "I'm Major Besser, the leader of the Civil Affairs group here. My job is to work with Afghans to see how the United States Army can help. I'd offer tea. Unfortunately, we don't have tea in this temporary base. Would you gentlemen like coffee instead?"

Baheer translated. The men accepted the offer, as he knew they would. It would have been rude to refuse the offer of hospitality. These men were not rude like the Americans. Killian left to fetch a tray of steaming paper cups, offering one to everyone. Baheer tried a sip and immediately had to struggle not to spit it out. He could tell by the looks on the faces of the other Afghan men that they did not like this coffee either. It was black as night, smelled like death, and tasted like ashes. Baba Jan, the perfect model of proper courtesy, could not even pretend to like it, but he drank it.

Major Besser sipped his drink. "Coffee keeps our Army running."

Baheer translated, wondering how this Army ever did anything with this sludge for fuel.

"It's good to meet you men," said Major Besser. "How can I help you?"

Baba Jan said, "Tell him, we are so happy that they are living in our neighborhood."

Baheer struggled to hide his surprise at this lie. He told the major, "They welcome you to our neighborhood."

The major nodded.

"Tell him we don't mind them staying here, but there are some problems."

Baheer translated Baba Jan's words for the major, but he worried Baba Jan was being too bold.

"First," Baba Jan said, "when you enter or leave your compound, you block the whole street. Second, your generators run constantly. They make too much noise. We see the outside wall is complete on your base near the airstrip. If you don't mind, would you please move there? We don't wish to be rude. You needn't leave immediately. Perhaps you can take your time and move in the next two weeks." Baba Jan was done.

The other neighbors had been nodding while Baba Jan spoke. Nobody paid attention to Baheer. That was good because it was too long a speech for Baheer to remember and translate.

"Sir," said Baheer. "They say, because of the street blocking when you come and go, and the constant noise of the generators in the neighborhood, they would kindly request you to move to your new constructed base outside the city."

"Oh. That's why you've come?"

Was the major surprised or angry? Baheer couldn't quite tell.

Major Besser sat back, took a sip of coffee, and then smiled. "Tell them we will leave this compound in two days."

Baheer translated this to Baba Jan and the neighbors. Baba Jan seemed surprised. The men smiled. Several of them nodded respectfully to Baheer.

The major said, "Thank you for bearing with us for so long. Our generators are too noisy. We're sorry for disturbing you." He let Baheer translate.

Baheer was puzzled. What had the major meant about bears? He ignored that part, telling the Afghans that the Americans were grateful and also sorry about the noise.

Almost everyone in his group said "Tashakor." It seemed they were not expecting this from the Americans. Baba Jan looked shocked.

Major Besser asked if the men needed anything else. They said no.

"Please thank him for his time and for this . . . coffee," Baba Jan said.

Baheer translated and everyone stood up.

Killian smiled at Baheer. "I better start packing."

Baheer laughed a little.

"Please come see us again if we can help with anything," said the major.

Baheer translated, and all the men shook hands. Baheer was pleased to see Major Besser seemed to understand the Afghan custom, leaving no one out.

Baba Jan waited until the other men had left the sitting

room and then squeezed Baheer's shoulder. "Ask him if I may speak to him about something else."

Baheer did so and the major agreed.

Baba Jan looked at Major Besser as he spoke. "If you and your men need any help moving your equipment and supplies from here to your base, I have a large truck. I would haul everything for free."

Baheer looked at his grandfather wide-eyed for a moment, shocked at the lie. Baba Jan didn't own a large truck. But Baba Jan nodded at Baheer seriously, so Baheer translated. Before the major could say anything, Baba Jan spoke again. "My truck is in good shape, and my sons are excellent reliable drivers. I guess your supplies are coming in from Kandahar? We know the way well. Would it be possible for my sons to also haul materials to and from Kandahar for you?"

Again Baba Jan allowed Baheer to translate. He was amazed at his grandfather's boldness, and excited he was taking Baheer's suggestion from a few days ago.

Baba Jan continued, "I've heard from other truck drivers that the rate is two hundred American dollars per trip?" Baheer translated.

Major Besser smiled and nodded. "I think that's the rate. I don't handle the supply situation directly, but I can talk to the officer who does. I know he's looking for more good, reliable drivers. I accept your offer to help us move to our permanent base, but the Army would never let me accept such an offer for free. I'd have to pay you at least one hundred American dollars."

It took Baheer a while to translate all of that, and he worried the whole time that Baba Jan would be offended by the officer turning down his gift of free help. Mostly, he struggled to concentrate on getting the translation right.

"Good," Baba Jan said, reaching out for another handshake. "My compound is next door to the west. Please let me know when you all are ready to move and when my sons might start driving to Kandahar for you."

Major Besser promised he would do as Baba Jan had asked, and a moment later the two of them left the sitting room and joined the other Afghan men in the street. Baheer was burning to ask his grandfather about their supposed truck, but Baba Jan shook his head.

As the group walked down the road, Commander Anwar said, "I didn't think they'd agree to leave so soon."

Habib Khan said to Baba Jan, "Haji Saheb, could you imagine going to the Russies and asking them to move? They'd have shot the messengers!"

"The Americans don't even know basic respect, though," said Haji Dilawar. "They're filthy. I must wash the taste of that coffee from my mouth."

Baheer thought the man was acting petty. The Americans weren't Afghans. They couldn't be expected to know proper culture.

•

Another neighbor patted Baba Jan's back. "I'm just happy they're leaving soon."

Commander Anwar put his hand on Baheer's shoulder. "We must thank our young translator. Without his help, we wouldn't have been successful."

The men agreed, shaking Baheer's hand, thanking him. They seemed genuinely grateful, looking Baheer in the eye like a man. He felt like one of them.

"My family will be so happy to hear this news," said another neighbor. "Two days!"

"Yeah. That's enough," said Baba Jan. "As the saying goes, no chicken, no feces," Baba Jan said. He bid farewell to the neighbors and entered their compound.

Baheer followed Baba Jan, bolting the gate behind him. Baba Jan smiled at Baheer.

When he said nothing, Baheer spoke up. "Baba Jan, we don't own a truck, do we?"

He laughed a little. "I guess I better buy one very soon. There's a lot of money to be made in driving the Americans' stuff around."

"But you said we shouldn't—"

"Haji Dilawar is right about their filthy way of living and their ignorant, disrespectful ways. But they're not out to conquer or destroy us like the Russians were. Any army that will apologize and agree to our request that they move is an army we can work with." He shrugged. "We don't have to like the infidels, but they do have money. We might as well earn some of it."

"Bale, Baba Jan," Baheer said.

"You did a good thing today, Baheer," Baba Jan said. "Their language is horrible. It sounds like metal clanging on metal. But you've studied and learned it well." He closed his eyes for a moment. "In only two days I'll be able to sleep in peace." He laughed as he headed toward his study. "Most powerful army in the world, and they move their base at the request of a boy."

Baheer felt accomplished and important. The Americans were very strange, but at least they were capable of understanding a logical request.

FARAH, AFGHANISTAN
September 15, 2003

Joe never imagined he would miss the Unsafe House, but he wished he was back there now.

"Little more kerosene," Joe said.

Sergeant Paulsen splashed more fuel onto the burning sewage in the two cut-off bottoms of fifty-gallon fuel drums.

Joe backed away as a fiery mushroom erupted. "No more," Joe said. "That sludge might burst out of there. I'm dirty enough. I don't want a burning poop-soup shower."

"Roger that," Paulsen said. "Keep stirring, Killer."

Joe stirred the burning mixture with a metal pole.

This was a rotating duty at the Provincial Reconstruction Team base, more commonly called the PRT. Until the septic system was installed, they did their business in plywood

Porta-Johns. Signs were posted telling soldiers to urinate in the PVC pipes angling down into the ground and not in the crappers, but people didn't obey. This made burning off the waste take longer. They couldn't dump the stuff in the desert, at least not anywhere near their base, for fear of disease, so they had to stir it to help it burn off. The process smelled terrible.

First Sergeant Dalton had ordered poo-burning shifts begin at 0200 while he slept. Even though it was an insane hour, the one good thing about this duty was that it didn't take the full guard shift, so after an hour or so, they could go back to sleep.

Major Besser and the officers in charge of their unit had stuck to their pledge and moved from the Unsafe House to the PRT two days after Baheer and all the men from the old neighborhood had asked them to do so.

The Afghans had argued the Americans should move because their base was complete.

It was not complete.

There was the outer wall, a deep well, and one set of concrete-block buildings that would eventually be walled off from the rest of the PRT to serve as office and meeting space for the Civil Affairs soldiers. Eventually Afghan translators would be housed there, too. There was no septic system or latrines, no machine shop for vehicle maintenance, no proper barracks, and no kitchen or DFAC. Cookmaster had to prepare breakfast and supper on his little electric stove outside.

The days were always crushing hot, dust blew everywhere, and flies buzzed over everything.

The guard towers were unfinished in the corners of their football-field-sized square, and the steel doors were not installed on the north and south gates. That meant two soldiers were always posted on either gate, and two more manned a Mk 19 atop the big steel shipping container in the center of the PRT construction zone.

There was a lot of time to think while gazing into a barrel of flaming crap.

"This isn't what I thought war was supposed to be like," Joe said quietly.

"You didn't expect to be up in the middle of the night stirring burning poop soup?" Sergeant Paulsen asked.

"No. They didn't train us for this super-important duty." Joe laughed.

"Well, the good news is, Sergeant Walden says the latrines will be ready for use tomorrow, so this will be the last night we'll be burning off the contents of the Porta-John."

"Flush toilets," Joe said. "A miracle. But, I mean, at first I thought war would be all about hunting down the Taliban and Al-Qaeda, fighting real terrorists. But then I looked around this place, saw all these poor kids, got to know people like Baheer—you know that English-speaking kid who lived next door to the Unsafe House?"

Sergeant Paulsen nodded. "Shows up on the jingle trucks all the time now."

"Yeah, well, I met people like that. Other Afghans. They're nothing like what our training back at Fort Hood made me expect. So, OK. We're on a reconstruction mission. Help protect Civil Affairs soldiers so they can help the Afghans. But all we've done so far is pull guard duty while our base is built."

"Base is about done," Sergeant Paulsen said. "Rumor is we'll be starting convoy operations soon, driving all over Farah Province, maybe down south into Nimruz and north into Herat Provinces, providing security so CA can do village assessments, meeting with the town elders to see how we can help."

"Sure." Joe stirred the bar around, opening up a rich vein of fuel in the poo ash so the fire flared up good. "But let's say the rumors are true for once and we do go out on some missions. The *Daily Iowan*, the University of Iowa student newspaper, is one of the best college papers in the country. I thought if I could bring them some stories about what's really happening in this war, it might be a good way for me to get on as a reporter or columnist for the paper. But what am I going to write? Even if we go on these missions you talk about, escorting the CA while they talk to a village chief doesn't tell anyone anything about how the war is going and how we're doing against the Taliban."

Sergeant Paulsen was silent for a moment, then asked, "Why do you want to be a journalist? Why do you want to write the news?"

"You remember how on 9/11 everybody—well, everybody who wasn't in New York, at Ground Zero, or at the Pentagon or something—was watching coverage on TV? Those reporters and desk anchors were bringing everybody the information as it happened, about how we were suddenly at war again. That's what I want to do, tell the story of war in a way that really matters to people."

Paulsen poured on a little more kerosene. Flames shot up. "And it's hard to see how what we're doing connects to the larger movement of the war."

"Yes, Sergeant." Joe took a step back from the heat. "I'm burning poop!"

"And this is a war," said Sergeant Paulsen. "Isn't burning poop part of the truth of war?"

"A stupid truth. Nothing anyone wants to read about. It's disgusting."

Paulsen shrugged. "War is disgusting. Weren't you reading that book of Ernie Pyle columns when we were back at Fort Hood?"

"Yeah," said Joe. "He was a master. But he was writing about World War Two, the most intense war in history. Way more dramatic than—"

"No he wasn't," said Sergeant Paulsen.

Joe was confused. "What? Have you read it?"

Sergeant Paulsen nodded. "In college. Majored in history. Took a World War Two class. And Ernie Pyle was not writing about the war."

"*Every* story in there is about the war. Army engineers rushing to build a bridge on a cliff in Italy. Sailors on a Landing Ship Tank." Joe struggled to remember the details. Army time was different than normal time. He'd read that book a lifetime ago. "Tail gunners in a bomber crew and how they—" Joe stopped, watching Paulsen smile. "He wrote about the people," Joe said. He waited for Paulsen to swoop in with laughter or some kind of snarky "gotcha" speech. Instead, Paulsen was quiet. Joe continued. "The infantry guys, the regular common soldiers. How they lived. How they survived."

"You're infantry, Killer," said Sergeant Paulsen. "You don't have to storm a beach at Normandy. You're in a forward area, not back on the safe Air Force base at Kandahar. What you're doing here is important. And even when your duty stinks—ha ha—it's still a part of the story. It still matters. Figure out the right stories to tell about this time."

Joe watched the light flicker on Paulsen, who stood shadowed on the opposite side of the fire. As a sergeant and team leader, he could have easily ordered two of his men to do this nasty duty themselves, while he relaxed on a guard position. But Sergeant Paulsen never pushed the worst of the duties onto others, never asked of his soldiers something he himself was unable or unwilling to do. He was in charge, but he worked with his soldiers. Joe promised himself in that early morning hour that he would find a way to tell the story of his team leader.

———◇———

The next night, instead of having a squad-level nightly meeting, every soldier who wasn't on guard duty gathered outside the CA building. The Delta Company commander, Captain Higgins, motioned for everyone to quiet down. He was standing next to three American men, all in civilian clothes. "Listen up, men! I gathered you all here because I want to introduce you to some new personnel we have here at the PRT. You'll see them going around in civilian clothes with relaxed grooming standards, meaning they're allowed to grow beards if they wish. These men work in Tactical Human inTelligence, or THT."

Baccam elbowed Joe. "THT? Shouldn't tactical human intelligence be THI?" he whispered.

Captain Higgins continued. "I'm going to let them take it from here."

One of the THT guys, a redhead with a thin, patchy beard, waved at everybody. "Good evening. My name is Jase. In order to preserve our covers for the kind of intelligence work we do, we don't use our rank or last names. So, again, I'm Jase." He motioned to his right at a skinny man wearing a Miami Dolphins hat. "This is my buddy Andy. And the big guy with the black shaggy beard is Eric. Our Afghan American interpreter, Ahmad, is a civilian, but he's an American citizen with the high level of security clearance needed for the kind of operating we do."

Mac coughed loudly, trying to cover his laugh. "Did he just say 'operating'?"

"Operating" was the word used to describe being engaged in highly classified super-spy stuff, deep Special Forces action. Joe had a lot of respect for the National Guard, but not a lot of people working with the Guard could accurately be described as operators.

Jase looked over the group in silence for a moment, nodding with his hands on his hips as though expecting everyone to be impressed. Finally, he continued. "I've been asked to tell you all that one of our regularly scheduled delivery trucks was stolen en route to the PRT. Our asset, the driver, was beaten up but survived. From what he tells us, it sounds like the Taliban stole his truck at random but got real lucky. Because that truck was hauling a lot of ammunition and explosives. So everybody needs to remain alert out there for IEDs."

The big black-bearded THT guy, Eric, spoke up. "Some of the intelligence streams from our various assets are coalescing around the idea that Israeli intelligence operatives may be in the area planting IEDs to kill Americans. We're still working to confirm that, but be advised."

Joe whispered to Baccam. "Why would our allies come all the way over here to kill us?"

Baccam shook his head. "The guy's crazy."

"Or they heard from some angry Muslims who don't like Israel and just made some stuff up. And be advised?" Mac whispered. "About what? We're supposed to keep a lookout for Israelis? It's not like they'd be in uniform."

"And that's all we have," said Jase. "Except that if you come across any information that might be of use to us, please come let us know."

The meeting broke up with the guys more confused than before.

———◇———

One day near the end of September, Joe was stuck on front-gate guard duty with Baccam. Of all duties on the PRT, guarding the front gate was the worst. The four corner guard towers were finally completed and they had air-conditioning and a plastic chair. A soldier could sit and sip coffee, eat snacks, and listen to music or audiobooks. But gate guards had to search incoming jingle trucks for bombs, pat down visiting Afghans checking for the same, and spend the whole hot shift in heavy body armor and helmets. Third and Fourth Squads had finally come out from Kandahar, so they had better guard rotations, allowing for better sleep. But that also meant that gate guard was six hours of hard work, and although Joe and his fellow soldiers were settling into their new life, there was still a risk on gate duty. If a truck bomb was launched against the PRT, the gate guards would be toast.

That day Joe and Baccam had the front gate. After patting down dozens of Afghans coming in for construction work that morning, they had three jingle trucks to search. Joe walked with an interpreter way out to the wire perimeter where Afghan guards had stopped the trucks.

The interpreter was about to tell the driver that he needed to climb down out of the truck to be searched when Baheer leaned out the passenger-side window. "Salaam, rafiq!"

"Baheer!" Joe called back. To his interpreter he added, "Hey, man. This guy's good with English. You can head back to the PRT and relax. We won't need you for this one." As the interpreter returned to the base, Joe shifted his attention back on Baheer. "I didn't recognize the truck. All the blue. And are those flowers painted on the side?"

Baheer said something to the driver and they both exited the truck and climbed down. "Business is good, so my grandfather say we must buy a second truck."

Joe brushed his boot along the dusty chains on the bottom edge of the vehicle. "Sweet jingle chains, man."

Baheer laughed. "Ah, yes. They are extra jingle, I think."

Both Baheer and the driver—his uncle, Joe thought Baheer had once told him—put their arms out, expecting a pat-down. Joe quickly searched them and then used a mirror on the end of a pole, looking under the truck, searching for weird wires or explosives. After inspecting the cab, Joe grabbed his radio and called the truck in clear.

"*Roger that, Ernie Pyle,*" Sergeant Paulsen radioed. "*They're still unloading the first two jingle trucks of the day, so that driver's going to have to wait awhile. Stay with the truck just to make sure nobody messes with it before it's clear to roll in.*"

"Roger that," Joe radioed back.

212

"We are stuck here," Baheer said. He explained the situation to his uncle, who yawned, stretched, and said something back. "My uncle wants to know if it is OK if he goes to sleep in the cab. He's tired from the long drive."

"Sure," Joe said. As the driver went back into the truck, Joe said to Baheer, "Your English is getting even better. How do you learn so fast? I mean, I can't imagine you had much of a chance to study English while the Taliban were in charge."

"I began to learn it in Pakistan."

Joe nodded. He'd read about thousands of Afghans fleeing to Pakistan or Iran during the wars. "The camps at Peshawar? I read those were terrible."

Baheer spoke slowly, as if concentrating on the right words. "The . . . how you say? 'Refugee'?"

"Refugee camps, yeah."

Baheer smiled. "We were refugees. But we didn't live in Peshawar. The refugee camps were very bad. My grandfather said to us not to go near the camp people."

"Why?" Joe asked.

"Many diseases in the camps. The kids there were going to mujahideen schools."

"That's good, right?" Joe asked. He'd read about the Mujahideen, the Afghans who had fought the Soviets. A lot of the Northern Alliance Afghans who had helped America remove the Taliban from power were Mujahideen. "Those guys were tough. Killed tons of those dirty Commie Russians."

Baheer shrugged. "It's hard to know. Mujahideen schools were no good. They make their own math books. Two plus two? Their book says two guns plus two guns equals four guns."

"They're not wrong, I guess." Joe laughed.

Baheer laughed, too. "Everything with them is more fighting. It must stop."

"Yes. It must. I guess that's why we're here," Joe said. "So you learned English in Pakistan?"

"Yes, there I was studying English. But now, I go to school here in Farah. And I am working to better my English."

"Why?" Joe wondered. "Why are you learning English? Do you want to work as an interpreter?"

"I am too young," Baheer said. "I have been thinking about this a lot. You will laugh. My idea is a silly dream."

"No, I won't," Joe promised. "I want to be a writer. I'm a sucker for silly dreams."

"My grandfather reads many great books, Afghanistan's and Iran's great old books. He talks about how good my country used to be. And why it is bad?" Baheer shrugged. "I think the Taliban? They were ignorant. They could not read. They knew nothing, especially not the Holy Quran. So, maybe . . . maybe we need school. We will know more, build more, do better. The Taliban *hate* girls going to school. I say send the girls to school! The Taliban say one thing, then we do the other thing. I want to maybe be a teacher, or Insha Allah, I want to make a new school that teaches English and also Afghan culture." He laughed. "But right now, I just study and help with the trucks."

Joe was about to ask more about Baheer's dream school, but Baheer continued with his own question: "What city are you from?"

"You wouldn't know if I told you." Joe laughed a little. "I'm from a tiny town called Riverside, in a state . . . er . . . a province called Iowa. In the middle of America. All green corn fields. The opposite of this desert."

"You are a soldier there?" Baheer asked.

"It's hard to explain," said Joe. He did his best to tell Baheer about the Army National Guard, and how, since 9/11—especially since the war had expanded to Iraq—the Guard had been activated a lot.

"You study at university?"

"Journalism." Joe saw that Baheer didn't seem to understand. "I'm learning to write for newspapers and magazines." He thought maybe he could show Baheer. "Here, I'll show you my notebook. Wait, can you *read* English or only speak it?"

"I speak it better than I read, but I can read it a little," Baheer said.

Joe reached into his pocket for the notebook so he could show Baheer some of the news stories he'd been trying to write, but when he pulled it out, an envelope from the last mail call fell to the ground. The wind picked up at that moment, and the paper skittered along the ground.

Baheer rushed for it, snapping it up and handing it back to Joe. "What is this?"

Joe smiled. "That is a letter from a very beautiful girl at my university that I started talking to before I had to come here."

Baheer looked up to the cab as if to see if his uncle was listening. He took a few steps away from the truck and spoke quietly. "And this is allowed? It is OK with her family for her to write you this letter?"

Wow. He's not even allowed to communicate through letters with a girl? Afghanistan was growing on him, but Joe couldn't help but pity Baheer for growing up in such a gender-segregated society. He hoped that with the Taliban out of the way, some of that would start to change. "Yes." He was careful not to sound condescending as he explained. "A letter is innocent. Not for you?"

Baheer shook his head. "No, no! We do not speak to girls outside of our family." He glanced nervously up at the truck again and spoke even more quietly. "We do not even speak *about* girls outside our family."

"Wow," Joe said. "I don't want to sound like I'm bashing on your country, but I'm sorry to hear that. Lindsey is pretty great. I hope to ask her out on a date when I get home."

"What is this date?" Baheer asked.

"Oh." *How can I explain this?* "It is when two people go to dinner or to a movie, and they talk and get to know each other. And maybe they will have feelings for each other. You know, romantic feelings? Like, eventually love."

Baheer shook his head again. He looked super embarrassed, like Joe had just been talking about the most pornographic stuff in the world.

"We do not have dates here," Baheer said. He was quiet a long time. He wiped his sweaty brow. "I am going to tell you a secret. You must tell absolutely no one. There is this girl I have seen when I walk to school. I do not know her name. That would be unthinkable for me to know her name. To me she is Mystery Girl. I would like to communicate with her, but this is not done."

It almost seemed like Baheer was asking Joe's permission, and although Joe was glad Baheer felt he could trust him, Joe wasn't sure how strongly he should advise him. "Well, I'm not going to tell you what to do. It's a . . . well, a complicated system you have here. But you say stuff like 'this is not done.'"

"It isn't!" Baheer said. He immediately checked himself and looked back to the cab of the truck to see if he'd been overheard.

"Yeah, well, about a year ago if you'd talked about people openly listening to music or girls going to school, you'd also have said 'this is not done here.'"

Baheer looked at him, then looked away. That seemed to be the end of that subject. Joe wondered if Baheer knew what he meant. "It's a new Afghanistan, man." Maybe the old ways had to change.

Finally, the jingle trucks inside the PRT compound had

been unloaded and rolled back out. Instead of walking all the way back to the gate, Joe climbed in and caught a ride as Baheer's uncle drove them up the path between the coils of wire, winding sharply back and forth around high concrete barriers, a set of obstacles designed to force vehicles to slow down so they couldn't drive straight through the gate. "I don't know how it is with you all, if you have to stay home after a certain time, but next week, next Saturday, a bunch of us guys are going to watch this movie *Star Wars*. Have you heard of it? It's this old movie about spaceships and light swords and stuff, at eighteen hundred—six o'clock. We have a TV set up and someone bought the DVD at the bazaar back in Kandahar. We just gotta wait till next week so we're not on guard duty. You'd have to be searched again, but my commanders said you could join us."

Baheer smiled. "I have not heard of this movie. It has always been hard for us to watch movies. Mostly we like Indian movies. The singing. The dancing. Amazing."

Joe laughed. "Yeah. I've seen parts of those." *So cheesy and melodramatic.* "Whatever you're into."

"Tashakor, but I am pretty sure we have a delivery to make at the United Nations compound near the bazaar next Saturday night. I am very busy with my studies and helping with the truck business. It helps when I am a translator."

"All right, buddy," Joe said as the truck stopped at the gate. He opened the door and climbed down. "Good talking to you. See you next time your truck comes in."

15

FARAH, AFGHANISTAN
September 28, 2003

It was almost one o'clock when Baheer's English teacher, Ustad Ahmadi, finally entered the class. Afghans were not as obsessed with clocks as Americans. Many Americans would yell if a truck was even ten to fifteen minutes late. Afghans did things more when the time was right, not when a watch or alarm clock said it was time. Still, their teacher was extra late today. It wouldn't have mattered to Baheer except it was one of those bright September days with a clear sky and weather—no wind, not too hot or cold—that would have pulled him toward sleep even if he were fully rested.

He was not fully rested. After Baheer returned home from the farm the night before, his father had told him he'd received word that the Americans had somehow acquired a civilian flatbed truck. "Maybe they took it in a raid on the

Taliban or from some highway robbers," Father had said. "The point is, they have no use for it and are willing to sell it. I'll need you to help me deal with them."

Baheer had studying to do, but Baba Jan had pointed at Baheer, his hand noticeably missing two silver rings with precious stones he'd always worn before the family bought their first truck from Omar's father. "Your English is good. The Americans listen to you. If your father and your uncle Kabir try to deal through the Americans' interpreter, we'll be cheated."

The deal had taken longer than they'd expected, and when they got the flatbed truck home, Father needed his help checking it over to see what repairs might be needed. It was late by the time Baheer was done working and studying.

"OK students. Go to page fifty-four!" Ustad said. Baheer sat up straighter and shook his head, trying to focus through his fatigue. "Today we are going to talk about all three forms of conditional sentences. Sometimes these are called 'if clauses' and . . ." He took almost half an hour explaining the rules, writing a formula on the blackboard for each form. Baheer and the other students took notes. This was great material. Ustad Ahmadi had a clear way of teaching that let Baheer see when he had recently said something in English in a way that was not quite right.

Rahim sat next to him, but sitting was all he did. He took no notes, asked no questions. Rahim's English sounded more and more like a conversation with a very small child. *He is wasting his opportunity.* Already Baheer's learning was helping him and helping the family. Sometimes Baheer was too busy translating for his uncles on truck runs to American bases to get stuck with farm work. But more than that, he'd been able to help get the family into the truck business. Baheer knew the American curse words, knew how the soldiers talked, and how much they hated the Taliban, all useful for getting better terms from them.

The night before, when he was bargaining with the Americans for the flatbed truck, Baheer told the truth, about how he hated the "mother-ducking" Taliban, too. His intentional error made the American soldiers laugh and shake Baheer's hand. He told the truth about how he wanted to use the trucks to help the Americans and build up Farah Province. In the end, the stupid rich Americans had agreed to Baheer's ridiculously low first offer. Most Americans were good people, but all of them were terrible at bargaining.

His new skills in English and in mathematics were helping to make life better for Baheer and his family far faster, and with less physical pain, than farm work. That was one reason he loved the private English classes he and Rahim took every day after the regular school day. He watched Ustad Ahmadi at the front of the room, so passionate at teaching. Baheer knew in that moment that, somehow, he would teach at a school or university. He might open his own school, Insha Allah. By helping people learn, he would be transforming them into their better selves, into people who were the opposite of the Taliban, people who had hope and knew kindness.

This, Baheer thought. *Classes like this are the best hope for Afghanistan.* He'd thought this before. He'd said this before. Lately, he'd made the mistake of voicing these ideas around Rahim, who had only mocked him.

"Baheer, it is your turn," Ustad said.

Pay attention! Baheer told himself. *You're bad as Rahim.* Every day, Ustad asked one person to present, in English, a news story he'd heard from the BBC News radio channel.

"Yes, sir." Baheer stood up with his notebook. On the chalkboard he wrote "September 28, 2003."

"Last night's BBC News was about George Bush, the president of America, and Tony Blair, the prime minister of England. They discussed working to build a new Afghanistan.

"More important, yesterday, the Farah Department of Education inaugurated a new building in Merman, Nazoo Girls' High School, which was partially funded by the PRT, er, the Provincial Reconstruction Team at Farah. This is the first and very famous high school for girls in the city. Fifty girls have started their studies there. But because there were no experienced women for principal, a former boy school's teacher is principal. Nevertheless"—Baheer hoped he'd used that big English word correctly—"more and more girls are going to school than ever before. I hope someday all the girls and boys can go to school. Thank you!"

The students and teacher clapped, except for Rahim, who merely yawned. Baheer returned to his spot on the floor.

Rahim leaned closer to him and whispered, "Man, there's a war going on and you talk about girls in school."

Finally, after their teacher's warm encouragement and a brief reading assignment in English, class was dismissed.

After the private English class had ended, Baheer and Rahim headed toward their bikes. As usual, Rahim hurried much faster than Baheer. *Good. Race home as fast as you can, Brother.* Baheer didn't like those rare days when Rahim stayed with him the whole way home. Then Baheer couldn't even glance at Mystery Girl.

They'd never spoken, and yet he and Mystery Girl seemed to understand each other. As if in answer to his thoughts, there she was, walking beneath the twisted old tree next to the dry irrigation ditch. And there was that warm, nervous feeling in his chest. As she passed, no more than a meter and a half away, he could almost feel a spark of electricity coming from her. He heard her giggle, just a little bit, and the sweet sound almost made him drop the bike he was walking.

But there was more than that. She'd been carrying an English textbook. She was studying English, just like him. He remembered Killian's letter from an American girl he liked. Killian had said it was a new Afghanistan, suggesting, without outright saying it, that Baheer should write a letter to Mystery Girl. But he'd told Killian the truth. That was not done in Afghanistan. If anyone else found the letter, the resulting punishment would be extreme. But if he could write to her in English, very few people would be able to read it. If questioned, she could say it was her homework. English was a perfect secret code.

Baheer smiled and turned to look back, but Mystery Girl was gone. He rode away on his bike, excited about his new plan.

Back at home, he dropped off his bike and changed into his work clothes, finding Rahim already changed and Maryam waiting for his notes from school.

"What took you so long getting back?" Rahim asked. "I've been waiting a long time. The main irrigation channel on the north end has collapsed a little, and it won't dig itself out."

"I'm hurrying," Baheer said.

Maryam smiled at him. "I hope you wrote everything down," she said. "Last time you left out key points, and then you were annoyed when I had to ask you questions."

"I didn't get annoyed." Baheer handed over his whole schoolbag.

"I was annoyed," Rahim said. "I was, because it's all so much of a waste of time."

Maryam snatched Baheer's schoolbag and squeezed his arm. "Thank you, dear brother," she said. "And you, my other dear brother. You need to find a break. Working that farm like a mule is making you grumpy."

"She may be right," Baheer said when the two of them

were out on the street. "I'm sorry if I haven't been helping enough. I'll try to do better."

"No, I'm sorry." Rahim clapped Baheer on the shoulder. "It's just that we never seem to catch up on the farm. And school . . . for example, today in English class. Three types of conditional clauses? I don't understand." Baheer was about to offer to help, but Rahim quickly continued. "I hate the stupid language. What's wrong with our own language?"

"Nothing, but knowing English—"

"I don't want to talk about it," Rahim said kindly. "Is that OK? I need a break from it."

"Sure." Baheer stopped outside the door to the compound the Americans had once occupied. "I only need to stop here quickly to see how the new truck is doing."

Rahim sighed, but Baheer was already knocking. A moment later their father opened the door, grease smeared on his cheek and his clothes dusty and stained. "Assalamu Alaikum!" He waved with a large wrench. "My son, I don't know how we managed to get this truck all the way back to Farah last night. Bullet holes have this thing leaking all over."

Their first truck took up a lot of room in their compound but still fit. When they had bought their second truck, they needed more room. So the family began renting the old American compound. Now they had three trucks, barrels of fuel and oil, tools, tires, and even some freight waiting to be transported that they were storing there. For the first time in months, Father and his uncles seemed cheerful and hopeful. And with the trucks just on the other side of the wall from their own compound, it was easier to guard from thieves or intruders.

"I didn't know you knew how to fix trucks," Rahim said to Father.

Baheer nodded. Their father was an excellent carpenter. He could make wood do anything, take any shape. But working on this old flatbed truck seemed completely different.

Father spun the wrench around a couple of times. "For a man to make it in Afghanistan, he must have many skills and can't be afraid to try new things." He started back toward the truck, patting a dusty bullet-hole-riddled fender. "But don't worry. We will get this truck repaired. Your uncle Kabir thinks we'll be able to profit more from the rug business using our own trucks. He's working on the numbers in the house. Your grandfather is in there, too, talking to Haji Dilawar about something. I don't know what, though." Father pointed toward the house in the other half of the compound. "He has some contracts in English that he would like you to try to read."

"Come on, man." Rahim tugged at Baheer's sleeve. "We have work to do at the farm. You can't translate now. We need to work while we still have daylight."

Baheer shook himself free as he led the way to the house in the other half of the compound. The place had been transformed since the Americans left. He stepped up on the concrete porch. The sandbags had been removed. The trench over by the wall had been filled in.

"It's illegal. It's dangerous. It's un-Islamic," Baba Jan said inside the house.

Baheer stopped himself just as he was reaching for the door handle. He met Rahim's raised-eyebrow look.

"Illegal?" said the other voice.

"Haji Dilawar," Baheer whispered to Rahim, who shrugged.

Haji Dilawar continued, "Who is to say what is legal? Who writes the law? The puppet government of the Americans? My friend, did we worry about what was legal according to the government the Russians imposed on us? Never! What is different, I ask you? Infidels are infidels."

What could they be talking about? Baheer wondered. Something was very wrong here.

"We came right here to this compound and asked the Americans to leave after two weeks. They answered with respect and said they would move in two days! You were there! The Russians would never have done this. The law aside, it is dishonest and dangerous."

"There is no danger," said Haji Dilawar. "My brother's friend was paid to transport supplies for the Americans. The Taliban paid him three times what the Americans paid for him to drive his truck down to Zaranj in Nimruz Province to a giant compound on the north side of the city. They took the cargo, beat up the driver a little bit, gave him a black eye and split lip only. Then, when the Taliban broke into the shipping container and found out he'd been transporting explosives and ammunition, they paid him an additional five hundred American dollars!"

The Taliban have a whole truckload of American explosives? Nothing good can come of this.

Rahim gripped Baheer's arm hard. "We should go. Now," he whispered. "This doesn't concern us. We don't want to know about this."

"The Americans would suspect him," Baba Jan said.

"What if they did?" said Haji Dilawar. "They can do nothing. So many trucks get robbed, nobody could sort out which were real robberies and which were drivers plotting with the Taliban. The Americans *still* paid my brother's friend. He made five times as much money for the one delivery."

Rahim pulled Baheer hard, away from the door. "Now!" he whispered with fury. "No good Afghan listens to the conversation of others this way. And we don't want to know anything about this."

They were already to the truck-lot side of the compound. "Rahim, did you hear what he—"

Rahim pushed him a little, glancing nervously at their father, who was working under the flatbed truck. "No," Rahim said bitterly. "And neither did you!"

Rahim reached for his arm again, but Baheer batted his hand away. "Stop it. What's the matter with you?"

His brother called to their father, "We're going to the farm now!"

"OK," said their father. "I will lock the door in a moment."

Baheer had to run a little to catch up with his brother. "But this is terrible," he said quietly. "If they've stolen—"

"Be quiet!" Rahim said. "Like I said. We don't know anything about it. We're not involved. You think you are so smart in school, almost to the head of the class line. Fine. Be smart about this and forget it. It has nothing to do with us."

Was that true? Surely Baba Jan was right. Stealing trucks, being dishonest in business dealings. These were not the ways of a good Muslim. What did the Prophet Mohammad (peace be upon Him) say about keeping deals with infidels? All Muslims should keep their transactions clear regardless of who they are dealing with. Baheer couldn't remember the exact words, but Baba Jan had once quoted something like this. Surely Baba Jan wasn't about to let the family try to make extra money by turning over their cargo to the Taliban? It was wrong, and far too dangerous.

And no matter what the Taliban claim, they are about as Islamic as the Americans. Baheer kicked a rock, sending it skittering through the dust along the road. *No, the Taliban are somehow less Islamic than the Americans. The Americans don't torture innocent Afghan kids like the Taliban.*

"I know what you are thinking, Brother," Rahim said after a long silence between them. "You want to tell the Americans what you imagine you know."

Had Baheer been thinking that? Not in any serious way.
"I wasn't—"

"It's bad enough to make money transporting American supplies. But if you tell them what you believe you heard, and the Americans use that information to attack the Taliban, the Taliban will find out somehow. They'll find a way to punish you and our whole family. We thought they were gone forever, but we've both heard the stories of Taliban cells returning to Farah Province and other parts of Afghanistan."

"I never said I was going to tell anyone anything," Baheer said. "But what can the Taliban do? The Americans have them on the run. They will not come after—"

"Baheer! You are the dumbest smart person I have ever met!" Rahim grabbed Baheer by the shoulders, standing close and looking him in the eye. "I don't like the Taliban either. I'm certainly not sad when the Americans bomb them. And I don't want the Americans or anyone else getting hurt. But we can't be in the middle of this. It is too dangerous. I know you think the Americans are your friends, but they pretend to like you only because you act like they do. You dress in their clothes for school and you speak their language. Those soldiers—what's his name? Killan?"

"Killian," Baheer corrected.

"Killian," Rahim said. "He talks to you only because he is stuck here where his government sent him. You yourself have said that he talks all the time about going back to America. When he goes, he will forget about Afghanistan and about you." Rahim thumped his own chest. "I am your brother. You and I are brothers, together forever. As your brother, I am asking you—I am asking you, in the name of the Prophet Mohammad (peace be upon Him), *please* do not tell anyone what you heard today. We owe the Americans nothing. They are not our friends. This is not our fight."

"Sure. Of course." Baheer's words cut through a flood of conflicting feelings and ideas.

16

FARAH, AFGHANISTAN
October 4, 2003

That night, Joe and a bunch of other soldiers were gathered in the new recreation building, all with their cardboard trays from the chow hall. They sat on the floor or on upside-down buckets if they could find them, waiting for the last of the guys interested in watching the movie to get their food and join the group.

An explosion rocked in from the distance like a sharp crack of thunder.

The crude jokes, laughter, and stupid conversations froze silent.

Joe closed his eyes and didn't move, a bite of chicken on his fork inches from his mouth. *Come on. Not tonight. Can't we just watch the movie?* First Squad was on Quick Reaction

Force. If there were any emergencies that required a rapid response, they'd call for QRF.

But nothing happened. The guys went back to talking, Joe ate that bite of chicken, and they started the movie. But just as on the screen the Rebel Alliance shut down the main reactor on the blockade runner, they heard the leaders shouting from across the PRT and radio traffic on the half dozen handhelds in the room lit up.

"*Let's go, Del-tah!*" First Sergeant Dalton shouted over the radio. "*Full battle rattle! QRF to your vehicles!*"

"Didn't even get to eat," Baccam said. Soldiers left their food trays on the floor and the movie still running as they sprinted out of the rec building to their stations.

Outside, the Tactical Human inTelligence guys were gathered around Captain Higgins.

"Sir," Jase said. "If you want, we can put on our Afghan clothes and go into town. We could blend in with the local nationals and see what they're saying about what's going on."

"Blend in?" Mac said quietly to the squad. "They're bright white and don't speak the language. Do they think the Afghans won't guess that they're Americans?"

"Um, no thanks, Jase," said Captain Higgins. "Better stay here. But, um . . . wow. Thanks." The captain rushed toward the command center. The THT guys wandered off to do whatever it was they did.

When a squad was on standby for QRF, they left all their gear, save for their individually assigned weapons, in the QRF Humvees. As Joe and the rest of First Squad were finishing scrambling into their armor vests, Lieutenant Riley ran up in armor and a helmet, 9-mil. strapped to his thigh. Their chief medic, Master Sergeant Dinsler, another medic named Specialist Gooding, and one of their Afghan interpreters were with him. The lieutenant pointed at the vehicles. "First Squad! Let's go! Mount up!"

Staff Sergeant Cavanaugh shouted, "Alpha Team, Humvee one! Bravo Team, number two! Have your night-vision goggles ready!"

Joe fought to keep his hands from shaking as he clicked the four-inch single-eye night-vision scope onto the flip-down mount on the front of his Kevlar. He was suited up, but he wasn't sure he was ready.

"Move it!" Sergeant Paulsen shouted. "Baccam, drive. Killer on turret. Mac—"

"Ride behind the driver and try to stay awake," Mac said.

"What do we got?" PFC Zimmerman asked as the squad scrambled into their armored Humvees.

Not knowing mission details was not unusual. Their job was to provide security for the CA soldiers who would be rolling out in a small civilian SUV. The squad rarely knew *why* they were going somewhere or what the CA guys would be doing, only that they had to protect them and the vehicles. The system had annoyed Joe at first. The journalist in him was always hungry for information, but he was getting used to not knowing much by now.

What I'm not used to is scrambling to roll out on QRF after an explosion has gone off somewhere. No time to think about it now. Do your job, Killian. Move!

Joe put his foot on the front bumper and heaved himself onto the hood of Humvee two. Two steps and a jump put him on the roof of the vehicle, and then he dropped into the circle hole of a turret, leaving only the top half of his body still visible outside. He unzipped and removed the light blue nylon cover from the Mk 19 in front of him on Humvee two's roof, dropping the cover onto the empty rear passenger seat. He unslung his M16 and lowered it into the vehicle, too, before gripping the handles of the Mk 19. Ahead, Alpha Team's Humvee spit gravel, racing toward the gate, with Shockley on the .50-cal. machine gun that pointed forward. The Toyota Land Cruiser with the two medics, the Afghan interpreter, and Lieutenant Riley followed.

Baccam peeled out after them. Joe pulled the turret release lever and twisted his body to rotate his Mk 19 to cover the rear, steadying himself with one hand on the gun's handle and the other on the support strut that held the turret hatch open. Down in the Humvee, Mac yanked the charging handle on top of his rifle to chamber a round. Joe flipped up the Mk 19 feed tray cover, set the chain of 40-millimeter grenades in place past the feed pawl, and slapped the cover back down, the standard posture for their missions so far.

"Killer," Paulsen called out. "Lock and load. Keep the safety on till you need to fire."

"OK. Here we go," Joe whispered. The situation must be really serious if he'd been ordered to chamber a round. That procedure on the Mk 19 was a bit tricky, requiring solid manpower. If a soldier didn't give it full strength, the link holding the lead grenade to the chain of grenades wouldn't break right, and the weapon would jam up. He pulled the charging handles back until the bolt locked to the rear. Then he hit the butterfly trigger, sending the bolt slamming forward to grab and position the lead grenade. The second pull was much harder. He yanked the charging handles with everything he had, breaking the grenade away from the others. With the bolt locked in the open position, the weapon was ready. He checked the safety switch below the trigger to make sure bumping the trigger wouldn't accidentally fire a bunch of grenades.

The sun had nearly set. "Quiet, everyone!" Sergeant Paulsen shouted. "Delta Actual, this is One, Bravo. Go ahead, over." Silence while Paulsen listened to whatever came over the net. "Roger. One, Bravo out." He shouted to everyone, "The UN compound was bombed. Multiple casualties."

A fresh wave of dread hit Joe. Baheer was supposed to be helping with a delivery to the UN compound tonight. *If these Taliban monsters . . .* Joe shook his head. *Focus. Do the job.*

Paulsen continued. "We're gonna close the street in front of the place. Lead vehicle will stop beyond the compound,

Land Cruiser will park in front, and we'll stop short of the compound. Killian, the commander doesn't want you shooting a bunch of grenades in the tight space downtown. Leave the gun ready in case the Taliban show up way down the street and we need heavy firepower. We'll all dismount and establish security perimeter. The medics may call some of us to go inside and cover them."

Joe let out a long breath. That was one bit of good news in this mess. He'd been wondering what he was supposed to do with a grenade-launching machine gun downtown right next to the bazaar. The Mk 19 wasn't a surgical-precision fire weapon.

The convoy passed the mountain of fifty-gallon drums at Farah's main fuel distribution point, the cemetery with its crude headstones and human-shaped mounds, and the police checkpoint, and then they were onto the paved bazaar road, passing more and more people and vehicles as they went along. A few more turns and they were on the right street, with the UN compound four blocks away.

Bright flash.

A boom!

The Humvee braked hard, throwing Joe toward the front of the vehicle, his ears ringing from the explosion. His back hit the turret lid, his head snapped up, and then he bounced forward, his front armor plate crashing into the rear of his gun.

"Secondary explosion!" Paulsen shouted. "Scan your sector, Killer, these guys aren't done!"

As their Humvee rolled ahead again, Joe regained his footing and watched behind his convoy. More than anything, Joe wanted to turn around to see what was happening. He wanted to see if Baheer's family's jingle truck was at the UN compound. Screams. Shouting. He couldn't look. He had his sector to cover.

"Get ready to dismount fast!" Paulsen shouted as the vehicle slowed. "Now! Go!Go!Go!"

Joe grabbed his M16 and was out of the turret, scrambling down. He jumped, having just missed stepping on a bloody human hand, shredded at the forearm. *This can't be real, can't be happening. Focus, Joe!*

"I'll cover down the street," Joe said, glancing to his guys so he could get his interval right.

A Land Rover burned in front of the UN compound, its top shredded. The explosion had collapsed part of the compound wall. More blood, debris, and human . . . stuff . . . littered the street.

Joe chambered a round in his M16, keeping the safety on. "You wanted real war, Joe?" he whispered to himself. "This is too real." It was getting dark, but the burning vehicle lit the place up too bright for night vision to work, and it cast a bunch of areas in shadow, giving the enemy concealment.

Like that day he and Paulsen had hurried to the roof, Joe's heart thundered through his body, his breathing came heavy, and his thoughts flew: *Are they coming?When are they coming? We got no cover out here. Shoot fast if anyone makes a move.*

A crowd of Afghans gathered on his side of the perimeter. Joe tried to hold them back. "Boro! You people gotta leave! Taliban could hit us again!" *Where's an interpreter when I need one?* The terp they'd brought with them must have gone into the compound with the medics to offer assistance.

The problem was, this road was the center of Farah's shopping district. Joe could tell from the pointing and sacks of goods that people had been shopping and were now trapped by the soldiers' barricade.

One man tried to walk through. "Road's closed! Back up!" Joe hurried in front of him to push the man back. "Boro!"

"Mac!" Sergeant Paulsen yelled. "Get inside with the medics. Got a radio?"

"Roger that, Sergeant!" Mac answered.

"I need help keeping these people back," Joe called to the others.

"Baccam, shift over there," said Sergeant Paulsen.

A jingle truck slowed to a halt behind the crowd, engine still running.

"No way that truck comes through here!" Sergeant Paulsen shouted. "Shoot the tires. Shoot out the radiator. Whatever you have to do. They are not driving that thing through here. In fact we need to back that truck up. Could be loaded with explosives."

The passenger door on the jingle truck swung open, and Baheer swung out, surveying the area.

Joe perked up. *Thank God! He's alive.* "The truck's no bomb, Sergeant Paulsen," Joe shouted back to his team leader without taking his eyes off his sector. He beckoned to Baheer. "Come here! I need your help. I need a terp."

"I need to get home," Baheer said.

Joe wanted Baheer as far from the area as possible, but without Baheer's help, even more people would be in danger. *Move fast. Get all these civvies, including Baheer, out of here.*

"Come on," said Joe, looking Baheer in the eye.

Baheer appeared nervous, taking in the horrible scene. Then he ducked back into the cab, and when he emerged, his head and most of his face was wrapped in a shawl.

What's he doing? "Baheer! Help me help your people! Please. Tell them they cannot pass through here. The Taliban might attack again. If they do, people here are going to get hurt. Tell them to leave. Now." Joe bit his lip and tried not to think of the boy on the roof as he brought his weapon up a little. "Tell them I have orders to shoot anyone who tries to come through here."

Baheer made his way through the crowd to Joe's side. "You would shoot—"

"No, Baheer, but just tell them that to make them leave. Now translate! Hurry!"

Baheer talked to the crowd. Some men argued. "Hey!" Joe showed his rifle.

Baheer kept talking. Gradually the crowd retreated.

"Thanks, man," said Joe. "Can you help out my guys on the other side of our perimeter?"

"Let me get my uncle out of here." Baheer ran to his truck and shouted up to the cab. The driver argued with him for a moment but then finally seemed to calm down, and the truck began a six-point turn so it could head back the way it had come.

"Bah—" Joe stopped himself. *Maybe Baheer doesn't want to be recognized here.* Joe shouted to his squad, "Our friend is coming through! He speaks English." To Baheer he added, "Go quickly. Tell anyone on the other side the same thing you said here, then get home!"

"Bale," Baheer said.

"Hey." Joe grabbed Baheer by the shoulder. "Tashakor."

Baheer nodded and ran, already shouting at the crowd down the street. Soon Joe didn't hear him anymore, and Joe assumed he must have cleared them out.

Eventually someone extinguished the vehicle fire, and Joe scanned the empty street through his green-tinted night-vision scope. The place settled into an eerie quiet save for warnings from his leadership to stay alert and the voices echoing from the compound. "Put pressure right there! Hold it! You gotta really press on it! Hold that IV bag up, I'll run . . . there. That's gonna need a tourniquet. He's gonna lose that leg. Twist that, Corporal! Tighter!"

———◇———

Hours later, Corporal MacDonald returned, blood soaking his uniform sleeves, the front of his armor vest, and his pants down to his knees. A red-brown streak swept across the right side of his face.

Joe risked looking away from the dark empty street before him, flipping his night-vision scope up to look at Mac in the little light out there. The guy looked like a zombie, exhausted, wide-eyed, kind of in a trance. *I'm so glad I didn't have to go in there.*

"You OK, Corporal?" Baccam asked.

Mac pulled a canteen from its pouch near his waist, unscrewed the top, took a long drink, and poured water on his face, trying to scrub the blood off. He took another drink.

Then he bent over and threw up.

17

FARAH, AFGHANISTAN
October 6, 2003

A cool breeze brought a chill to the gray evening as Baheer stood on the roof of his house, watching his cousins Patoo and Roma kick a ball around the back courtyard. They kept trying to get Maryam and Sapoora to play, but the two older girls preferred to sit beneath the mulberry tree talking about whatever girls talked about. Baheer backed up a little and sat down on the dome roof to avoid being seen. He didn't want to play either. The last time he'd come up here to get away from his family and to think, he'd been filled with hope about school.

Now Baheer's insides were seized by a mixture of guilt, doubt, fear, and—as had been a constant for the past two days—the horror of what he'd seen outside the United Nations compound Saturday night. So much fire. So much blood. He'd stepped right over a human hand. Five Afghans and a United Nations woman from Germany had been killed by the blasts. If the Taliban had timed the second explosion better, they would have killed several Americans.

If Uncle Feraidoon and I had made our delivery a little earlier, we'd be dead, too. Aloud, Baheer whispered, "Did I know about this? Could I have stopped it?" *A week! I knew about the Taliban's stolen explosives for a whole week and I did nothing!* But he didn't know if the explosives used at the United Nations compound were the same ones the Taliban stole from the man Haji Dilawar had spoken of to Baba Jan. The Taliban blew stuff up a lot. "This isn't my fault," he whispered.

"What's not your fault?" Baba Jan said from behind him. Baheer jumped. He'd whispered too loudly. Baba Jan chuckled. "Sorry. I did not mean to startle you."

"No. no. It's OK," Baheer said. "I'm fine."

"I do not think you've been fine since Saturday night." Baba Jan grunted as he sat down next to Baheer. "That bombing was a terrible thing. I give thanks and praise to Allah the Most Merciful for sparing my son and my grandson."

"Not everyone was spared," Baheer said very quietly.

"No," Baba Jan agreed. "You know I have worked hard all my life. My sons work hard. And now you work hard. I have insisted upon this because it is every man's duty to make a better life for his family if he can. Allah says in the Holy Quran chapter Al-Jumu'a in verses 9 and 10, 'O ye who believe! When the call is proclaimed To prayer on Friday

(The Day of Assembly), Hasten earnestly to the Remembrance Of God, and leave off Business (and traffic): That is best for you If ye but knew! And when the Prayer Is finished, then may ye Disperse through the land, And seek of the Bounty of God . . .' Seek of the Bounty of God. Even on our day of prayer, Friday, we are encouraged to work hard . . ."

This was a new idea for Baheer, but before he could deeply consider it, Baba Jan continued, "But we have to have faith in Him, the Almighty."

"You have provided a better life for all of us, Baba Jan," Baheer said. "Tashakor."

"But the one thing I have never been able to provide for long was peace." Baba Jan stroked his gray beard. "Food, yes. The chance to go to school, yes. And we have been blessed sometimes with a bit of extra money, so I have paid zakat and given money and food in charity in the name of Allah as he asks us in chapter 2, verse 110, 'And be steadfast in prayer and regular in charity.'" He was quiet for a moment. "We can plow the fields. We can read all the books. But we cannot seem to stop the fighting." From the courtyard below echoed the sound of the girls laughing and screaming as they played. "It is never easy to see these violent things. When I was younger I saw what a Soviet helicopter gunship had done to a line of cars filled with Afghans. When the cursed infidels had finally flown away, we rushed from our hiding to see if we could help those who had been shot. Oh. I nearly wept. There was nothing we could do for those people. There were no people left. We were far too late."

"It wasn't your fault, Baba Jan," Baheer said. "You could not have stopped the helicopter." Not like Baheer might have helped stop the United Nations compound bombing.

Baba Jan patted Baheer's back. Baheer was surprised. He was not normally a very affectionate man. He did not give hugs or make other such gestures very often. "No. There was nothing I could have done, and I believe that made it worse. I am still troubled by this memory from almost two decades in the past. I am an old man, my grandson. My generation failed Afghanistan."

"But your generation, your brother, helped stopped the Russians!" Baheer said. He could hardly believe what he was hearing.

"Only after ten exhausting, bloody years that devastated our country. And after we won, we failed to build a good, strong, hopeful Afghanistan. It is up to your generation now, Baheer, to make our home better. There must be something better than war or life under the Taliban. Insha Allah."

Baheer sighed a little, relieved his grandfather had said that last part. No man who had made a terrible deal to allow the Taliban to rob his trucks would then hope for life free of the Taliban.

It was the time of year when the dark of night came early, so Baheer couldn't be sure, given how so much of his grandfather's face was cast in deep shadow, but he thought he'd seen Baba Jan wipe a tear from his eye. He rose to his feet and coughed a little. "Don't stay out here too late. We have a truck parked next door waiting to be delivered to the American base as soon as they open in the morning."

"Bale, Baba Jan," Baheer said.

———◇———

Baheer rode in the truck with his father early the next morning, after prayers and breakfast. He hoped the Americans would not take too long unloading the truck or else Baheer would be late for school. And yet being on time was his smallest concern. As the truck passed the second roundabout on the bazaar road, he began to wish the drive would take longer, giving him more time to consider his decision, but their truck soon rolled to a halt inside the PRT's outer wire perimeter, just as the soldiers were coming on gate guard duty.

Killian was not among them. Baheer had learned the soldiers rotated through different kinds of work every four days. Four days on guard duty, four days driving around doing things in town, four days driving to do things far away. Outsiders couldn't easily keep track of the system, and he was pretty sure the Americans liked it that way.

Well, OK then. Killian isn't out here. That's a sign that I'm not supposed to tell him or the other Americans what I know. Rahim must have been right. This is not my war.

But even as he thought about that, he knew they were the thoughts of a coward. The Taliban weren't Muslims. They were evil. When they came for Uncle Kabir, Baba Jan had dared them to fight him. He had dared to tell the Taliban they were wrong when they shaved Uncle Feraidoon's head on the road to Farah. How was this war not about him if those harami Taliban had killed so many Afghans Saturday night? They would have killed Baheer, too, if he had arrived just a little earlier.

Finally one soldier and an Afghan interpreter showed up beside the truck. The soldier carried a rifle slung on his shoulder and a mirror attached to a pole. "Good morning," he said. The interpreter translated this, unnecessarily. "We need to search you and your truck before we can bring you in to be unloaded," the soldier said.

Before the interpreter could translate further, Baheer and his father were already out of the truck with their legs and arms spread, waiting to be patted down. By the time the search was complete and the truck cleared to drive into the PRT, Baheer had made his decision. The soldier was surprised to hear him say, in English, "I need to speak to PFC Killian, please. It's important."

———◇———

"Dude, are you serious?" Killian asked after Baheer had told him what he'd heard Haji Dilawar saying. He'd learned the word "dude" mostly meant "guy" and could be an expression of either friendship or amazement. The two of them were talking by themselves between two shipping containers while the rest of Killian's squad unloaded the truck.

"Of course I am serious," Baheer said. "Do you think I would joke about something like this?"

"No." Despite the chill in the air, Killian wiped his brow.

"This is a big deal, Baheer. The UN compound bombing, do you think—"

"I don't know anything about it," Baheer said. "I only know what I heard Haji Dilawar say. And nobody can know I've told you this."

"What do you mean?" Killian asked. "My commanders will want to know how I know about this. I can't *not* tell them."

Maybe he'd made a mistake. Maybe he should have listened to his brother and stayed out of this. "Listen to me. My family drives trucks to transport American supplies sometimes. That is all. I do not work with the Army like one of your interpreters or something."

"All right," Killian pulled a small notebook and pen out of his pocket. "I get you. Just tell me everything again so I have all the details right. Otherwise my commanders will want to ask you more questions."

"OK," said Baheer. "This is what I know."

————◇————

Two days later, Baheer experienced the now-familiar stomach flip and damp hands as he dismounted and walked his bike near the twisted tree by the dry canal. For months now, he and Mystery Girl had passed each other in this place, exchanging only glances and smiles, more than what was allowed by custom. Today, he would take an additional step—a jump—forward.

If he were caught, people would question his upbringing, his family's manners, and his personal integrity and character. If she were caught, everyone would question the girl's virtue and bar her from going to school. From what Baheer had learned from Killian, relationships between American boys and girls were completely different. In Afghanistan, girls were sometimes killed for even the suspicion of having been talking to a boy.

Maybe this is a bad idea, Baheer thought. *It's not too late to give up on this plan. Just keep on walking. Destroy the letter.*

With shaking hands, he pulled the paper from his pocket and unfolded it so he could review it one more time. The message needed to be perfect.

Dear Mystery Girl,

I don't know if your gaze toward me means anything. But, I hope it does. You have very beautiful eyes. I wanted to talk to you for a long time, but you know our society. They would say terrible things about us. That's why I am writing a letter.

By the look of your books, it seems you are a student. I think this is very good. I am wondering how you convinced your family to let you go to school. My sister is older than me and would like to go to school. I would like to help her. But how can I help her? Maybe you know.

I will understand if you choose to ignore this letter, but I hope you will write back. I have many things to tell you.

Sincerely yours,

Baheer wanted to write his name, but got scared of the consequences, even though, in English, the letter was basically in code. But if an English reader found the letter, then it would be very bad if he'd left proof of his name. And maybe he'd read all her signals wrong. She could complain to someone, showing his name. So Baheer did not write his name on the note. He wanted to know her, but even if she didn't mean anything by her signals, she might at least write back, helping him find ways to send Maryam to school. If she wrote back, kindly, then maybe he could tell her his name in the future. Now that the letter was ready, getting it to the Mystery Girl was the biggest challenge.

Baheer's hands were so sweaty, he worried he'd ruin the letter. He carefully refolded it. Everything he had been raised to believe told him what he was about to do was wrong. But this girl was amazing.

Then he saw her.

Mystery Girl almost smiled as she walked in Baheer's general direction.

He held the folded letter in front of his body carefully so that she'd be able to see the flash of white, but anyone else around might not notice. He didn't dare try to hand it to her. Their fingers might touch, and if anyone saw that, they'd be in terrible trouble.

Only two meters remained between them. *Now! Do it now! Drop the letter so she will see it fall and will be able to pick it up.* He felt almost as if his hand was wired into an unbreakable grip on the letter. *Don't be a coward!*

Mystery Girl lowered her gaze as she came to within a meter of Baheer. Baheer dropped the letter on the ground in front of her as he passed.

He looked back a moment later. Save for Mystery Girl, the entire street was empty. She casually stepped over the folded piece of paper.

Baheer felt like he might be sick. *She doesn't want anything to do with me!* Or maybe she somehow hadn't noticed the letter?

Baheer turned back one more time. Mystery Girl stood with her foot covering the folded paper, looking around to see if anyone else was watching. She was risking her entire life if she picked up that letter. Baheer knew it.

I'm a fool! What right do I have to put her in this position? If only he could get the letter back somehow, reverse time only a few minutes and stop the mistake.

Mystery Girl picked up the letter and quickly slid it into her English book. She smiled. Baheer smiled. And suddenly his doubts melted away. They both continued on their separate ways, but with the help of the letter, they were perhaps not as separate as before.

18

FARAH, AFGHANISTAN
November 2, 2003

C ongratulations, Specialist Killian!" Sergeant Paulsen
pinned two specialist rank insignias to Joe's collar. When
they were in place, he pulled back his fist like he was going to
punch the sharp posts on the back of the rank pins through
his shirt and into his flesh. This was something of a tradition
for promotions in the Army, but at the last second Paulsen
checked his punch and instead secured the backings that
would keep the rank pins on his collar.

The other tradition from which they were breaking was
the promotion ceremony formation. With so much work to
do on deployment, and some ridiculous concern about snip-
ers firing over the walls at officers being saluted at the front
of all those soldiers at attention, there were almost no for-
mations on the PRT. They'd had one when the PRT base was

dedicated as officially open for business and another when command of the Provincial Reconstruction Team had transferred from the Navy engineer in charge of designing and building the base to Army lieutenant colonel Santiago. Now, gathered with him in the Civil Affairs main meeting room, it was only sergeants Cavanaugh and Paulsen along with all of the THT guys except for Ahmad, their interpreter.

Staff Sergeant Cavanaugh shook his hand. "Congratulations, Specialist."

"Thank you, Sergeant," Joe said. "But I don't understand what we're doing in here."

It was the nicest room on the PRT. It had been furnished with padded wooden couches and a smooth coffee table. Wood, especially if it was nicely finished, was rare in Afghanistan. All the rest of the limited furniture on the base was plastic or metal. The CA room also sported large colorful Afghan rugs, as well as Afghan and American flags on the walls next to photographs of interim president Hamid Karzai and that Lion of the Panjshir guy who had been killed by Al-Qaeda right before 9/11. This room was used for soldier-conducted worship services and for meeting with important Afghans.

Jase, the THT leader, rubbed his patchy red beard and nodded. "That's because this meeting requires a little secrecy."

Sergeant Paulsen held out a small, flat blue box. He opened it to reveal a medal with a green-and-white ribbon.

Sergeant Cavanaugh opened a big green folder and read, "This is to certify that the Secretary of the Army has awarded the Army Commendation Medal to Specialist Joseph Killian for exceptionally meritorious achievement while assigned to the Farah PRT in skillfully developing useful relationships with valuable sources of critical intelligence. Specialist Killian's acquisition of important information directly contributed to the success of counterinsurgency operations in Nimruz Province, Afghanistan, and the recovery of important weapons, explosives, and ammunition that had been seized by the enemy. Specialist Killian's outstanding performance of duty reflects great credit upon himself, his unit, United States Central Command, and the United States of America."

I'm getting a medal for telling them what Baheer told me? That's crazy. Medals were supposed to be for combat, weren't they? Maybe if he'd stormed a machine gun nest or shot up a bunch of Taliban, he'd deserve a medal. But, what had Sergeant Cavanaugh said? Something like "developing useful relationships with intel sources"? They made him sound like he was some kind of spy.

There was a round of handshakes and congratulations before Jase motioned for everyone to take a seat. Jase looked at his fellow THT spy-wannabes in a conspiratorial way, like they were all expecting him to dive into the most important national security secrets. "The people I report to . . ." He held up a hand. "And I *can't* reveal to you who those people

255

are—were *very* impressed with the information you provided us."

"Well, Baheer provided the information," Joe said. "Is that why I was promoted? Because of this? This was nothing."

Jase's best buddy and fellow THT guy Andy curled the brim of the camouflage Miami Dolphins hat he was always messing with, the fluorescent lights overhead shining off his glass-smooth shaved head. "Those of us such as ourselves"—he motioned to his fellow THT guys—"who work in intelligence, especially in human intelligence—HumInt"—he pronounced the word *Hew*-mint—"know that it's rare to score such dramatic results. Based on your security clearance all we can tell you is your information convinced Command to redirect aerial reconnaissance assets to the location you described. What they saw corroborated your HumInt source. The ground assets that conducted the raid neutralized over a dozen Taliban insurgents and recovered almost all of the ammunition and explosives stolen from our truck a few months ago."

Eric was the largest of the THT men, someone who took their relaxed grooming standards to the limit with a mane of shaggy black hair and a thick beard. "We believe the Taliban may have been planning to use those explosives to attack Israelis in Tel Aviv or to destroy nuclear power plants somewhere in the United States."

Joe and Paulsen exchanged a look of disbelief.

"That sounds pretty ambitious," Sergeant Paulsen said.

"How did the Taliban plan to get the explosives across multiple international borders and through sec—"

"That's classified," Eric snapped.

"You don't have the necessary security clearance that we have." Jase leaned toward Joe. "What you need to know at your level is that in addition to your actions earning you a medal and a promotion, you have saved many lives."

"Perhaps millions of people," Eric confirmed.

Sergeant Paulsen spoke up. "Well, the Taliban weren't going to use all those explosives for anything good. It's great that we took that back."

"That's why we need to continue to cultivate your HumInt," Jase said. "Now our sources tell us that your HumInt asset is here on the PRT right now."

Andy spun his Dolphins hat on his finger. "We actually knew he was going to be here today before he showed up."

Sergeant Paulsen held his fist to his mouth and coughed to cover his laugh.

Are these guys serious? Do they really think they sound like super spies? Joe couldn't stop himself. "Do you mean you checked the schedule of arriving shipments and saw one of his family's trucks was due to arrive today?"

"We can't reveal our sources," Jase said, failing to meet Joe's eyes. "But we'd like you to bring the HumInt asset you've cultivated into this room. We need to see what else he may know."

Eric tugged his bushy black beard. "Even things he may not know that he knows."

Joe and Sergeant Paulsen exchanged another baffled look. This time even Sergeant Cavanaugh shook his head. Baheer didn't want to be involved in any of this. He'd only told Joe what he'd heard because he didn't want another explosion going off like that bomb at the UN compound. *There must be a way to get out of this.* "I'm just an infantry guy," Joe said. "I don't know much about intel work."

Jase smiled. "Before I was reclassed into Tactical Human inTelligence, I was an Army truck driver."

"Office clerk," Andy said.

"Medic," said Eric.

"But our country needed us for this job, and now it needs you to help us," Jase said. "We have our orders. And now so do you."

Baheer had made Joe promise to keep him out of stuff like this. "If you order me to bring Baheer in, you'll be revealing the fact that you outrank a specialist." It was a pathetic attempt, but he had to do all he could for Baheer's sake.

"Specialist Killian," Jase said. "Almost everybody out-ranks you."

The metal door to the building opened, flashing the dimly lit room in bright sunlight. Then the door closed with a hard, metallic clang. In marched the tall muscular form of Lieutenant Colonel Santiago. Everyone sprang to their feet.

"As you were," Santiago said sharply. He surveyed the room in an instant. "Where's the Afghan kid?"

"We were just sending—"

Santiago cursed. "Go get him! You're wasting time."

A long string of fierce obscenities sent Joe out of the room into the bright morning and running across the PRT to where they were unloading Baheer's family's jingle truck.

"Rafiq!" Joe shouted the word for "friend" and waved to Baheer.

"Salaam!" Baheer called back with a smile. He frowned for just a moment but then pointed at Joe, fingering his own imaginary collar with his other hand. "You have new pins there, I think."

"Yeah, about that," Joe said. "I was promoted to the rank of specialist."

"Oh, this is good news," Baheer said. "Do you have some free time? I have a new football, er, soccer ball in the truck. We could kick it around a—"

"Actually, rafiq." Joe jerked his thumb back toward the CA building. "I need you to come with me. The PRT commander and some other guys are waiting for us back there. We need to hurry."

Joe met Baheer's worried eyes for a moment. "I'm sorry, rafiq. I did everything I could."

"What do you mean?" Baheer said. "Killian, what's happening?"

Back in the meeting room of the CA building, everybody stood up and greeted Baheer with a smile. Even Lieutenant Colonel Santiago mostly succeeded in putting on a happy face.

"Welcome, Baheer!" Jase said. "Come on in and have a seat." Jase made all the introductions. "And of course you already know Specialist Killian."

Joe's cheeks were burning. He could see Baheer's discomfort, even fear, in the way he looked around and fidgeted with the bottom of his shirt.

"Is there a problem with one of my family's deliveries, sir?" Baheer asked.

"No. There's no problem. In fact—" Jase reached down into a backpack beside his chair and pulled out a thick stack of cash, slapping it on the coffee table before Baheer. Joe watched it with wide eyes. *Are they all ten-dollar bills? A stack of tens that big has to add up.* "I myself and these other two you see with me in plain civilian clothes work for people who are very interested in learning as much information as they can in order to protect American soldiers and Afghan local nationals. They were very impressed with what you were able to find out about that truck full of explosives that the Taliban stole. You saved a lot of lives, Baheer. You're kind of a hero. So we want you to have this, just to say thank you. There's a thousand American dollars there."

Baheer stared at the money for a long time. He shot a glance at Joe, then looked at the money again. "Sir, I cannot accept this money. My family only wants to drive trucks and be paid for our work."

"Sure." Jase reached over and slid the money closer to Baheer. "We want you to keep on truckin'. But we'd also like you to know we're your friends, and if you hear anything else about the Taliban, stuff that might help us save more lives, please let us know."

"I don't want to work for you," Baheer said. "I only want to help my father and uncles drive trucks. We are not soldiers, sir. We're not in the war."

"Of course," Jase said. "I don't want you to work for me. In fact it would work best if you keep driving your truck, and just let Specialist Killian know if you hear anything."

Lieutenant Colonel Santiago had been watching Baheer closely. He sat back in his chair and steepled his fingers. "That thousand dollars is close to something like fifty thousand afghanis," Santiago said in his deep voice. "Take the money. It will help your family. There's no pressure here. You're not in trouble with us if you find nothing. But in the last two months, the other PRTs around the country have reported over a dozen suspicious truck robberies just like the one you told us about. Your family works driving trucks. Maybe you'll find something else that might help us. Maybe we'll have more money to give you."

They're making him feel like garbage. Why can't they just let him go? Joe watched Lieutenant Colonel Santiago, the highest-ranking officer at the PRT, in all of Farah Province, a man everybody knew was not to be messed with. He might chew Joe out or put him on a tedious work detail for speaking up, but Joe knew he couldn't just sit there.

"Baheer has made his feelings about this pretty clear," Joe said, his cheeks flaring hot. "He doesn't want to be involved in intelligence work. He's no spy. It's too dangerous." *And if anything goes wrong we can't protect him.* But he didn't say as much since Santiago glared at him with his icy, intense stare.

"I have no information," Baheer said. "I cannot take this money. It is, how you say? I saw in a movie once—it is blood money. I will not accept. My family and I only want to continue driving our trucks to transport your supplies. Please, sir. That is all, please, sir," Baheer said.

Lieutenant Colonel Santiago stood up and everybody rose with him. He looked intently at Baheer for a long moment before pushing the cash back to Jase. "I understand your fear. I do. But you really did a great thing, telling us what you did. You saved many lives. I think you're a good man who will be willing to save more lives if you get the opportunity. Thank you for helping us and for helping your country."

"I'm so sorry," Joe said to Baheer a moment later, as he walked him back to his jingle truck. "I tried so hard to get them to leave you alone. I explained you didn't want to be part of . . . of their stupid spy games. But there wasn't much I could do when the PRT commander showed up."

"It is OK," Baheer eventually said. "I knew this could happen when I told you about the stolen truck. Hopefully it is over."

———◇———

"This is going to be the worst, most lonely Christmas of my life," Joe said several weeks later as he walked with his squad across the PRT toward the front gate. They were just seven guys (Sergeant Hart and Specialist Shockley weren't interested) on their way to the Christmas Eve all-denomination worship service.

"That's pretty optimistic," said Corporal MacDonald. "You might have much worse Christmases after this."

Baccam slapped his back. "And you're stuck living with us. Cookmaster says he's got a big pan of baked beans to serve with our Christmas dinner tonight. You listen to and smell all our farts all night and then try to say you're alone."

"I spent last Christmas living under a bridge of a freeway overpass," Specialist Quinn spoke up. "This Christmas I get a big meal, a bed. We got a heater in our room." The Mighty Quinn hoisted up his SAW, looking along its sights as if he were aiming up at the distant mountain visible over the top of the wall. "Rumor is they're taking volunteers for deployment extensions. I'm gonna stay here in Afghanistan as long as they let me. I'll just keep doing this, reenlisting, stay deployed. I'll save up my money, and when we win this war and they make me go home, I'm gonna buy a few acres along the Cedar or Iowa River, buy a trailer house on the bank, up on blocks for when it floods. Then I'll get some job. Whatever. And at night I come home and fish right off my deck."

The squad walked along in silence for a long moment, the only sound the ever-present generator near the gate and the crunch of their boots on the gravel floor of the PRT. It was the most any of them had ever heard the Mighty Quinn say at one time before.

"Except for the part about staying in the Army longer, that sounds like the most perfect plan I've ever heard of," Mac said.

Joe and the guys laughed.

Specialists Dodge and Welch were on gate guard duty. Joe felt bad for them. It was a miserably cold day to be out there.

"Hey, Killer!" Dodge shouted. "This guy here says you invited him or something? We're supposed to be shutting down the gate! I'm not staying on duty longer for you! You get up here and take care of this!"

Joe jogged up to the gate, grabbing the barrel of his ever-present M16 so it didn't keep flopping into his side as he ran. "Yeah! I'll close up. Merry Christmas, you guys." Outside the gate, Baheer stood shivering in the dark, holding a cloth bundle in his hands.

"Happy Christmas!" Baheer said, moving to place his feet between the two stacks of sandbags to be searched.

"You kidding?" Joe shouted. "Come on! I'm not feeling up any dudes this Christmas." He pointed at the cloth-wrapped bundle Baheer carried. "Unless that's a bomb."

"It is the most new-baked naan I could get," Baheer said. "Still warm a little."

"Awesome," Joe said. Afghan naan had turned out to be one of his favorite foods in the world. He'd had naan once in an Indian restaurant in Iowa City, but it wasn't as light and soft and good as Afghan naan.

"Baheer!" Mac shouted when the two of them came back inside the compound and Joe locked the gate. "Merry Christmas, man! You still hanging out with this sad-sack Killer, here?"

"He says you Americans are supposed to have a big Christmas feast tonight." Baheer held up his bundle. "I brought naan because I know you people will never get your food right. Probably just MREs."

The squad laughed. Joe was pleased to see Baheer had figured out the art of giving the guys crap.

"Yeah, your favorite. Pork MREs." Joe laughed.

Baheer shrugged, grinning. "Yeah, you eat up that pig meat. If you want to go to Dozakh. It will not bother me."

"I think he just told us to go to Hell," Mac said. "He'd be a good soldier."

In the CA building's main meeting room, the mood was a little more serious. Master Sergeant Dinsler was preparing to lead the worship service.

Joe and Baheer sat next to each other on plastic chairs dragged in for the occasion.

"Everybody sit tight while I hurry and get the worship-music CD I forgot in the barracks." Master Sergeant Dinsler laughed. "I remembered the CD player but forgot the disc."

This was Joe's chance. "Speaking of CDs." He unbuttoned the cargo pocket on his pants and pulled out a sweet new Sony Discman portable CD player and four mix CDs he'd had Krista burn on the computer at home.

"Yeah, and you better appreciate this," Mac blurted out. "They weren't even going to fly our mail out here in time for Christmas. Some general ordered a flight last minute. Chinook lands and the crew must have been pretty mad to have to fly on Christmas Eve 'cause they started throwing our sacks of mail and packages out onto the ground. Rotor wash blowing letters and cards all over."

"That is terrible," Baheer said.

"Yes!" Mac said. "It was terrible. So Shockley and I go right up on the back ramp of the bird, right in this officer's face." Mac held out his hand in the classic Army knife-hand gesture. "Hey! I don't care what you rank! You throw our stuff all over Afghanistan, I'm gonna throw you!"

Baccam laughed. "Shockley was all, 'You serve the cushy life on the big airbase! We're in a forward area! What's the matter with you? These are people's Christmas presents.'"

PFC Zimmerman shook his head. "Corporal MacDonald

and Specialist Shockley getting along and working together. A Christmas miracle."

Joe handed the gift to Baheer. "Anyway, it's a CD player, top-of-the-line Discman with bass boost and anti-shock. Headphones and four CDs with really good American music old and new."

Baheer looked it all over with a smile. "Tashakor, rafiq."

"Are batteries available in Afghanistan?" Joe asked. Why hadn't he thought of this? Would Baheer just run out of batteries and the Discman would be useless?

"Yes, we have batteries." Baheer laughed. "Sometimes you Americans think Afghanistan is a different planet. Yes! We have batteries."

The master sergeant and three of the Afghan interpreters who lived next door to the CA building returned, and the worship service began. Joe looked around the room as they opened in prayer. All of the Americans, save for two Catholics, were Protestant of one denomination or another. This was their usual situation, and it wasn't hard to work around. The Catholics simply mumbled as the Protestants finished the Lord's Prayer. What was unusual was to be joined in prayer by four Muslims.

". . . And we ask, Lord, by whatever name each of us calls you, that you please bless our mission, and please protect us as we all work together to stop evil and help the good people of Afghanistan build a better society for themselves. Amen," said Master Sergeant Dinsler.

"Amen," said the soldiers.

"Ameen," said the Afghans.

Next they sang "Silent Night" and even one of the interpreters joined in.

"I am sorry," Baheer spoke up after the song. "I am trying to listen to the words in the song. What does this mean? What is this Christmas? I know it is important to Americans, but why do you celebrate?"

"I'll tell you what Christmas is all about, Charlie Brown," Mac joked. He summarized the story of Mary and Joseph finding no room at the inn as well as the birth of Jesus and his manger for a crib.

Baheer moved forward in his seat so fast, he nearly dropped his Discman. "Yes! Mary is mentioned in our Holy Quran. We call her Maryam. But in our Holy Quran Mary is not with Joseph. The Quran story of the birth of Jesus is very different. In the Holy Quran the baby Jesus speaks to a crowd of people even when he is still a newborn." The interpreters nodded their agreement.

Joe watched the eagerness with which Baheer spoke. Since 9/11 there had been a lot of discussion about Islam, some condemning it as a violent cult, others defending it as a religion of peace. *How in all this time have I never heard anyone talk about the Quran including a story about the birth of Jesus?*

The four Afghans seemed to compete for who could tell the most about similarities between the Bible and the Quran. "We have 'Yaqub' for Jacob and 'Abraheem' for Abraham."

As the group continued to marvel at the similarities and laugh about the differences between the two sets of scripture, Joe grew quiet, sitting back to watch and listen. Before he came to Afghanistan, he never would have thought something like this would be possible. "Before 9/11, I never thought very much about Islam. Then suddenly these handful of—" He stopped himself. "These people who attacked us were talking about Islam."

"Those evil men are not Muslim!" Baheer blurted out. "The Holy Quran says—"

"I know!" Joe said. "I know that now. But back on 9/11, I never could have imagined that all of us could pray together like this. And it would be . . ." He struggled to find the right words. *Come on, Joe! You're supposed to be a writer!* "I mean, this has been so easy."

"I know, right?" Baccam said.

"Why can't the rest of the world just relax and get along like this?" Joe asked.

They were all quiet for a moment after that. Finally Master Sergeant Dinsler smiled. "That's a good question, Specialist. And before we head over to the chow hall for our Christmas dinner why don't we close out our worship with a prayer about everybody getting along?"

—◇—

Their deployment continued through January, and the soldiers were surprised when it finally rained. In the engineering and construction of the big, squared, walled-in PRT compound, nobody had thought about drainage. Why would they, when for many months they had hardly seen one cloud? Their shortsightedness caused a lot of trouble when, in a cold, heavy late January rain, soldiers had to scramble with pickaxes to create drainage holes in a few places at the foundation of the wall.

The rain also changed the desert in ways for which the soldiers were unprepared. Many convoy missions to distant villages were foiled or severely impeded by Humvees getting stuck in soupy mud that had looked reasonably solid on approach. Even when the desert appeared dry, it often tricked them, sucking their wheels down into deep, powdery sand that would swamp their vehicles almost as bad as the mud.

Because of all this, long-distance convoys were suspended, and soldiers were restricted to local missions. It was on one such mission that First Squad found themselves in early February.

Jase and his THT guys stood around outside their Toyota Hilux pickup, all of them wearing sunglasses, khaki or green civilian pants and sweatshirts, and 9-mil. handguns in drop holsters strapped to their thighs. The guy who went by the name Andy wore his camouflage Miami Dolphins hat.

As usual, Jase spoke for the group. "One of our local HumInt assets made us aware of an underground concrete bunker, sort of a giant cave, packed with unexploded ordnance. Now we have hired some Afghan workers to move all that UXO out of the cave and load it onto trucks"—Jase paused and nodded at Joe—"trucks owned by your friend's family, which will then transport the UXO north to Herat to be destroyed by US explosive ordnance disposal units." He put his hands on his hips. "All you guys have to do is provide security and make sure none of the workers run off with any explosives or ammunition."

"Right," Sergeant Paulsen said. "Specialist Killian, why don't you run to the terp building and grab us an interpreter for this—"

"Oh, no, Sergeant Paulsen," Jase interrupted. "We're cool. We got Ahmad, our terp."

"You sure?" Paulsen asked.

"Yeah. Let's roll. It's no problem."

When First Squad arrived on site and surveyed the bunker, Corporal MacDonald said, "I think we have a problem. All these months we've been in Farah, and the whole time this arsenal has been down here?"

The large cave was dug down into the earth, leading to two big chambers. Old, rusted mortar rounds were stacked along one wall of the entry tunnel. In the first chamber, piled from the floor to the high domed ceiling, were wooden crates containing old, never-touched-after-the-factory Soviet mortars. A smaller second room contained belts of rusted machine gun rounds, loose bullets, more corroded mortars, and even old, cracked Soviet antipersonnel mines.

Specialist Quinn groaned. "Oh, this is going to take a long time."

Nobody in First Squad was a mortar man, but their basic working wasn't hard to figure out.

"It's worse than just taking a long time," said Corporal MacDonald. He held one of the big steel turkey-drumstick-shaped mortars by the narrow end in his left hand, and with his right, he tried to unscrew and remove the cone-shaped fuse sticking out of the fat tip of the other end. "I take it if this fuse gets knocked around too much, it will explode the mortar."

"Yeah," Joe said. "So, we just twist them. They'll screw right out to disarm."

"In a perfect world, maybe," Mac said. "But these Russian mortars were made with the cheapest communist labor on the orders of a government who didn't care anything for the workers or anyone else. They're old. This fuse, and some of the others, are corroded, even cracked. Do you want to bet your life that trying to force these old fuses out won't set them off?"

"We do have a problem," Joe said. "I'll radio for—"

Mac slapped Joe's hand away to prevent him from reaching his little civilian Motorola.

"No radio signals down here!" Mac said.

"Come on, Corporal," Baccam said. "It's not even a tactical radio. Not high powered or anything. No way it could set off any—"

"Oh, did you learn that in your Army class about handling crappy, worn-out, twenty-year-old Soviet explosives?" Mac asked. "I must have been on a special work detail the day they taught that class. I say we follow Corporal MacDonald's Explosives Handling General Order Number One. Never assume everything is safe, especially when you're in an underground ammo dump in Afghanistan where if anything goes wrong you could be instantly vaporized in the biggest explosion this war-torn province has ever seen."

Joe shrugged. "So basically, what you're saying is, no radios down here."

Minutes later, up on the surface in bright sunlight, Joe and Mac talked with Sergeant Paulsen, Sergeant Hart, and Staff Sergeant Cavanaugh.

"Well, the safest way to ship them is to take the fuses out," said Cavanaugh. "We don't want a mortar with a fuse shifting around in the back of the truck and blowing the whole thing up. These drivers are trusting us."

"The drivers are Baheer's family," Joe said. He surveyed the empty field around the entrance to the tunnel. "Or at least that's the plan, if the trucks ever get here. Not like we'd want to put any drivers in danger, but he and his family haul a lot of stuff for us, and they might feel pretty disrespected if we tell them they have to haul dangerous fused mortars."

Mac pointed at the crowd of Afghan men thirty yards away. "The workers who will be hauling the stuff out of the cave are trusting us, too. I say we remove all the fuses that come out easily, but if they're stuck, we don't try to force them, risking an explosion. If they're stuck, we should leave the fuses in."

"I'm with that plan," said Sergeant Paulsen. "That way, *maybe* the fuse gets bumped on the truck ride. But maybe not. On the other hand, if we try forcing those bad-shape fuses out, we're *certainly* messing with them and risking an explosion."

"Leaving the bad ones in is the best of two bad options," said Sergeant Hart.

Joe shook his head. Here they were, talking about the odds of least casualties in the event of an explosion, with Baheer's family deemed the most expendable in the present situation. "Why don't we call EOD down here to blow everything up in place?" Joe asked. "That way we don't have to risk anyone."

Sergeant Paulsen pointed to a bunch of nearby compounds. "Detonating everything in that cave would set off an explosion big enough to level all those houses. Plus it's underground. So we wouldn't just be dealing with the explosive yield of all the weapons down there, but the explosion would expand underground, building up pressure, until finally all the dirt above the cave blasted up into the sky. We'd be raining down rocks and bricks and who knows what else on everyone who lives around here."

Cavanaugh looked around. "Where the heck are those THT guys? This is supposed to be their mission. I was told we were here to provide security and that's it. They said they'd be running everything."

Sergeant Paulsen shook his head. "You won't want to hear this, but they said they were worried, with all these Afghan workers around, that their covers would be blown." He pointed to the THT guys about a hundred and fifty yards away sitting on their pickup in the shade of a distant wall. "And they took our only interpreter."

Cavanaugh bit his lower lip and blew out through his nose. "Absolute morons," he whispered. He was quiet for a long moment. Finally, he nodded, coming to a decision. "Mac, we go with your plan. Paulsen, Hart, you help me supervise the loading of the trucks up here. Remember, part of our mission is to make sure nobody runs off with any ordnance. Mac, Killer, you supervise the workers down there. Keep them going. Killian, you're good at talking to these people. I need you to go down there and explain to the Afghans our plan for the mortars with bad fuses."

Joe frowned. "Roger that, Sergeant, but I don't actually speak Dari or Pashto. A few words maybe, but I don't have the first clue how to talk about fuses or mortars. Maybe Baheer will be coming with his family's trucks."

"Just do it, Specialist!" Cavanaugh shouted. "We don't have time to wait for the trucks and hope your friend comes along. We'll start stacking the stuff up here, ready to go on the trucks when they arrive. I'll try to get the THT interpreter down there, but in the meantime, just do your best."

Joe and Mac waited until they were down in the cave before they said anything. It wouldn't do to complain in front of their squad leader.

"Over six years in the Guard," Mac said. "My enlistment expired back in December. I'm involuntarily extended. And in all my time serving, this here is the dumbest situation I've ever been stuck in."

"What are we supposed to do?" Joe agreed. "Pantomime how to defuse, or I guess when *not* to defuse old mortar rounds?"

That is exactly what they did. "Hey!" Joe shouted. "Rafiq! Rafiq!" He slung his rifle on his back to free up his hands, and he picked up a mortar. "OK. If the fuse comes out easy—" He unscrewed the fuse from a mortar that looked to be in good condition. Then he gave a thumbs-up. "That's good. Good. But"—he found a crappy-looking one and began to twist the fuse but grunted and pretended the fuse wouldn't budge—"if the fuse won't come out, we leave it in there. You understand?"

The Afghans looked at him like he was crazy. And he was. This was a crazy stupid situation. He heard Mac trying to explain the same thing to the workers deeper in the cave. It took about three more tries, three more ridiculous pantomimes, but finally one of the workers near him smiled and nodded.

"Bale!" the man said. He demonstrated the concept, talking it through to the others in his language. Another worker brought an older-looking mortar round to him, made a minor effort to unscrew the fuse, and then appeared to ask the man for his opinion.

"Nay," said the man.

The bad mortar was passed along the human chain with its corroded fuse still installed.

They understood. Joe let go a sigh of relief. *We might just survive this after all.*

The work went smoothly, until an Afghan man in a Western suit and tie showed up. Someone said he was one of the governor's men. Immediately he started talking to Joe, unloading an urgent stream of words that Joe couldn't understand.

"I don't—" The man kept talking, gesticulating more intensely. Joe tried again. "I don't . . . I can't understand you. Ingleesi?"

Mr. Angry Suit stopped one of the workers who had been passing along an old mortar with the fuse stuck in it. He tried to twist the fuse out. When he couldn't, he pointed at it, saying something loudly and making a motion like the fuse and round should be separated.

"No, we're not going to do that," Joe said. "It's more dangerous to try to force out bad fuses than to leave them in and—" Angry Suit shouted. Joe took a step toward the man. The Suit carried no weapons. He didn't seem to have any of the governor's armed guards with him. "I don't know who you are, and I don't care who you are connected with." Joe pointed toward the exit. "Get out of my mission!"

Next to Joe, a worker tried to unscrew a fuse and found it stuck.

He slammed the thing down repeatedly on a four-foot stack of mortars. *Bang!Bang!Bang!* Like a hammer.

"STOP!" Joe screamed. His heart pounded as he watched the fused mortar that could have—should have—blown up the whole cave. "This mission is over! Everybody get out of here! Now!"

The Afghans seemed to understand that much, and the group filed back up to the surface.

Mac walked beside Joe, blinking in the bright sun outside. "Did that guy do what I think I saw him do?"

"Yup."

Both Joe's team leader and squad leader asked him what was going on. He no longer cared how much trouble he would be in for not answering or obeying orders. He said nothing, but started his march across the dirt field.

"You going to chew out the THT idiots?" Mac asked, trying to keep up.

"Yup."

"Oh, I am *so* right with you," said Mac.

Nobody knew what any of the THT guys ranked. That was a part of their stupid wannabe spy program. But since Joe was only a specialist, it was a good bet they all outranked him. Practically everybody outranked him.

The lead THT guy, Jase, had been lying on the hood

of their pickup, his back on the windshield. He sat up and smiled. "Hey, Killian. How's it going with—"

Joe cursed him out. "I don't care what you morons rank! I'll knock out all your teeth right here!" His anger gave him more courage than he otherwise would have possessed. He was grateful for Mac's presence by his side. "You put us on this mission, and then you take the terp away so that I have to *pantomime* how to handle explosives! I'm stuck in a shouting match with one of the governor's guys because you completely worthless moronic brain-dead incompetent freaking *cowards* of *non*soldiers took away my interpreter!"

"Hey, easy there," Jase said. "It was too high profile for us to be over there. The workers would start to recognize us as—"

"No Afghan is stupid enough to believe you white, non-Pashto-speaking idiots are anything other than Americans! You are not spies! You are worthless!"

Across the field, Mr. Angry Suit was arguing with Staff Sergeant Cavanaugh.

"You pull something like this again, I swear I will knock you out. I will beat you unconscious. They can court-martial me!" Joe said. The THT guys were weaker than he thought, saying nothing, even though he was way out of line. "Where is the terp now!?"

"We sent him back to the PRT," Jase said. "We didn't think we'd need him anymore."

Mac cursed and took a step forward, but Joe stopped him. At the edge of the field, Baheer's family's jingle trucks rocked along the bumpy road, rolling closer. Joe whispered a little prayer of thanks. "No, hold on, Corporal. We're in luck. For once."

Please be in one of those trucks, Baheer. Please, please, please. Come on, buddy, you gotta be there.

As Joe and Mac approached the crowd around the trucks and cave entrance, they began to slow down. The three drivers were out of the trucks. Baheer was nowhere in sight.

"Oh no," Joe said. "We're screwed."

But then the passenger door on the blue jingle truck opened, and his Afghan friend climbed down and raised his arms in a stretch. Joe had never been so happy to see an Afghan before in his life. "Baheer!" he shouted and waved. "Just the man I wanted to see! Come on, buddy! You're drafted. I need an interpreter or people are going to start to get hurt."

"Of course, I am happy to help," Baheer said, as Joe put his arm around his shoulders and guided him toward the work site. "I was hoping you would be on duty today."

"Yeah, well I wish I wasn't," said Joe. He told Baheer about his problems with the THT guys and a lack of an interpreter.

"I think I understand," Baheer said. "I will try to talk to this man in the suit, but he looks very angry."

Joe stayed by Baheer's side as he talked to Angry Suit

Guy. The two of them rattled back and forth very quickly in their language.

"Chi mega?" Joe asked what the man said.

Baheer frowned. "He is from the office of the Farah Province governor. He thinks we must remove the fuse before we put the . . . the little bombs on the truck."

"Yeah, I understood that much," Joe said.

"He was the one who contacted the bearded Americans about this cave of old weapons," Baheer translated. "He wants to know where those men are now."

Joe put his hands on his hips. "Next time, do not deal with those men. They are fools." Joe patted his uniform. "Come to the soldiers in these uniforms. We will try to help you."

After Baheer's translation, the man laughed and started to calm down. "I told him also," said Baheer, "that the trucks belong to my family, and we support your idea about the fuses."

The man said something else and then reached out to shake Joe's hand.

"He accepts your plan," Baheer said.

Joe shook the man's hand. "Yeah, Baheer. I kind of figured that out, too."

A few minutes later, Baheer had fully explained and made sure every Afghan understood the method for moving the UXO. Finally, the chain of workers was back at it, and gradually the trucks began to fill up, ready for their convoy to the munitions destruction point near Herat.

"This is a good day," Baheer said. "A good mission. These weapons might have been taken by the Taliban. Soon all these bombs and bullets will be gone, and will hurt no one." He smiled. "I've heard on the radio that this is happening everywhere. Americans getting rid of all these old bombs, even clearing minefields. Thank you for this, my friend. My country can have a chance again, because of you soldiers."

Joe thought for a moment about how, when he first arrived in Afghanistan, he believed the whole place was worthless, its people ignorant savages. And he had hated his mission of reconstruction. He'd been wrong in his life before, but never had he been so completely wrong. Baheer wasn't saying those things just to butter Joe up, or because Baheer wanted something. He meant them. Sure, Joe wasn't out here hunting the Taliban, looking for firefights. But he could be proud of his mission. He'd help take thousands of uncontrolled, dangerous weapons and explosives out of the world today, making Afghanistan a little safer for Afghans and Americans. He'd almost died in the process, but the mission was worth that risk.

"Thanks, Baheer," Joe said, patting his friend's shoulder. "You really saved us on this one. I owe you."

19

FARAH, AFGHANISTAN
March 19, 2004

Spring had arrived, and with it slightly warmer temperatures, but it seemed to Baheer nothing could warm his spirits. He had once heard Killian complain about not having a life. At the time, he hadn't understood, but Baheer knew now what he meant. Baheer prayed, ate, went to school, worked on the farm, worked for the family truck business, studied, slept a tiny bit, and then it all repeated.

The trip to school used to be something he looked forward to with excitement. Now he simply rode his bike, his eyes fixed on his wheels churning the muddy road below. Months ago, he'd given up hope of ever seeing Mystery Girl again. Thoughts of her used to make him smile, but now he was certain his letter had caused some terrible trouble for her.

I'm a fool! I've ruined her life! There are rumors of girls being so severely punished for much less an act than accepting a letter from a strange boy.

He worried in this way every time he passed the twisted tree by the irrigation canal, a canal now full of water from the winter rains. In one place, the ditch was overflowing, flooding the road ahead with a massive puddle at least fifteen centimeters deep. People had tried to place rocks and shovel sand beside the canal to contain the water, but all they'd done was create a path of stepping stones, which was his only chance of passing through without getting wet up to his ankles. He slowed and stopped the bike.

There was Mystery Girl, carefully making her way along the path, risking glances at him, and smiling a little.

Impossible! Is it really her? After so many months? But of course it was her. He'd thought of her face and those magic eyes so often that he'd recognize her anywhere.

When she saw Baheer coming, she stepped up the little slope to the twisted tree, turned over a stone between two of the tree's roots, and placed a paper under it. She did it all so smoothly and gracefully that she hardly stopped moving. Baheer walked his bike slowly, waiting for her to get far enough away. Then he pretended his bike had a problem and stopped next to the rock to check on it. When he was sure he was not being watched, he lifted the stone, snatched up the paper, and stuffed it into his pocket.

She'd written back! How was he supposed to wait until he

could be alone to read the letter? Throughout the school day and then later on the farm, every so often, he would touch his pocket to check if the paper was still there.

That night, with his flashlight under his blanket, Baheer opened the letter. She had folded it impossibly neatly and had also drawn flowers on the four corners and red curved lines from each flower to the other. Baheer felt embarrassed. His clumsily folded letter had no such decorations and was garbage compared to hers.

Hey Mystery Guy,
It has been very long time since I have seen you.
I am sorry. Soon after the bomb at the United Nations, my father told me not to go to school from tomorrow. My mother asked, "why?" He said that today one his friends had told him that Taliban has sent threats of killing girls or spreading acid on their faces if they go to school. That night I cried till morning.

Baheer looked up from the letter, his hands shaking. *Why? Why every time there was something good, did the Taliban have to try to destroy it?* He really wanted to kick every harami talib in his back. Baheer remembered the saying of Prophet Mohammad (peace be upon Him): *Acquiring knowledge is compulsory for both men and women.* How did men make threats like this and still call themselves Muslims? Baheer continued reading.

For a long time I begged my mother to try to convince my father about school. She promised to do so. But she tells me, with my father, Patience. Yesterday, I went to my father before he would leave to his shop in early morning. I told my father that I won't leave going to school even if these monsters tear me into pieces. He did not agree first, but when my mother told him to change my school to the one newly build close the boys' school, he nodded. He transferred me in one day through his connections in the Education department. Last night, he allowed me to go to school and that I should only go to school and return straight back home.

"Yes!" Baheer waved his fist as a football player does after scoring a goal. "I knew it. She is a strong girl," Baheer whispered to himself like a crazy man. He continued reading.

I was very happy my father change his mind because I wish for school and because I wish to reply to your letter.

I will answer your letter. Yes. I have been giving you signals. I am very happy you have write to me. I always had a question, "Why would you go to farm when all the kids would go to school?" That's why I want to know that. I was showing my books to you. I mean, I am going to school. Why you are not going? But, when one day, you showed me your books, I feel happy. I thanked Allah that you start school.

And thank you for your saying "my eyes are beautiful." My mother also tells me this. You look very good person. Study as much as you can.

We must be careful. I hope to read a new letter from you, my Mystery Guy. You said me about your sister. I thought, my life with school is the same. Actually, my mother was a great support. First, you can speak to your mother to convince your father. When my mother spoke to my father, first, he rejected. But I did not give up. Luckily, my father agreed after that. But, my mother played important role. I can't tell the full story here.

Sincerely,

Ayesha

Her name was Ayesha. It was his mother's name.

Relax. There is more than one girl named Ayesha. It is not as though it is a sign from Allah. But it did make him think. The Mystery Girl—Ayesha. He barely knew her, and yet he felt proud of her. Baheer hadn't faced the kind of obstacles to education that she had, but he knew something of the challenges.

And so did his sister, Maryam. She worked so hard to learn all she could from the notes he brought home, but she deserved a chance to go to school. He'd told Maryam so many times that he would do all he could to help, but had he really tried? No. He needed to be brave like Ayesha and try harder to help his sister.

The next night, the family was drinking green tea in Baba Jan's room at his house as usual. Maryam entered. "Nabegha!" Baba Jan called her a genius, his words sounding like a celebration. "Come here."

Maryam sat close to Baba Jan. "Come now, my brilliant little walking book of poems. Recite something new you've memorized," Baba Jan said with warmth in his eyes.

"Bale, Baba." She smiled. She looked up and down, a sort of trick she had as she recalled poems.

Baba Jan leaned back and closed his eyes.

Ask him. Ask him about school for Maryam, you coward! Baheer tried to work up the courage to say something. *The school is on the other side of the wall from yours. So many other girls are attending.*

She began reciting Maxim 81 from Sa'di's *Gulistan*:

A sage was asked: "Of so many notable, high, and fruitful trees which Allah the Almighty has created, not one is called free, except the cypress, which bears no fruit. What is the reason of this?" He replied: "Every tree has its appropriate season of fruit, so that it is sometimes flourishing therewith, and looks sometimes withered by its absence. With the cypress, however, neither is the case, it being fresh at all times, and this is the quality of those who are free."

Place not thy heart on what passes away, for the Tigris

Will flow in Baghdad even after many Khalifas have
passed away.
If thou art able, be kind like the date tree,
And if thy hand cannot afford it, be free like the cypress.

Baheer knew this poem. It was about not being bonded
too much to temporary or meaningless things. *If Maryam is to
be free, shouldn't she be allowed to go to real school?*

Baba Jan patted Maryam's shoulder before he kissed
her cheek. He smiled. "Wasn't this from the last chapter of
the book?"

"Yes. Baba Jan. I have finished reading it."

"This is my nabegha." Baba Jan looked all around the
room.

"Baba?" Baheer said. His heart pounded. Baba Jan's anger
was not something to be taken lightly.

"What, bachem?" Baba Jan asked.

"We can send her to school, where she can learn even
more than this." The words were out almost before he'd
made the decision to take the risk and speak. They could not
be taken back.

Baba Jan did not say a word. All his aunts and uncles
stared silently at Baheer. Uncle Feraidoon shook his head
sadly, as if Baheer were condemned.

Baba Jan looked around the room. He was silent for a
long time. "No," he said quietly. "I can't let her go."

Baheer wanted to ask why, but he couldn't. Fortunately, he didn't have to ask.

"I'd like to say yes, but our people are not yet open-minded. All the relatives would start talking bad about me. They would say that I let my girls go wild in the downtown." He shook his head. "I can't let that happen. I can't let my dignity and honor be questioned."

"I will take her to school every day on my bike," Baheer said. "The school is right on the other side of the wall from ours."

"No. It's the bottom line. No." Baba Jan's voice changed and Baheer could see the anger in his eyes.

Baheer could not understand how a man like Baba Jan, with all his appreciation for literacy, who was obviously delighted with Maryam's learning, could be so stubborn about letting girls go to school. His stated reasons didn't make sense to Baheer.

Maryam didn't say a word. Who would, when Baba Jan was angry? The whole time, Maryam looked down, rubbing her fingers.

Everyone remained silent for quite a while. Eventually Maryam ran off. Baheer followed her quickly.

He caught up to her just before she entered her room.

She turned to face him, forcing a smile. "It's fine."

"I'm sorry. I will try again. Don't worry," Baheer said.

"I knew he wouldn't let me go to school. I'll try to at least keep reading around the house." She ran into her room.

The next day Baheer and Rahim arrived on the farm as usual, but as soon as they opened the compound gate Baheer knew today was anything but normal. "Oh no."

"What happened here?" Rahim said.

The vineyard was smashed, plants chopped, torn up, and thrown everywhere. Irrigation channels were crushed and filled in. The diesel pump for the well was shattered into pieces on the ground. "Someone did this on purpose," Baheer said.

"This destruction is too much work for one man," Rahim said. "And look at the many footprints."

Baheer dropped to his knees in the torn-up dirt and shredded plants. All the work they'd done for the spring planting. Destroyed.

"Who would . . . Why?" Baheer asked.

"People know our family has been working for the Americans, and someone doesn't like it," Rahim said. "This is a message. We better go tell Baba Jan."

At first the brothers rode their bikes home very fast, but before they'd gone even halfway, Rahim slowed down. "There is no use in rushing now. The damage to the farm is already done."

As they rode home, Baheer couldn't get the image of their destroyed work out of his mind. Was Rahim right? Had the farm been attacked because they worked for the Americans? Cold dread tightened his chest. *Was it because of our trucks or was it because of the information I turned over to Killian?* "No, no, no," Baheer whispered. *What if this is all my fault?*

Back at home, the two of them rolled right across the compound on their bikes. Baheer's legs were shaking when he dismounted outside Baba Jan's house.

"But Haji Dilawar is a good man," Uncle Kabir said inside.

"Of course he is," Baba Jan said. "I do not say he is much involved with them, but his brother is more deeply connected to the Taliban than Haji Dilawar says. I wouldn't be surprised if Haji Dilawar is storing weapons for them."

"We don't know that," said Uncle Feraidoon. "We should not speculate."

Rahim grabbed Baheer's arm hard and yanked him inside. "Come on," he said sharply. "Enough of this."

"What are you boys doing here?" Baba Jan said sharply as soon as they entered. "You should be on the farm. Anyway, don't sneak up on conversations."

"Bale, Baba Jan," Rahim said. "But we have bad news." Rahim waited for Baheer to explain, but Baheer could only look from his brother to his grandfather and back again.

What if this is my fault?

Finally Rahim explained what had happened on the farm. "I think we were attacked because of our work for the Americans." When Rahim was finished, Baheer expected an eruption of fury from Baba Jan or the other men gathered in the study, but instead a cold silence fell on the room.

Baheer read the looks of worry and even fear on the faces of his father and uncles. Baba Jan stared off as if looking into the far distance. He stroked his beard. "It is early in the season," Baba Jan said at last. "With enough hard work, we can still produce a good crop. As to who did this, of course we cannot know, but if it is as you say, Rahim, we will not be intimidated. We will continue our business. The Americans may be infidels but they have dealt with us fairly, paying well."

Baheer's cheeks flared hot as he remembered the stack of American money he'd refused. Should he have taken it? His family could use it now. He took a deep breath. No. If he truly believed in working for a new and better Afghanistan, he would not do so with dirty spy money.

"If the cowards who destroyed our farm thought we would wither like the plants they ripped up, they are wrong." Baba Jan stood up. "Now, let's get changed into our work clothes and go salvage our farm."

Baheer, Rahim, and the men of the family worked hard restoring the farm that night, as long as the light lasted. Through the next week, with every spare moment the men could muster, they worked to return the farm to working order. "This is the way men should be!" Baba Jan would sometimes shout. "We cannot fail! We'll get a great crop yet!"

Everything Baba Jan said was meant to uplift them, but it only made Baheer feel worse. Finally the family managed to return the farm to normal, but Baheer never escaped the shame and fear that he was responsible for the destruction.

"Oh man, I'm sorry about that, rafiq," Killian said the next Saturday, after Baheer had told him about the trouble on the farm.

Uncle Kabir had driven the truck to the PRT that day. The search was complete and now they were second in line within the compound to be unloaded. When this happened, and Killian wasn't sleeping off a guard shift or away on a mission, the two of them, and sometimes other soldiers, kicked around a football, what the Americans called a soccer ball. But today Baheer was not excited about playing. He half-heartedly kicked the ball back to Killian.

Killian stopped the ball with his foot. "I wish we could get out there, find all these Taliban scumbags and force them to stop messing with everybody. I understand this is a war, and they want to kill us soldiers. That's fair. That's what war is. But why won't they just leave their own people alone?" He kicked the ball back hard.

Before the ball reached Baheer, that THT guy Jase rushed in and stopped it, cheating by using his hands so he could try to bounce it from one knee to another. "Hey, there's my buddy Baheer!" The ball fell to the dirt. "How you doing?"

Baheer couldn't fake enthusiasm anymore. Not with this THT guy. "I do not have anything to tell you."

Jase put his arms up in front of him. "Whoa! This isn't an interrogation. I was just checking in to see if you'd heard anyone saying anything interesting. Maybe you've talked to other truck drivers who—"

"He said he has nothing to tell you, Jase," Killian said, putting extra emphasis on the man's name in a way that somehow sounded insulting. "Leave him alone."

Jase's smile faded a little and he stood up straight. For a moment, he looked like he might try to fight Killian or at least yell at him. Killian did not have the highest rank, and Baheer knew that most of the time Killian was as respectful of those with higher rank as Baheer was of his parents, uncles, aunts, and grandfather. But there was no respect in Killian's eyes now. He glared at Jase.

"Let's go check on your truck, Baheer," Killian said after a long tense silence. Killian picked up the football, and the two of them left Jase behind. "I hate those THT guys," he said when Jase was too far away to hear.

"I know!" Baheer said. "Every time they see me here, they ask what I know." Baheer looked around to make sure nobody was looking. "For months they ask me what I know about the Taliban. I know nothing! A week ago, my grandfather and uncle were talking about Haji Dilawar, a friend of our family who lives on the other side of your old Unsafe House from my family's side. They were saying they *think* his brother is too close to Taliban. They *think* . . . they *guess* Haji Dilawar stores weapons in his compound. This is nothing! And that's all I've heard besides rumors and news of what Taliban cells have done around Farah Province and the country." Baheer took a breath. He couldn't afford to be loud. Those THT jackals could be anywhere. "Sorry, Killian. I should not become angry."

Killian was quiet for a long moment. "You know . . ." He stopped walking. Baheer stopped as well and looked at him curiously. "Way back at the Unsafe House, I wouldn't tell you my first name."

"That is OK," Baheer said. The Americans *did* have to be careful about their security. And Killian had orders from his commanders not to share too much information.

"Joe," Killian said. "My name's Joe. Joseph actually, so I guess you might call me Yusuf." He reached out for a handshake. "But my friends call me Joe."

Baheer laughed and shook his hand. "It is nice to meet you, Joe Killian."

20

FARAH, AFGHANISTAN
April 15, 2004

The squad was staged up, vehicles prepped and ready, waiting outside the chow hall. Armor, helmets, and all their gear was gathered beside them. They'd just finished chow about an hour earlier, and now they waited to roll out to wherever they were supposed to go. It was the medics' show. Master Sergeant Dinsler had ordered them all to stand fast while he was working out some last-minute details.

The THT clowns came out of the chow hall. Jase seemed to light up when he saw Joe. "Hey! You guys fixing to go out on a mission?"

"Oh no," Mac said. "You know First Squad. We just love getting all our gear out so we can stand around the Humvees, just for fun."

Jase didn't seem to understand Mac's joke was at his expense. He laughed.

"Hey, Specialist Killian, can I have a word?" He motioned for Joe to walk with him.

Joe looked to Sergeant Paulsen, who nodded. "Don't go too far. We're gonna roll out pretty soon."

Why couldn't Sergeant Paulsen just have refused permission? Joe sighed and walked off a few yards with Jase.

"Good job with that HumInt asset," Jase said.

"Sure," Joe said. "Now will you finally leave Baheer and me alone about it? We're not spies."

Jase moved closer and spoke quietly. "I can't tell you everything that happened."

"Good."

"But some good results. Keep cultivating that HumInt asset."

"I told you what he told me as an example of how little information Baheer has. And that Dilawar guy is a friend of Baheer's family. He was supposed to be left alone."

Jase frowned. "Well, the guys who made the decision about how to deal with the information aren't the kind of guys who take orders or ask permission from specialists in the Iowa Army National Guard. I'm just saying, good work. Keep it up."

What did these guys do? I should have kept my big mouth shut.

"What was that all about?" Baccam asked when Joe rejoined the squad. "Still playing spy?"

"No," Joe said. "Hopefully it's about nothing."

Finally Master Sergeant Dinsler and Farida, the new American female civilian interpreter, emerged from the chow hall. It was time to roll out. They didn't normally do a lot of night missions, but on this four-day rotation of local duty, they had been going out every night driving around on "presence patrols." These were regularly scheduled cruises for the sole purpose of letting any would-be Taliban know that the Americans were just fine going out at night. Other than those patrols and tonight, there had only been one unexpected night mission, that time they'd been called out for the UN compound bombing. That seemed like a lifetime ago.

Joe rode in the gun turret behind the Mk 19, covering the convoy's six as they rolled out of the PRT. He marveled at how comfortable and routine this had all become. Even after the UN bombing, the near attack on the Unsafe House, and assorted highway robbers and other minor issues they'd encountered on long convoys, this had all become a routine, a job, a way of life. Sure, he had his night-vision on and scanned his sector, watching for trouble, but he wasn't all that worried about an attack.

What had happened to him? How could all of this possibly have become normal?

And if this was his new normal, if this soldier guy was now his identity, how would he live after he finally returned home? How do you go from wearing armor and manning machine guns to writing papers and studying for midterm exams?

Do I even want to go back to college? If I want to be a writer, maybe this is the best place to be, riding around with rifles and machine guns and stuff. When Joe had first been called up for this war, it had seemed like a big interruption in his progress toward his writing and journalism dreams. But he was living his best writing material right now. Maybe he should be like Specialist Quinn and request a second deployment, hook up with another unit and stay in Afghanistan.

They pulled into the local hospital compound and, after their two Humvees stopped, Sergeant Paulsen called Joe down from the gun. "We're not going to be firing a bunch of grenades around in this enclosed area." Paulsen handed him the AN/PRC-148 radio, a little black box the size of a big TV remote control with a black coiled cord leading to the hand mike that clipped to the front of his vest.

"Go inside with the medics," Sergeant Paulsen said. "We'll stay out here to guard the vehicles. If you need help, give a call and we'll be on our way."

"Help in a hospital?" Joe said. "Not like I'll be scrubbing into surgery. I won't need an assist."

Paulsen laughed. "Yeah, well, we gotta stay connected just in case there's trouble."

"Ready?" Master Sergeant Dinsler asked. He and Farida the interpreter stood in a little shaft of moonlight that shined down through the trees. A warm breeze shuffled the branches, shaking and mixing light and shadow, so that the two of them seemed to shimmer like ghosts.

Joe escorted them into the big concrete building through a flimsy screen door that snapped shut behind them, making him tense up on his weapon for a moment. "This is a hospital?" he asked.

The master sergeant nodded. "Best in Farah," he said. "Sad, isn't it?"

Paint peeled off the walls of the dimly lit rooms, and they moved through shadow as they made their way down the hall.

Farida spoke to an Afghan man where the hallway split in two different directions. He answered her. She pointed to the left. "Women's ward is this way."

Joe raised an eyebrow. It would be interesting to have the chance to interact with Afghan women. Someone said Farida had been born in Afghanistan but had lived in America since she was two. There was a big difference between Afghan and Afghan American women. Afghan girls were allowed to play outside and didn't have to be covered up, but once they hit puberty they were, most of the time, hidden behind walls or under a burqa.

Joe wiped his brow. It might have been a nice night outside, but the inside of the hospital was hot and humid. The concrete building had cooked all day in the sun and then held on to that heat into the evening. He'd been naive to hope Farah's chief medical facility might have air-conditioning.

They passed one room where a sour-sweet stench hit his eyes and nose like a slap in the face.

"Oh, that's putrid," Farida said.

The horrid odor rose from a pile of red-brown blood-soaked rags on the floor of a room to their right. Flies buzzed over the messy mound, and Joe was glad the room was fairly dark, because he was pretty sure he saw maggots wriggling around in there.

They emerged into a large room about the size of his high school English classroom, but slightly narrower and with a higher ceiling. The only light came from a couple of dim light bulbs hanging from wires at either end of the room. Some of the concrete up there had crumbled away, exposing rebar.

The beds were arranged side by side along either wall, with an aisle down the middle. They were nothing more than thin foam mattresses with dingy blankets resting atop stacks of wooden shipping pallets. Only four of the beds were occupied, two of them with mothers who, themselves sick, nevertheless tried to console crying children. A third bed had someone lying on her side, covered in a thin sheet.

There weren't even screens on the open windows. Flies buzzed and crawled about everywhere.

Master Sergeant Dinsler led them down the aisle to the far end of the room, where an Afghan girl about his age, maybe a couple of years younger, rested on the slab, dressed in a long-sleeved pink-and-purple-flowered dress.

Those Afghan girls sure are talented, making all their clothes by hand. "How do they—"

Joe froze. Something tightened in his stomach, and despite the heat in the room, a cold terror filled him. "Oh no," he whispered.

His eyes had deceived him. Or his brain didn't want to recognize the true sight before him. The girl wasn't wearing a pink-and-purple dress. She wasn't wearing a dress at all.

She had been burned. The outer layer of her skin had turned a dark yellow-tan and peeled away, clumping into brown-red-purple charred clumps on her arms, lower abdomen, and neck, leaving exposed a light pink underflesh. The fire had missed most of her face, but her neck was charred and her lower left cheek singed. She'd once had shoulder-length midnight-black hair, but much of it was fried into clumps around her burned left ear. She'd been burned terribly from her neck at least to her waist. Green pants covered below that. A towel covered her breasts, though the edges still showed, a furious, painful pink.

He stared at her, open mouthed. She didn't cry. She made no noise, but the look of agony on her face was unmistakable, like the fire had pushed her beyond the mind's capability of understanding pain.

Somehow, she seemed to notice him looking at her, and her eyes met his, as if to say, *Well, what do you think?*

Master Sergeant Dinsler leaned close to Joe and spoke quietly. "The hospital sent a messenger to the PRT. He said they had a burn victim but lacked the resources to care for her. He asked us to try to help her."

Another Afghan woman sat by the burned girl's bedside. Farida spoke to her and then to us.

"The girl's name is Shaista. This is her mother," said Farida. Her mother? She did not look even close to old enough to be Shaista's mother. Farida continued, "Her mother says she was burned in a cooking accident."

"But you don't believe her?" Master Sergeant Dinsler asked.

Farida shrugged. "I don't know. It's possible."

"Ask her if she has had any medications," said the master sergeant. "Ask her if she is allergic to any medications."

"It's possible she's had no medications in her entire life," Farida said. "The Taliban wouldn't allow women and girls to get medical attention, even if it were available, and—" She gestured around the room. "Look at this place."

Nevertheless, Farida did as she was told and found out basically nothing had been done for Shaista. After getting permission to help, the master sergeant ran an IV and issued medicine to help with the pain and to fight infection.

Farida and Shaista's mother talked a lot. Farida learned the girl was only about sixteen. She was married.

Married? At sixteen? What was happening here?

After a while Farida turned to Joe. "Can you get her mother out of here?"

Joe shrugged. What was he supposed to do? He couldn't physically push her out of the room. Half of Farah would probably riot if they found out he'd touched her. He looked to Master Sergeant Dinsler for confirmation.

304

"Just step closer to her, motion toward the door. Be firm when you suggest she step out of the room for a moment. Farida will translate."

"She'll be more likely to listen to a man," Farida said.

Joe took a deep breath, sorry at once that he'd done so, due to the horrible burn smell.

He approached the woman at Shaista's bedside and pointed to the door. "Ma'am, please step out of the room. Come with me."

As soon as Joe moved closer, the mother stepped back, a worried look on her face. When she heard Farida's translation, she looked from Joe to Shaista and back again. Then she nodded and hurried from the room.

Farida looked down on Shaista with a pained expression on her face. She reached out to pat Shaista's shoulder, to comfort the girl, but immediately stopped herself. "Shaista? Shaista?" She continued in Pashto, but Shaista didn't seem to hear.

After a minute or so, Shaista spoke, slowly, careful not to move.

Tears welled up in Farida's eyes. "She says she doesn't like her husband. She's his second wife."

"Did his first wife die?" Joe asked.

Farida and Master Sergeant Dinsler glared at him. "It's called polygamy," Farida snapped. "Now be quiet."

Shaista continued to speak slowly and softly. "She says her husband and his first wife had no kids." To the soldiers,

Farida explained, "So of course, it's automatically viewed as the wife's fault and he marries Shaista. His first wife becomes more of a servant. Then he and Shaista couldn't have kids."

"Ask her how the fire happened," said Master Sergeant Dinsler.

Farida said something in Pashto. Shaista answered. Farida looked up, shook her head. "She says only that she does not like her husband."

"Do you think she burned herself?" asked the master sergeant.

Farida wiped a tear from her eye. "Some Afghan girls commit suicide that way. Some are burned to death by their ignorant families who believe she's dishonored them in some way, like if she's been with a man before she was married. It doesn't happen a lot, but it happens enough to be a known phenomenon."

"I've read about it," Dinsler said.

Joe looked at Shaista. This was sick. This was wrong. The very best-case scenario here was that she'd been burned in an accident. Otherwise either her life was so miserable that she thought being burned to death was better than living or her family was mad at her for some primitive reason and set her on fire.

"The name Shaista means 'beautiful,'" Farida said.

Joe was sure she had been beautiful once. He could see it in what remained of her face and hair. Only sixteen. She'd never been given a chance.

Like so many of the other women and girls in this country. *What the heck was wrong with these people? How could they let something like this happen?*

"There's not much more we can do for her tonight," said the master sergeant.

"We can't leave her here!" Farida waved a fly out of Shaista's face. "Not in this dump."

"When we get back to base, I'll try to persuade Lieutenant Colonel Santiago to ask for a medevac. But a lot of his answer will depend on what her family says. We can't fly her away without their consent. They'd say it was an abduction, or that *we* burned her. Rumors like that can hurt our position throughout the entire province."

That was it. Master Sergeant Dinsler nodded toward the door. Farida and Joe followed him out.

Joe keyed his radio. "One-One Bravo, this is Ernie Pyle, over." He was calling for the First Platoon, First Squad, Bravo Team leader, Sergeant Paulsen.

"Go ahead, over," Paulsen radioed back.

Joe called again. "We're coming out. Time to return to base. We're done here."

"Roger. We'll prepare to RTB. Out."

Joe was the last of his group to leave the room. He stopped at the door and looked back at Shaista. She did not move her charred body but met his eyes. "I'm so sorry. Khuda Hafiz," he said. Goodbye.

He caught up with the other two outside on the concrete

porch in front of the building. A big Afghan man with flecks of gray in his black beard stood calmly, smoking a cigarette. Farida stopped and said something to him in Pashto.

The man replied evenly.

Then Farida started in again. Joe couldn't understand her words, but he understood she was furious. The man tried to say something else for a moment, but she stepped closer to him, shouting, pointing. The man yelled something back at her, but she wasn't having it. She screamed at him.

Other Afghans, security guards, a couple of men who worked at the hospital, were watching the exchange with shocked expressions. This simply did not happen in Afghanistan. Women never spoke with men outside of their families. They certainly didn't shout at them.

"This scumbag is Shaista's husband," Farida explained.

"Her husband?" Joe asked. "He doesn't seem too concerned about—"

"No, why should he care!" Farida said. She launched into another tirade, this time even closer to the man. The man's fists clenched, and his neck muscles tightened.

You have a duty. You must protect your people at all costs, Joe reminded himself. *If that man tries to hit her . . .*

Joe held his rifle a little higher and stepped closer to the two of them. He didn't aim his weapon at Shaista's husband, but held it up across his chest, still pointed down at a forty-five-degree angle. The man saw it, got the message, and backed up.

And for just a moment, Joe was sorry that the man had backed down. *Hit her. Just try to hit her, and I swear, at this range, I'll put four rounds through you before your worthless dead body hits the ground. Come on, guy. Do it.*

But Master Sergeant Dinsler gently pulled Farida away, leaving the man not mourning the probable loss of his wife, but shaking with anger from Farida's outburst.

Back at the PRT, Baccam caught up to Joe after they'd parked the Humvees and put the covers on the machine guns. "What happened in there?" he asked.

Joe shook his head. "Man, I don't want to talk about it right now. Tomorrow maybe. This is the worst night of my life."

———◇———

The next day was another beautiful spring day in Farah, but Joe felt no relief, no comfort in routine or from experience with his job. He couldn't even summon joy from the knowledge that his tour was nearing its end. He felt it would be an eternity before he ever left the country. Master Sergeant Dinsler passed the word to him at breakfast. Shaista had died shortly before dawn.

Without a word, Joe dumped his full breakfast in the trash, threw on his gear, and trudged out to his duty post. He was stuck on gate guard that morning. Already three jingle trucks waited outside the wire to be searched before they could come in and unload.

This time he was on the rotation with Corporal MacDonald. "Want me to search the trucks?" MacDonald asked.

"No!" Joe said quickly. "I'm doing it. You stay here and pat down sweaty man crotches." Then he remembered Mac did outrank him. Technically, he was an NCO. "I mean, if that's OK, Corporal."

"Sure, man," Mac said. "Go ahead."

Joe took his sweet time searching the trucks. Spring was well underway and would erupt into Afghanistan's brutal hot summer any day. It was already getting hot under his armor out here in the sun. The second driver complained, asking through the interpreter why the search was taking so long. "Shut your mouth!" Joe shouted at him. "I will clear your truck to enter when I am good and ready! Translate *that*," Joe shouted at his terp.

But before he could finish his search of the second truck the passenger door of the third truck swung open. "Killian," Baheer called, the usual cheerfulness absent from his voice. He was on the ground, quickly heading for Joe. "I must speak with you."

"You know, this isn't actually a good time," Joe said.

"You told the THT about Haji Dilawar. You told them he was Taliban," Baheer said.

Joe let out a long breath. *I do not need this right now.* He couldn't stop seeing Shaista's burned body, the defeated look in her eyes. He couldn't lose the smell of that filthy hospital and burned flesh.

"I didn't . . ." Joe's armor and weapon felt heavy enough to pull him right down into the endless Afghan dust. Jase and the other THT guys hadn't left him alone. "I thought if I handed over that useless information—just speculation really—that you'd given me, they'd realize you couldn't help them anymore and they'd finally stop bugging us."

"Americans or somebody came to Haji Dilawar's compound, kicked down the door. They took him away."

"Well then he was probably some Taliban scumbag who deserved it," Joe said. "Nothing I can do about it now."

"I did not tell you about Haji Dilawar so you could tell THT," Baheer said.

"What do you care?" Joe shouted. "What? Are you sad that we stopped some Taliban guy now?"

"You are not understanding," Baheer said.

Joe wanted to scream. He wanted to punch something or someone. There was so much terrible, evil stuff, and he was supposed to be here fighting against all that, but he couldn't make it right. "I do understand that last night we were called out to what you people call a hospital. There was a girl there, younger than me, who had been married to this guy, had to be forty. She was all burned up. The guy didn't even care. Wasn't concerned at all. Now she's dead."

Baheer looked down for a moment. "These things happen," he finally said.

"How can you be so casual about it!" Joe shouted. It felt good to yell, one small action he could take in the face of helplessness.

"What is the meaning of 'casual'?" Baheer tried.

311

"You don't even *care!* In what kind of sick and twisted culture is it perfectly normal for a girl to burn herself to death rather than live in her sick arranged marriage to a guy old enough to be her grandfather?"

Baheer frowned. "This is not fair. You are—"

"You're right, it's not fair! Shaista deserved better." Joe kicked a rock, sending it skittering across the dirt.

"I trusted you, Joe," Baheer said. "You shouldn't have told THT—"

"You're more upset because some Taliban lover was arrested than you are about an innocent girl who was burned to death?" Joe took an angry step toward Baheer.

Baheer stepped up too. "You don't live here! This is my home, not yours! You'll go home to America soon and Americans will say you're so brave for coming here. The war will be over for you, but not for me! Not for me! My grandfather! My father! My whole life, we live this war! Someone found out I told you about the stolen truck of explosives. They trashed our farm. They're going to blame me for Haji Dilawar's arrest. You have big guns and an army! You're leaving soon!"

"I can't wait," Joe said.

The gray-uniformed Afghan guards at the checkpoint outside the wire had heard the shouting and were watching now. Joe didn't care. He didn't care about anything.

"You think your America is so perfect!?" Baheer shouted. "I watch the news. I see the stories of children in your country shooting guns in schools! I see rich Americans in big castle houses and others live on the ground like a dirty dog. No food!"

"America is better than Afghanistan by every objective measure. There's no comparison."

For a moment Joe thought Baheer was about to throw a punch. Good. He welcomed it. He wanted to fight. Scream. Punch something, someone, anyone. But Baheer regained control. "Then why are you even here? Afghanistan did not attack you! Why don't you all leave?" He turned and stormed away to his truck, climbing inside and slamming the door.

Joe watched him go, wondering for a moment if he should apologize. But then the image of that burned girl flashed in his memory again and rage burned through him.

21

FARAH, AFGHANISTAN
May 1, 2004

What are you doing?" Rahim asked that morning as Baheer was buttoning up his school shirt. "I thought you said you had permission to miss school this morning because you and Uncle Kabir were going to drive to pick up supplies for the Americans from the airport in Herat."

Baheer finished with the last button. He frowned, looking at his brother, surprised to find Rahim the first one dressed and ready for school. "The cargo flight into Herat was canceled." He shrugged. "Who knows why. This is hardly the first time a canceled American flight has messed up plans." *They think they are so powerful and advanced, but they can't even figure out simple flights.*

"You know what will happen," Rahim said. "The Americans will change their minds again, and then they will be upset you are not already in Herat. Maybe you and Uncle Kabir should just go up to Herat to be ready for when the plane arrives."

Baheer frowned. *Why is Rahim suddenly so interested in the business?* "That's crazy. They'll let us know when to expect the shipment to come in. We're lucky they told us the flight was canceled before we drove all the way there."

"I know, but . . ." Rahim paced the room.

"Are you OK?"

"Sure," Rahim said. He tugged at his collar. "I just hate these stupid Western clothes, especially as it is starting to get hot. I sweat so much. I just wish we didn't have to go to school today. Maybe we could—"

"Today the Americans are supposed to be coming to the school with a whole truckload of supplies. Paper. Pens. Chalkboards. Even desks. Can you imagine not having to sit on the floor in class?"

"No," Rahim said quietly.

"I only wish we could have got the contract to deliver the supplies, but we went for the Herat deal instead because it was higher pay." Baheer grabbed his book bag and headed for the door. "Come on. We don't want to miss the big event."

Later, at school, Baheer thought about the progress he'd made. He was currently second in the line, eager to finally earn the top place. His last chance to move up and secure the front of the line for the start of next year was in the final exams that would start next week. He had been studying with every spare moment he could find, and he felt good about his chances of moving into first place. Baheer turned to look down the line, to see how far he'd come. There, near the back of the line, was Rahim, wiping sweat from his brow as he watched Baheer. *Maybe he's jealous of my accomplishment? Well, then he should have actually studied.* After the recitation from the Holy Quran, the principal talked about the exam times and other small matters.

Baheer's thoughts wandered, drifting, as they often did, to Ayesha. She was determined to go to school, despite whatever risks her father imagined. Now, Baheer could see her every day without needing to go way out by the twisted tree because she was attending the school next door. With the new construction on the girls' compound entrance, they even had to temporarily come and go through the front section of the boys' compound. Baheer had been delighted to see Ayesha at least twice already right here in school. He had been very careful to act as though he didn't notice her at all.

And if Ayesha and other girls could attend school, if more girls like Ayesha were being educated, maybe Maryam could study without risking her reputation as Baba Jan feared. Baheer knew he couldn't admit to knowing a strange girl as part of his argument for convincing Baba Jan to let Maryam go to school, though. Such an admission would have the opposite effect from what Baheer hoped.

If they were ever going to beat the Taliban, there would need to be more men like Ayesha's father who could accept the risks and allow the girls to learn. Good people couldn't continue surrendering to threats. Both women and men should be given the chance to study and contribute to build a more peaceful and compassionate society. That was what Baheer was working toward. That was his life's work.

But he couldn't call on the courage of others, unless he could first summon some of his own. He'd thought about the problem of good people continuing to surrender to the threat of the Taliban, and what had he done? He'd yelled at Joe, a good friend who had helped Baheer improve his English so that he could help his family make more money with their trucks. Even if Joe could be an arrogant American jerk sometimes, he was, or at least he had been, sincerely trying to make things better for Afghans everywhere. He was still mad at Joe. *Maybe if Joe at least says he's sorry, things could be OK between us.*

Baheer knew he had to talk to Baba Jan again, and this time continue his efforts to persuade the man to allow Maryam to attend school.

As the principal's remarks came to an end, the two school guards opened the compound's main vehicle gate. At last the Americans had arrived. Two Humvees and a Toyota Land Cruiser entered the compound and parked in a line near the assembly area.

Like Baheer had seen them do many times before, the soldiers quickly exited their trucks and circled around for security. An uncomfortable mix of dread and anger twisted around in his stomach. Would Joe be here? He really did not want to face him after their argument. The Americans had helped Afghans regain their country, but their kindness was often matched by their ignorance and arrogance.

Joe was the last to exit the tailing Humvee, running to join the rest of his squad in the circle of men around their vehicles.

"Hey, Baheer! Americans!" Omar shouted with joy. He had worked hard, too, and now stood right behind Baheer.

"What is so exciting about it?" Baheer said.

"Man, they are here. They will give us something. They always have candy at least."

"Probably Jolly Ranchers," Baheer murmured.

"What?" Omar asked.

Baheer thought he may have finally understood Baba Jan's old reluctance to trust Americans and embrace Baheer's study of English. Americans weren't so great. They weren't superheroes. Far from it. "If we want to build this country we have to study and work hard. We have to do things on our own. These rich and arrogant Americans can't build it for us," Baheer said.

Omar waved away his concern. "I don't care. They are here to help us."

While Baheer and Omar had been talking, a big truck rolled in. It began pulling forward and back, trying to get closer to the school building. When it was finally parked and its engine shut down, one of the Americans released a lock and swung open the cargo doors. The entire shipping container on the truck was packed floor to ceiling with chairs and desks. There were a few pallets loaded with boxes of paper and pens.

"Look at all that!" Omar said. "How can you not understand they are great?"

Baheer understood that if his family had been awarded the contract to ship these supplies instead of a deal to pick up a load in Herat, they would have earned good and much-needed money. Instead they were given an empty apology for a canceled flight.

"Yeah. These chairs will build Afghanistan. These chairs will let girls go to school. Chairs are going to stop the killing. Yes. These chairs will bring peace and stability in our country."

Omar was usually a joker, but for once he was serious. "Come on, man. Do you really think we'd even have this school if not for what the Americans did?" He nodded toward a line of girls being led from their compound toward the main gate. He didn't dare do more than nod. The boys had strict instructions to behave with honor when the girls came through. "Do you think they'd be in school if not for the Americans?"

Baheer's breath caught at the sight of Ayesha leading the line of girls. He wasn't prepared to admit out loud that Omar was right, but in the very depth of his heart he knew. This was true. The Americans did help. But they were still often jerks.

———◇———

All three of First Squad's vehicles were parked in a line in a big open courtyard inside the school compound. Alpha Team's lead Humvee, with Z on the .50-cal. machine gun turret, had set up closer to the big white concrete-block school building. The CA's Toyota Land Cruiser was parked one vehicle length behind that, and Bravo Team's Humvee another length behind that. Joe had been picked to drive, so Baccam manned the Mk 19.

"I'm so not into this today." Joe rubbed his eyes. The nightmare about Shaista had robbed him of sleep again.

The CA was jokingly calling this Operation Mega School since it was the biggest school-supply drop they'd ever coordinated. Baheer had often told him about the primitive conditions at his school. Finally, the kids would have some desks and chairs instead of just sitting on the floor, and there was enough paper and stuff to last for a while. But what difference would any of this make in a country where it was not uncommon for girls to be burned like Shaista had been?

Rumor was, Joe's unit would be rotated out and sent home next month or maybe the month after. He was done with Afghanistan.

"Had a dream last night," Baccam called down from the turret. "A freaky one. We were on some mission that had totally fallen apart. We were driving down this narrow alley between mud-brick walls, bullets flying at us. Being chased by the Taliban. And our Hummer rolled up to a dead end. Sergeant Paulsen was like, 'Shoot the wall!' so I blasted it with the Mk 19. Then we were just running and gunning through the village. It was nuts."

"Sounds worse than mine," Joe said.

An Afghan man, some official of the school, began speaking to all the boys in the nearby courtyard.

"Bale!" the boys shouted at once. Joe knew this meant "yes."

"Good news," Sergeant Paulsen said, stepping toward his team from his part of the security circle around the vehicles. "Our terp says the principal has just volunteered the kids to unload this truck for us. There are a million kids. They'll form a human chain and this will go fast and easy."

Joe watched the line coming, Baheer among its leaders. Baheer offered no greeting, and Joe didn't wave. Instead he turned around and went back to the empty task of covering his sector.

———◇———

As Baheer marched toward the jingle truck, he saw Joe turn away. Baheer did not like Joe's attitude. *If it was not for our school and people, I wouldn't agree to help with this.*

Baheer led the line, followed by Omar, but Rahim moved forward and said, "Hey, Brother. Maybe you and I should go see where these materials will go in the classroom. There are enough people to unload the trucks."

"There will be a teacher or someone inside to decide where things will go. Come on. Get in the line and pass things along." Baheer picked up the first chair and turned to hand it to Rahim, but before he could release his grip, a loud metal clang shook the air.

A small pickup was ramming the front gate, bending the steel doors and breaking the hinges.

"Get down!" Rahim pulled Baheer to the ground.

The pickup exploded. The gate went flying. The shockwave was hot and strong, knocking everybody down. Baheer grabbed for his brother, trying to cover him with his own body.

Everyone was screaming, but after the explosion, it was like all sound had been swallowed. Baheer froze when he saw Omar lying on the ground next to him, looking up at the sky.

A big piece of steel had sliced diagonally through Omar's chest and shoulder. He was dead.

"O Allah!" Baheer shouted.

Baheer's brain was not working. He couldn't think of what to do except to find cover. Hands shaking, he grabbed Rahim by his collar and pulled him behind the jingle truck.

In the next instant a big bus rolled in, parking horizontally to form a wall in front of the gate. They were all trapped. Some of the students were rolling in blood.

Men don't cry. Baheer recalled his grandfather's words.

Gunfire erupted from within the bus. The Americans shot back. Everyone shouted. Baheer looked to his right, noticing that the girls who had been leaving class were caught in the middle of everything. They were crying, screaming. Some of them were hurt and on the ground. Baheer couldn't move. Bullets were raining down. A few hit the ground a couple of feet from where his brother and he were hidden.

———◇———

Joe felt like someone had punched him in the chest when the explosion had knocked him down. *You're alive, Joe! Do something!* He patted his legs, arms, chest—all there, shrapnel in vest.

"Baccam, light up that bus!" Paulsen screamed from the ground where he'd dropped to start shooting.

"Grenades in the school compound?" Baccam yanked the charging handles on the Mk 19, the first step in readying it to fire.

A cacophony of gunfire, dozens of white flashes in the bus windows. A bullet hit the ground near Joe's leg. Another. One sparked off the Humvee.

"Get cover!" Joe yelled.

"Get this jingle truck out of my way!" Z screamed from behind his .50-cal.

"Baccam, NOW!" Paulsen screamed.

Joe scramble-crawled. "Hold your weapon!" he said to himself. And somehow, he was behind the Humvee, on his feet, crouched behind the vehicle's sloped back end.

"Joe!" Paulsen shouted. "Radio! Call it in!"

Joe threw open the passenger door, the inside of the Humvee loud with dozens of bullet impacts, like the thing was being pounded with a bunch of hammers. He grabbed the radio handset and hit the transmit button. "Seattle Base, this is First Squad! Emergency! Emergency! Couple dozen Taliban attacking school. Bunch of people hurt! We need QRF and medics now! How copy? Over!" *Come on, guys. You better be monitoring the radio.* If he had to wait, he'd punch someone.

"*First Squad, Seattle Base. Evacuate the school and RTB. Over.*"

Joe hit the transmit button again. "Negative! We can't return to base. They're blocking the gate. We're trapped at the school compound. Get QRF here now! Over!"

"*Roger that, First Squad. Be advised QRF is inbound to your position. ETA ten mikes. How copy? Over.*"

"Ten minutes!" Joe tossed the radio handset. Ten minutes was an eternity in a fight. "That's how I copy!"

He rushed to the sloped back of the Humvee, flicked his weapon's fire-selector switch from SAFE to SEMI, and opened up on the bus. Pulling the trigger as fast as he could, he turned that M16 into a machine gun, emptying his magazine in about seven seconds. He squatted down, his back against the Humvee as he pressed the release button to drop the empty mag and fumbled to pull another from his ammo pouch.

A Toyota pickup rushed through the gate behind the cover of the bus. It rolled out at an angle off the bus's back end into the courtyard. The rear of the pickup was packed with Taliban fighters. Bullets rained down on Joe's Humvee.

"Don't let 'em get around behind us!" Cavanaugh called.

A second pickup rolled into the compound at the opposite angle past the front of the bus, some of their fighters shooting at a group of girls, some at the squad.

Mac cursed. "How many of them are there?"

———◇———

Baheer stayed on the ground between the jingle truck and the front Humvee, the two vehicles parked side by side. He called to his other classmates to get behind the jingle truck or the Humvees. Nobody could hear him, but he was trying. The gunfire was so loud, he felt he was stabbed in the ears with every shot.

Rahim screamed near his ear to be heard, "I'm bleeding."

A metal rod from the gate had lodged in his brother's shoulder. Blood poured out. So much blood! "O Allah!" The helpless prayer was all he could muster, but as if his prayer were answered, Baheer knew what to do. Another prayer for strength helped him tear away part of one of his shirt sleeves. "Press this on the wound to stop the bleeding. You'll be OK."

Rahim followed his instructions, and although Baheer didn't want to leave him, he had to help the others. Gathering the attention of the other kids who could walk, Baheer motioned for them to move behind the Humvees.

"Let's go toward the school building!" Rahim screamed, holding the blood-soaked cloth to his shoulder.

Baheer's group tried to run that way, but Taliban gunfire from the second pickup blocked their path. The sound of girls screaming could somehow be heard over the roar of the battle.

"You sick haramis! You shoot the girls, you filthy cowards! Shoot me, if you have the courage!" Baheer shouted as if they would care or hear him. A classmate right next to Baheer was crying. He'd peed in his pants.

Baheer tried to hold his nerves. He was terrified, scared of losing Rahim—or Ayesha, whom he'd seen screaming just before the second pickup had blocked his view.

A soldier in the machine gun hole of the Humvee behind them kept cursing. Baheer could just make out what he was saying. "He can't shoot! The truck's in his way."

Rahim pulled at his arm. "Come on! We can make it if we rush to the school!"

Baheer looked back to the truck driver slumped over the steering wheel. Dead. "Someone has to move that truck." Baheer said it without even thinking.

"Not us!" said Rahim.

Baheer looked his brother in the eye. "There is nobody else." He wasn't sure if he could move the truck or not, but he went for it.

"What are you doing?" Rahim screamed as he followed. "Let's just run toward the school."

Baheer climbed up to the driver's door. "If we run, we'll get shot. The truck will give us cover and once it's moved, the American machine gun can shoot back."

He opened the door. The driver had taken two bullets

in his head. With the strength that comes from desperation, Baheer shoved the man's body across to the passenger side, then moved his legs out of the way. Several bullets pinged the truck, and Baheer stayed low to avoid the enemy's sight. Rahim stood on the steel step below the door.

Baheer had only had one driving lesson, and it was over a year ago, but he'd seen his uncles and father drive trucks like this all the time. He did his best to remember, he and Rahim mumbling prayers the whole time. He turned the key to start the truck and then grinded the clutch a little, trying to shift into gear.

"Come on!" Baheer pleaded. "Pleeeease, you stupid truck! Go!"

Ahead of him, the other Humvee machine gun opened up. A slower *chunk-chunk-chunk-chunk-chunk*. Baheer cursed. "Stop for a second. I'm getting this thing out of your way."

The bus exploded from the inside, not explosions of fire, but bursts of shrapnel, glass, and blood. Baheer and Rahim ducked.

"Baheer, we can't stay here!" Rahim shouted. "Drive!"

Baheer fought to shift again. "Grab this shifter and help me pull!" Both Baheer and Rahim pulled it back. A second barrage from the American grenade-shooting machine gun. *Chunk-chunk-chunk-chunk*. The bus was being shredded.

Baheer felt the gears clunk into place. "Finally!" he shouted. "Here we go!" He stomped on the gas, but the truck lurched backward. Baheer hit the brakes hard.

"Just go!" Rahim screamed.

"There are hurt people behind me," Baheer said.

"They'll be hurt if they don't keep moving. Anyway, we can't drive in front of that grenade-launching machine gun," Rahim said.

Baheer reversed toward the school until the back of the truck slammed into the concrete porch. They jerked to a stop and killed the engine, but they still weren't safe. The Taliban turned their guns toward the truck. Rahim pulled Baheer out of the vehicle and down to the ground before the bullets could catch him.

———◇———

On the edge of Joe's consciousness, he knew the jingle truck had backed out of the way. He felt compressed air in his chest with the *PopPopPopPop* of the .50-cal. joining the fight.

BreathControl—RelaxedTriggerSqueeze—AimCenter Mass. No thought. No separation from his weapon. Joe shot and killed people—Taliban. He'd burned through another magazine, laying down fire on the bus. He slapped another magazine into his weapon, pushed the bolt release to send the bolt forward to seat a new round, and started taking down individual targets one by one.

But that first pickup was trying to flank them. If it did, they were dead.

Joe grabbed the grenade from the canteen cup clipped low on his vest. Unthinking, he bit hard on the tape holding down the spoon, the safety lever, ripping it away with a jerk of the head. He pulled the pin, squared up to the Hilux.

Give it some lead! Gotta hit this! One chance!

He didn't throw the grenade with the special windup they'd showed them in basic. He whipped it baseball style, one bounce short of the truck, and a roll right to the front left wheel.

The grenade exploded, shredding the tire, part of the wheel, maybe some of the engine, and the truck skidded to a halt.

"We're just trying to help a school!" Joe fired three times. At least one round hit the driver.

Baccam cursed. "They hit my gun! Right in the barrel! We got more coming in through the gate!"

"We gotta get out of here!" Paulsen shouted from behind the Land Cruiser. "We're pushing a bad position!"

"Baccam?" Joe called. "Make toward the school?"

The taliban in the pickup Joe had disabled were using their vehicle for cover and showering them with rounds. Joe moved back, opened the rear passenger-side door for a shield and returned fire.

"Shockley, what are you *doing*!?" Cavanaugh shouted. "Everybody get to the school!"

The big guy had slung his rifle and run toward the disabled pickup with the AT4, talking himself through the cocking procedure even as he did it. "Go! I got these guys!" Shockley yelled. He wasn't waiting, but slung that big green tube up onto his shoulder. Baccam pulled Joe toward the school.

The AT4 screamed! Fire and smoke shot out both ends, and the pickup exploded into fire, glass, shredded metal, and blood. In a second, Shockley chucked the spent weapon to the ground and brought his M16 to bear. He fired a couple more times at the remains of the truck, then pivoted toward the bus and gate where more of the enemy had taken up shooting positions. He fired—two steps back—fired—two more steps. *He's incredible!* Joe, Baccam, Mac, and Paulsen laid down cover fire from over the hood of the Land Cruiser.

A third pickup drove in, following the path of the one Shockley had just destroyed. "Shockley, *move!*" Paulsen shouted. He slapped a 40-millimeter grenade into the M203 grenade launcher beneath the barrel of his M16, slammed the breach closed, took a second to aim, and fired toward the new truck.

The enemy saw the danger and swerved to the right, away from the incoming grenade round. It exploded on the ground short of the target.

Joe, Baccam, Mac, Paulsen, and Shockley used the enemy's moment of distraction to fall back to Alpha Team's Humvee.

A talib on the new truck fired a rocket-propelled grenade. It screamed through the shot-out back window of the Land Cruiser and exploded inside, blasting all four doors and the remains of the windshield completely away.

"Get to the school!" Baheer yelled. He helped a terrified younger boy, lifting him off the ground and pushing him along. The girls' screams were almost quiet. *Where is Joe? What if he's dead?* The last time the two had talked, they had argued. Baheer had never apologized.

When he looked at the Humvee where Joe had been earlier, there was no one. "O Allah, please save him. He was here only to help our school."

The Land Cruiser was blown up. Baheer and Rahim ducked almost under the jingle truck to get covered.

More taliban were at the gate. "Wait here," he told Rahim. "I gotta shift the jingle truck into forward to drive ahead and block the gate."

"Stupid! Don't!" Rahim shouted.

"I have to. We have to protect our school."

Baheer climbed back into the truck. But when he got it started, bullets hit the front. Steam started rolling out. Baheer cursed the Taliban. The truck overheated and died.

"Thank Allah," Rahim shouted. "Let's go, Baheer."

Baheer abandoned the truck and noticed Joe and other soldiers running back his way. They were being overrun. The taliban had a better position. Then Baheer had an idea.

"I know the way to the roof," Baheer yelled to Joe. He led Rahim, Joe, and three other soldiers while the last American machine gun continued shooting back.

Just inside the main doors on the way to the principal's

office, there was a ladder leading up through a hatch. "Come on!" Baheer shouted and hurried up, Rahim and the others following close behind.

"Joe! You are bleeding." Baheer pointed to his arm when they'd reached the flat roof.

Joe looked surprised. How had he not felt the wound? He set his rifle down near Baheer's feet.

"I didn't think it was that bad," Joe said. "Adrenaline, I guess. Take my weapon and shoot back while I work on a bandage."

Baheer eyed the gun. "I can help you tie the bandage."

"Just shoot 'em, Baheer!" Joe shouted, pulling a bandage from a pouch on his vest.

Time slowed down for Baheer. He thought about how the Taliban had tortured and oppressed Uncle Kabir and Ayesha, and so many at school back in Kabul. Baheer knew this was never about Islam. It wasn't about school or education being bad. It was about control. School, education, new ideas—people who had free thought were harder to control. So first the Taliban came for the books. They attacked a school.

Baheer's shoulders heaved. He wanted to scream. Baba Jan had once quoted the Holy Quran, "If you kill an innocent human being, it is as if you have killed the whole of humanity, and if you have saved an innocent human being's life, it is as if you have saved the whole of humanity."

He should save the lives of the school kids, teachers, and

his American friends who were here to help. The Americans may be rich and arrogant, but they *were* trying to help.

As Baheer stepped up to the short wall at the edge of the roof he said quietly, "No! Enough! You're done! We will not go back!" He blinked the tears from his eyes. "You have to *stop!*" And he started shooting. It wasn't hard. Pull the trigger, the gun shoots. He missed with his first three shots but didn't care. His grandfather stood up to the Taliban to protect his family. Baheer would make his stand here. They would not stop his school or make this place an oppression zone like schools were during the Taliban time.

Baheer shot a talib by the gate. Right in the chest. He fell and shook around for a moment before going still. Baheer's mouth was dry. He shot again, killed another. He missed four more shots. Then he hit a third talib in the head by the bus.

By this time, two more American Humvees had swung in through the gate, the lead machine gun cutting down the remaining taliban by the bus.

The last pickup was disabled by the first American machine gun. Baheer stopped firing for a moment. Now the second new American Humvee rolled in, and its machine gun roared, blasting right through that pickup and every talib near it.

Baheer screamed, "Allah-o-Akbar!" and pulled the trigger again and again and again, helping the American machine guns destroy the last Taliban pickup. Finally the rifle clicked empty, but Baheer kept pressing the trigger.

"It's out of bullets. Stand down," Joe said.

Baheer ignored him. His breathing was super fast. He couldn't control it. His teeth hurt from grinding them so hard when firing. He was nearly crying. He kept pulling the trigger, aiming at the dead truck, even though he had no more bullets to fire and there was no more enemy to kill.

———◇———

Joe put his hand over Baheer's, the Afghan's skin sweaty, trembling. "Ease it down, Baheer. It's over." With his other hand, Joe gently lowered the barrel of the rifle. "Come on. Breathe. Try to relax. You're OK."

Baheer handed the rifle to Joe before pounding his fist over his chest, coughing. "My grandfather says, men don't cry."

Joe wiped his eyes. "I think we get a pass on man points after combat, rafiq." He felt the turn in his stomach, more saliva in his mouth. His legs shook. A cough. Then he heaved. He spit hot, sour-sweet bile. He stepped back, slung his rifle on his shoulder, bent over, and vomited hard, everything he had left in him. Hard trembles shook through his whole body, and he dropped to a knee, felt his own sick soak through his uniform pants. "Yep. We're all good."

Baccam produced a bandage from his own pouch and set to work, tying a proper field dressing on the other Afghan with Baheer. "What do we do now?" Joe asked breathlessly.

"Security and casualty treatment," Sergeant Paulsen said. "Killer, that bandage stop the bleeding for now?"

"Hurts, but yeah. I think so." All that time back at Fort Hood and Des Moines spent going over treating battlefield wounds. Joe had thought he was going to lose his mind from the tedium back then. Today he would have lost his life without that training.

"Good," Paulsen said. "Reload. Then you and Baccam stay up here. Keep scanning the perimeter. You see anything remotely hostile, you shoot it. Mac, let's go see who else needs help." The two of them headed for the ladder.

Baccam lifted his SAW. "I'll take overwatch on the gate and street. You scan everything else." He let out a long breath, eyes wide. He was shaking. "Anybody else feel like they're . . . kind of . . . floating? Like they've just slammed a case of energy drinks and can't calm down now?"

Joe smiled. A hard shiver went through his whole body. "Hadn't noticed."

He stepped away from his best Army friend to take up position over most of the school compound.

Cavanaugh groaned, trying not to scream, as Master Sergeant Dinsler tightened a field dressing on a leg wound. Specialist Gooding sprinted from one boy on the ground to another, dropping to his knees and yanking out a bandage, working to stop the bleeding. A couple of guys from Second Squad hurried to help the medic.

"Joe," Baheer said quietly. "I'm . . . I'm sorry for what I

said before at the PRT. I should not have become so angry with—"

Without thinking, Joe sprang to his feet and reached out to shake Baheer's hand, wincing as red-hot pain seared in the wound in his arm. He reached around to hug his Afghan friend with his good arm. "I'm sorry too, rafiq. I shouldn't have assumed . . . I mean, I know now, have known for a while, not all Afghans are the same. Most of you are great. And you know—"

Baheer put his hand on Joe's shoulder. "After this, I say we forget about it."

Joe nodded. "Thanks for getting us to the roof. Thanks for covering me after I got hit."

There was a lot more to say, about what had happened there that day and about their unlikely friendship. About this mission in Afghanistan. He had spent the whole time in this place trying to come up with the words to tell the truth about this war, but when his eyes met Baheer's, he found he had nothing to say. Sometimes words weren't enough. Sometimes they weren't needed.

Baheer nodded at Joe. He wanted to say goodbye or apologize for whatever he might have done wrong. But, he couldn't. He simply nodded and, taking his brother by the arm, left the roof.

Rahim reached the base of the ladder first and was waiting for Baheer to climb down. He was shaking with sobs by the time Baheer reached the floor.

"It wasn't—" Rahim gasped, crying. "It wasn't supposed to be this way. Baheer, I need to tell you something."

Baheer looked at his brother, this boy who hated school so much, who complained about the Americans and anything Western. Rahim had tried so hard to keep Baheer from going to school today. He'd been the only Afghan who knew Baheer had told the Americans about the stolen truck full of explosives, and he'd been so sure about the reason why their farm had been attacked. "I know," Baheer said quietly. "I know it was you, Rahim." Sometime in the course of the battle he'd sensed the truth that he'd been trying for months to ignore.

"No, you don't know! It wasn't what you think." Rahim was quiet for a moment. "Not completely. I didn't talk to the Taliban. The guy I know said he knows them, said they'd just scare the Americans off. A bunch of shots before they even reached the school. That's it! There wasn't supposed to be an attack like this."

"You tried so hard to get me to avoid school today."

Rahim shrugged, then groaned from the pain from his wound. "I thought it would be better if you just left town for the day, just in case—" He burst into tears, his whole body shaking.

Never before had Baheer experienced such a confused mix of emotions. He was disappointed in his brother, and yet pity crept into his heart as he watched Rahim crumble before him. Baheer threw his arms around Rahim, feeling his brother melt into the hug with anguished sobs. "I'm sorry," Rahim cried. "I'm so sorry."

Later, Baheer might be angry about what his brother had done, but for now he knew both of them were sad and exhausted and the day had furnished more than enough pain. He did not need to add to it with angry accusations.

Omar and so many others were dead. He remembered the girls who had been passing through the campus. *Ayesha.* He called her name. For once he didn't care if anyone heard him or knew he was looking for her.

He ran over to where the girls had been when the attack started. He saw one girl face down in the dirt. Next to her, lying on her back in a dark circle in the dirt near the school building, was Ayesha. The other girls had crouched on the ground around the corner.

"It can't be her," Baheer muttered.

"She pushed us out of the way, but she was shot," said one of the nearby girls.

Baheer fell onto his knees next to Ayesha. Then he finally cried. The girls circled around with him. He'd wanted to meet Ayesha. This was the only meeting the two of them would ever have.

FARAH, AFGHANISTAN
May 15, 2004

Faisal died a few hours after the Taliban attack on the school. Before he'd even taken the final exam, Baheer was already the top student in his grade. He had finally made it to the front of the line. He had worked hard to earn the position, had dreamed of standing there with pride. But now the Taliban twisted that dream into a nightmare, and he knew he would always feel like an impostor, standing in Faisal's place. And he would always feel guilty thinking about such things, knowing others had been killed and no longer stood anywhere, impostors or not.

Taking the final exam was even more difficult than he'd expected. He sat in the classroom at a nice new desk, and he should have focused on the exam material. Instead he couldn't help but notice the many empty desks in the room,

339

chairs unoccupied both because of the students who had died and because of those who, out of fear, would not return to school. Once during the exam Baheer dove to the floor at the sound of a loud bang. He returned to his seat a moment later, sweating and with a pounding heart, after he realized the sound had been caused by his teacher accidentally dropping a book.

No matter what Baheer was doing, his thoughts kept drifting back to Ayesha. How long would the image of her bleeding body be burned into his memory? How long would the sound of her screams echo through his head?

Was this how Joe had felt after he'd encountered the girl who had been burned? No. Baheer shook his head. Joe hadn't felt toward that poor girl quite the same as Baheer felt for Ayesha. Still, Baheer thought he understood his friend better now. He shared the crushing, consuming weight of that helpless anger, that frustration that burned in him every time he remembered the people lost at the school that day and the way nothing he did could bring them back.

He couldn't do anything about changing the past, but he *could* work for a better future. His determination to help make Afghanistan better only grew stronger.

After the test he left the school for the last time that term, riding alone because Rahim remained at home recovering, and because Ayesha would never again brighten his path near the twisted tree. At home, he went to Baba Jan in his reading room.

"I finished my exams today," Baheer said. "Forgive me if this sounds as though I am boasting, but I am certain I did well." He bit his lip for a moment. "I'm the best student in my grade now. I will be in front of the line next term. Insha Allah."

Baba Jan put aside the book he'd been reading. His eyes gleamed. He recited the same poem that had sparked in Baheer a great love for words when he first read it during his farm work: "Capable is he who is wise / Happiness from wisdom will arise."

Say it, Baheer said to himself. *How can you fight the Taliban at the school, but be too afraid to talk to your own grandfather?* Baheer squeezed his hands into fists. He would not be afraid anymore. Too many had died for him, for any of them, to continue cowering in fear.

"Baba, if wisdom is that important, why can't Maryam go to school?" Baheer knew what Baba Jan's answer would be, but he still asked. He owed that much to Ayesha. He couldn't let her death have no meaning. Girls had to be educated if they wanted to have a new, free, and prosperous Afghanistan.

Baba Jan looked around, the gleam in the eyes dulled. "What? After that terrible attack on the school? No."

"*Because* of the attack on the school." Baheer blinked his eyes. He would not cry. He would not back down. "Baba Jan, I fought them. I shot the taliban. They attacked children and little girls, all because they don't want anyone to learn anything." Baheer motioned to the books behind his

341

grandfather. "If those evil, godless men would kill to prevent us from reading books like these, shouldn't we do all we can to ensure they are read by as many people as possible? And Maryam is gifted. She has memorized so many parts of the books we love so much."

Baba Jan held up a shaking finger. "It is not this that bothers me. Yes, it is good that she reads, that all my grand-daughters might read. But to send Maryam or the other girls to school? Have them going about all over town? What will people say? It is our responsibility as men to protect the rep-utations of the women in our family."

Baheer's legs shook. Arguing with Baba Jan was always an intimidating experience. Baheer's grandfather was a man who did not back down, even from the Taliban. But now, nei-ther did Baheer. "Who cares about others? What matters at the end is what you think about it, Baba Jan. A long time ago, when we spoke on the roof after the United Nations com-pound had been bombed, you said it was the responsibility of my generation to build a new Afghanistan, one where we might finally have peace. How can we build something new and better without trying anything new?" Baheer coughed and shook his head. "Girls at that school believed, as you and I believe, as Maryam believes, in that new Afghanistan. The Taliban killed them. They died for that belief. I . . . I saw them, Baba Jan. Do we now back down in fear and hide behind our walls the way the Taliban want? Will we live in fear of the Taliban?"

Baba Jan's eyes went wide. "Do you call me a coward, little boy?"

"I'm asking you this because I know you are not a coward. And I am not a little boy."

Baba Jan did not speak. There was silence for quite a while.

Baheer tried more reasoning. "Last time you said the school is too far away. Now, it's right next to my school. Sure there was a security problem, but the Americans fought it off. I fought it off. I almost died for that school. Some did." He paused to regain control of his emotions as he thought of Ayesha. "Some girls did. We can't let that be for nothing, Baba Jan. We can't keep backing down from the Taliban. Please let Maryam and all the girls take the risk. We have to take the risk if our people are to have any chance of rebuilding our country."

For a long time Baba Jan said nothing. Finally, he nodded. "When I heard about the attack on the school I feared I had lost two of my three grandsons. I tell you, this old man would not have survived such a catastrophe. I thanked Allah for answering my prayers to save you." Baba Jan stroked his beard. "Your brother told me what he did, telling his friend about when the Americans would be at the school so his friend could tell the Taliban."

How had Rahim survived such a confession? Baba Jan must have been furious.

"Baba Jan, I think—"

"He told me what *you* did, too, both at the school that day and passing information to the Americans. It seems you both used questionable judgment. But if you made mistakes, Baheer, at least it was in the interest of protecting people and opposing the Taliban. Rahim?" Baba Jan shrugged. "He feels terrible about what he has done, and as good Muslims we must forgive him."

"Bale, Baba Jan." Baheer nodded.

Baba Jan continued. "I think . . . Rahim's terrible mistake was born at least in part from the same blind love of tradition from which I sometimes suffer. My entire life, things were not as strict as when the Taliban ruled everything, but still, there was a sense that it was not good for women and girls to go about doing all these things, school and such. I have heard Rahim say things like this, heard him clinging to old ways just as I hold on to my fear of people's petty gossip. The Taliban hold too tightly and too extremely to such ways, ways that are challenged by wisdom and education. You are right, my brave grandson. A new and better Afghanistan requires courage, people who will no longer back down to the Taliban and their ideas. You tell your sister that if she wishes to go to school next term, she has my blessing."

Baheer put his hand over his heart and bowed deeply. "Tashakor, Baba Jan."

Baba nodded. "Thank *you*, my grandson."

After the discussion, Baheer walked out into the sunny courtyard. It would be a hot day, but Baheer didn't mind it.

He spotted Maryam sitting on the porch at another house writing in a notebook. She was concentrating so intently on her work that she didn't notice his approach until his shadow covered her paper.

"It would be even better if you could practice that writing in school," Baheer said.

Maryam grunted. "Of course. Maybe someday."

"Not maybe. Definitely next term. Baba Jan said so."

She dropped her pencil and looked up at him in shock. "Really? You did it?"

"No. You did it. Your persistence, your prayers, and your hope did it. Allah helped both of us," Baheer said.

Maryam hugged Baheer tightly and didn't say a word. He felt her fast heartbeat. It was a feeling of great hope.

———◇———

It was another week before Baheer could make it to the PRT to see Joe. With Rahim still recovering from his wound, Baheer faced even more farm work and simply could not get away. When he finally did find some time apart from his duties, he wanted to share all his great news with Joe, his friend, his American friend.

"Excuse me, sir," Baheer said as he rode his bike up to one of the soldiers whom he had never before seen on gate guard duty.

"You speak English?" The soldier looked surprised, and a little alarmed by Baheer's approach.

"Can I meet Joe?" Baheer said.

"Who?" the soldier replied.

"Joe Killian," Baheer said. "Specialist Joe Killian."

Before this soldier could say anything, another soldier with a broad chest said, "Oh. You're Baheer?"

"Yes, sir," Baheer quickly said. *How could he possibly know my name?*

"Specialist Killian's unit rotated home a few days ago," he said.

Baheer's shoulders fell. He knew Joe had been discouraged about his mission after he encountered the burned girl. Maybe he would have been happy to know that his work and sacrifice, the work and sacrifice of all the other soldiers, was really helping Afghanistan. Maryam going to school might not seem like a world-changing event, but Baheer knew the opportunity to learn would change Maryam's world. And who knew what she, in her lifetime, could accomplish? Real progress was happening. Joe should know.

"But he left this for you." The soldier held out a big tan envelope with Baheer's name on it.

Baheer took the envelope and said goodbye to the soldier. "Thank you, sir."

Later that day, alone in his room despite the heat, Baheer opened the envelope. Inside was a book entitled *Bridge to Terabithia,* and a letter. He began reading it.

Date: May 19, 2004

Dear Baheer,

If you're reading this, I've cycled out of Afghanistan on my way home to America. I'm sorry I didn't get the chance to say goodbye in person. I hope this letter is better than not saying goodbye at all.

I'm super excited to be going home! I've been dreaming of the day when I'm finally released from duty ever since my deployment began. But what I did not expect was how much I would miss about Afghanistan, how much I would feel like I'm leaving home. I guess once you suffer for a place, bleed for it, breathe in its dust for a year, it becomes a part of you. I grew kind of fond of our little base built out in the garbage flats.

You and I have talked about the foolish ideas I had after my country was attacked on September 11, 2001 and when I first arrived in Afghanistan. I'm sorry for thinking those things. And I'm sorry for saying those things again when we argued shortly before that horrible day at the school. I didn't mean the things I said. I was just so angry about what had happened to Shaista. I felt so helpless and hopeless. I've made a lot of mistakes in my life, but I have never been so completely wrong, never so totally changed my mind as with my attitude toward your country.

I've told you about how back in America I'm studying to become a writer, a journalist, how I've been trying to figure out how to write about the war in Afghanistan. Telling the truth has been much harder than I thought it would be.

But one truth I know about war: War isn't about religion or resources. It's about control. And the real battle for control is in the schools and libraries. Throughout history it has always been the same mission. Whether we're fighting Nazi Germany, the Soviet Union, the Taliban, or some other terrible group, first they come for the books. They seek to control who can speak, who can express their ideas or their art. My friend, people like us always share the same mission. The forces of free thought and expression against the evil that would crush those things.

You and I were part of the same mission, and I hope you will carry on the effort. American bullets and bombs can help. They can send our enemy on the run, destroy a lot of them, but wars are won by teachers, librarians, and artists—the real peacemakers. Peace is more than just blowing up bad guys. Real peace comes from building something worth living for. Our Provincial Reconstruction Team tried hard to build up Afghanistan. Hopefully the new soldiers, our replacements, will embrace that mission as well. If they're annoying or rude at first, give them time. Try to remember they've been trained to fight, not to fix, that they miss their homes, and that they are very scared.

But the real task of building a better Afghanistan is up to you, and people like you. I know you understand this. I know how hard you worked to learn English and everything else. I saw you fight for that better future at the school. Keep working for something better. Afghanistan is rising—Insha Allah.

You saved my life that day at the school, Baheer. You probably saved us all. I won't forget that. I won't forget you. And I know I'll never forget my time in Afghanistan.

I wish you a great life and much success. I pray for the success of our mission.

And I know in Afghanistan you're lucky if you have electricity. The odds of you having a computer or the internet are even worse. But Afghanistan is getting better. So I'll leave you with my email address in the hope that we might stay in touch in the future. Email me any time at: J-Killian5@iowa.edu.

Good bye, rafiq. And good luck.

Yours,

Joe Killian

Baheer sat in silence for a while, thinking about all Joe had written, wondering how he'd ever manage to send him an email. Then he picked up the book. It was obviously in

English, and Baheer had never read a whole book in English. Could he do it?

He smiled. He'd love to try. Then he noticed the bookmark near the beginning of the book, at the opposite end from the start of an Afghan book, since English script and books ran backward. He opened to the bookmarked page and found a passage, a sentence, with two parts underlined. Baheer knew almost at once why Joe had pointed this out to him.

He felt . . . that it was the beginning of a new season in his life, and he chose deliberately to make it so.

Baheer nodded and laughed a little. "Well, OK, Joe," Baheer said quietly to himself. "You're right. And I will make this a great new season in my life."

IOWA CITY, IOWA, UNITED STATES OF AMERICA
July 10, 2004

Joe sat at a small table near the back of Terralon Coffee Shop on a Saturday afternoon, in front of his brand-new Apple iBook G4, trying, not for the first time, to write something coherent about the war from which he'd only recently returned. The last time he'd been in this place, he was still eighteen years old. But his teenage years had died long before he turned twenty. And now he felt much older.

His homecoming had been different than he always imagined it would be. When the Air Force "Freedom Bird," that C-130, at last left the rumbling dirt runway next to the PRT at Farah, Joe wanted to cheer. He'd expected everybody to whoop and clap. Instead it was quiet. Everyone stared ahead silently, exhausted or relieved or having trouble figuring out what the departure really meant.

After some time at the airbase at Kandahar and another week of boring, long lines for medical and legal stations at Fort Hood, Texas, they were finally flown back to Iowa, touching down in Cedar Rapids. A bunch of Army Guard privates were on hand to transfer all the bags from the plane to a bus, and then they headed south to the welcome-home ceremony in Iowa City. Some officers and politicians gave some speeches. The politicians who wanted to be reelected kept their speeches short. Joe didn't remember a word they said. He only wanted to be released from that formation and from duty.

Finally, Captain Higgins stood at attention before Delta Company in the hot sun, every man standing up straight with his hands behind the small of his back in the position of parade rest. "Company!" he shouted.

"Platoon!" said the two lieutenant platoon leaders.

"Atten-TION!" Captain Higgins called.

At once and in perfect unison, every man snapped his feet together, fists at his side, eyes forward, at the position of attention.

The captain saluted. "Dismissed!"

And just like that, a year and a half of total Army control was over.

That was a month ago, and Joe had been doing mostly OK since then. There were nightmares sometimes. He dreamed about the fight at the school, the dead kids there. He dreamed about Shaista and her terrible burns. But for the most part, he was fine.

The hardest part was trying to write about the experience. Ernie Pyle had written the most profound, relatable truth about World War II, and he had done so in a foxhole while being shelled. He hadn't made it home, killed by a Japanese sniper.

Joe had survived, and he took a deep breath, grateful for that fact. But why did he have such a difficult time writing about his experience in Afghanistan?

War is hard to explain. It defies neat descriptions or easy comparisons, and one war idea contradicts another and another, all of them equally true. But I think what I'll remember most from my time in war isn't the homesickness, fear, pain, or even the mission and what it was all supposed to mean. I'll remember the friends I made there. The soldiers with whom I served and the regular people there who struggled with us are some of the best friends anyone could imagine. War is about fighting to protect and to make life better for the people you care about. And maybe in that crazy, counterintuitive way, war is about love.

Was that too dramatic? He wasn't sure. War was a dramatic enterprise.

Just then, the person he'd come here to meet walked in,

and Joe stood up, his heart leaping in panic for just a moment as he reached to his side for his M16 and found it missing. He took a deep breath and let it out slowly. *You turned in your weapon as soon as you got off the plane in Texas*, Joe reminded himself. *You're not responsible for it anymore. You're free.*

"Hello, Joe," his father said, reaching out to offer a handshake. "It's been a long time."

Joe smiled and shook Dad's hand. "It has. I'm glad you're here. I have so much to tell you." A year ago, a much angrier Joe Killian would never have agreed to this meeting. But Joe was done with war—with all forms of war—and he was ready to live in peace.

His email dinged to indicate a new message had arrived.

"Got yourself a fancy new laptop computer there?" Dad asked as he sat down at the table.

"Yeah, sorry," Joe said. "I'll shut down the email so it won't . . ." He smiled when he saw the name on the new message in the inbox: Baheer Siddiq. The subject line read: SALAAM RAFIQ!

He'd done it. He'd actually found a computer with internet and made contact. Joe laughed, nodding. Well of course he had. He was Afghan, after all, and the people of Afghanistan were indomitable. Joe looked up and smiled, grateful for the gift of being free to live in peace.

NOTES FROM THE AUTHORS

Years ago, suffering from the brutality of Taliban-minded teachers in Naderia High School in Kabul, Afghanistan, I never imagined that one day I'd co-write a novel in English published in America. English doesn't even use my primary language's proper letters! Enduring the cruel farce of the education to which the Taliban had reduced my school, I wanted to get as far away from books as possible.

Like Baheer, I was given the choice between the shovel and the book, education or farm work, and remembering the beatings and Taliban inspections I'd received at school, I fled to the farm. Also like Baheer, I thought leaving school to work on my family's farm was the best option for my future.

But my family, especially my late grandfather, Haji Mohammad Munir Khan, through his example of reading and studying his many books of Persian poetry, Afghan history, and Islamic philosophy, encouraged me to hold on to the promise of education. He was an amazing man, and I wanted to be as wise as him. Finally, in the western Afghan city of Farah, I dared to break from the routine of farm work to try school again.

After 9/11, Afghanistan experienced many changes, and I found out school was no exception. Teachers were friendly, and students were appreciated for what they knew and how hard they worked to learn. I was able to earn good scores in my first term, and felt the difference, a change in my life, right away. I still remember Mr. Ahmadi, our English teacher, who encouraged me to study and who asked me to start teaching English at his private institute. It was the first of many opportunities education opened for me.

Eventually we found out that American soldiers had moved to town. A friend from school told me one of the soldiers was an English teacher and that people could talk to him over the wall. I thought this would be a great opportunity to practice my English. I was happy for the chance to meet this American teacher.

But when I finally had the chance to talk to him, I was disappointed. Instead of being kind like my teachers in Farah, this soldier was rude. It was a hot July day, and I wanted to stand in the shade of the front wall of the American compound, but Corporal Reedy ordered me to back away into the hot sun. Afghans are friendly and will invite people closer to get to know them. But Corporal Reedy didn't even invite me inside for tea. Eventually I realized that a large part of the Americans' rude attitude came from their obsession with security. They were new to Afghanistan, and very afraid. Yet, American and British people were all over Afghanistan. I thought it would be worth it to overlook their strange ways because English would offer me more economic opportunities and, if I'm being honest, a bit of prestige.

Over the next several weeks I kept returning to the wall to talk to the American soldier. Trent and I continued to meet regularly, even after the soldiers moved to their base outside of town. I practiced English. He tried to work on his Dari and Pashto. Eventually, he knew a few phrases and could talk like a baby in my language. Over the weeks and months our language practice developed into a friendship that we maintained over email and then social media, even after Trent returned to America.

Speaking to Trent and other American soldiers, as well as sharing a fictionalized version of my story through this book, was only possible through education. Learning broadened my perspective and offered more possibilities in my life, and I believe that it is through education that Afghanistan will realize a new and better future.

These new opportunities for both men and women were made possible due to the efforts of American and coalition soldiers after their arrival in Afghanistan in late 2001. Their presence in our society opened windows toward a new horizon that profoundly affected the lives of millions of Afghans. Before what the Americans called Operation Enduring Freedom, men, boys, and especially women and girls were deprived of education and other basic freedoms. We were deprived of hope. Now, twenty years after the American war in Afghanistan began, and over fifteen years since Trent and

I last spoke in Farah, my country still faces many problems. But we will not go backward. Today, many Afghan women go to school. They learn, they lead, and they teach other men and women. We are filled with a new creativity and hope.

Although I've received an education in English language and literature, co-writing this book was a real challenge. I often worried I would not be able to do it. Even after overcoming my fears, the difficulty of working on the book from opposite sides of the world was formidable. One of us slept while the other worked, and finally we made a story that is very close to our hearts. We wanted to show how our lives were changed by the 9/11 attacks and the war that followed.

Trent and I did our best to express the worldview transformation of an entire generation. Throughout history, the Taliban, Nazis, Soviets, and other evil forces have always targeted education because uneducated people are easier to rule. But now, the youngest generation of Afghanistan is educated and cannot be ruled by a group that doesn't even know how to hold a book. I hope *Enduring Freedom* will convey the message of hope and the wonder of education to the world. I pray it will offer a clearer picture of the difficult struggle our people share. We will prevail. Insha Allah.

Jawad Arash
Herat, Afghanistan
October 2020

A s I write this, I've been home from the war in Afghanistan for fifteen years. That's the entire lifetime of some of my readers, and yet I think of my time in that country every single day. Many of the scenes and concepts in *Enduring Freedom* were inspired by events that occurred during my deployment. I have written fiction inspired by these experiences before, but every time I tried to write a novel directly from the perspective of a soldier, it wasn't quite right.

I have been blessed to stay in contact with my friend Jawad Arash since I departed Afghanistan. One day, when talking about his desire to write fiction, we discussed his experiences with American soldiers and with the Taliban before them. I asked him how he found out about the 9/11 attacks on America and was fascinated by his answer. By the time he told me about his first encounter with American troops—the day he met me, when I was on guard duty at the wall of the Unsafe House compound—I knew we had found a story suitable for a novel.

Until *Enduring Freedom* I'd been unable to write a novel all about the Afghan war because the war isn't about the soldiers. Not entirely. The mission in Afghanistan is to build a country where people are freer and better able to resist extremist ideologies. It is a mission shared by millions of indomitable, peace-loving Afghans across the country. And just as the mission is not the soldiers' alone, this novel could never be only about Private Killian and his fellow soldiers. Joe's experiences are meaningless without Baheer's. The heart of the novel is in the seemingly unlikely friendship between the young men.

During different phases of PFC Joe Killian's deployment, he suffers from terrible fear and anger and harbors hateful, ignorant ideas about Afghanistan, Afghans, and Muslims. To my everlasting shame, I held those same ideas when I first reached Afghanistan. Like Joe, my beliefs quickly changed once I met the Afghan people. I talked with Jawad extensively about the representation of those old prejudiced ideas in this book. We reasoned that showing a character's heartfelt change from anger, hatred, and prejudice toward a more fair, informed, and friendly understanding of Afghanistan would be a more effective means of challenging the lingering prejudice that our readers might encounter in America than to present soldier characters who never faced that internal struggle for change. If we can accept that war can change a person, I beg readers to believe that my time in the war changed my attitudes completely. Nevertheless I remain ashamed of the prejudice I once harbored toward Afghans and Afghanistan, and I apologize for any offense the depiction of these ideas may have caused.

Jawad and I wrote *Enduring Freedom* because we wholeheartedly believe in the mission in Afghanistan, in the struggle to resist the evil forces of the Taliban while building a real, lasting, meaningful peace in which all Afghans, boys and girls, men and women, are free to pursue their own best destinies. We hope that *Enduring Freedom* will help readers better understand the importance of this mission, and that readers will be inspired to join this same struggle for freedom of thought and expression against those forces that would seek to limit and control people. Live free and read, people everywhere.

Trent Reedy
Spokane, Washington, USA
October 2020

—◇—

Acknowledgments

Just as the mission in Afghanistan requires the support of thousands working together with tens of millions of great Afghans to build a new and better future for Afghanistan and the world, so do authors rely on a great deal of assistance in writing books. As with all my books, I am indebted to far more people than my publisher will allow me paper upon which to name them, so I apologize to those wonderful people I am unable to mention here. Nevertheless, I owe special thanks . . .

To the many soldiers who helped me get through my time in the war. As a lifelong English Major, book lover, and writer, I was never a natural soldier, but First Sergeant Scott Wolf, Staff Sergeant Ryan Jackson, Sergeant First Class Matthew Peterson, and—well, an army—of soldiers taught me and compelled me to do my duty. I owe my life to these soldiers, and I will forever be grateful.

To Staff Sergeant Ryan Jackson and Sergeant First Class Matthew Peterson, for answering many questions about weapons and other military systems. And special thanks to Staff Sergeant Jacob Pries, for being on call constantly to answer tons of questions about everything from loading a Mk 19 grenade-launching machine gun to drill and ceremony regulations. Thank you so much!

To many other people who helped me during my time in the war. The complete list is too long to include here, but special thanks go to my mother Lu Ann Hennings, my brother Tyler Reedy, my sister Tiffany Klima, my mother-in-law Rosemary Straubinger, my late father-in-law Lieutenant Colonel Dennis Straubinger, Matthew P. Allers, Sheri Stewart, Stephanie Luster, Mary Bardsley, all those who sent me letters or emails, and all who sent packages. America's military could not succeed without—well, an army—of people back home supporting it. Thanks so much to all who support our military.

To Krestyna Lypen, the fantastic and utterly brilliant editor who helped Jawad and me hammer and then polish *Enduring Freedom* into shape. This novel was especially difficult to write because it was hard to closely weave together the experiences of Baheer and Joe, because the timeline of 9/11 through Joe's deployment was difficult to pace, and because Army life consists of episodic and unconnected experiences that don't easily fit a narrative story structure. Krestyna was very kind, patient, and insightful. Her ideas for the overhaul of this manuscript saved the book, and I'll forever be grateful.

To my agent, Ammi-Joan Paquette, who reassured and encouraged me as we navigated the uncertain task of finding a new publisher for the first time in nine years. Thanks for believing in this project from the moment I mentioned the rough idea. I'll never forget what you said on the first phone call about

Enduring Freedom before one word of the book had been written: "I want this book *yesterday*!" Now yesterday is today, and I hope we'll be working together for many tomorrows. Thank you, my friend.

To my dear friend, one of the very best writers in kid lit and the world, Katherine Paterson. Katherine, I will never stop thanking you for the way your novel *Bridge to Terabithia* saved my spirit and kept me going through the darkest part of my time in the war in Afghanistan. I was approaching my breaking point, and your beautiful story reminded me there is still hope even in the most difficult times. Thank God for you. Your book and the letters we exchanged saved me. Thank you for all your support in my pursuit of my writing career.

To my brave and brilliant co-writer, Jawad Arash. We did it, rafiq! A real book! Thanks for your patience with me and my fearful and misguided attitude during the early days of my time in your great country. Thank you for keeping me company during lonely guard shifts at the Unsafe House. Thank you for being willing to embark on the long, difficult journey of writing this book with me. Most of all, thank you for being a true patriot, a believer in the mission of promoting free thought, expression, and everyone's pursuit of their own best destinies. I admire the way you have faced so many obstacles, never surrendering, working with millions of indomitable Afghans to build a new and better Afghanistan. You will succeed, rafiq. We will win. Afghanistan rising. Insha Allah.

To my daughter, Verity. I'm sorry for all those times I could not play with you because I had to be writing. Thank you for your patience and for the many compliments about *Enduring Freedom* while you were engaged in pandemic-inspired in-home online kindergarten and I was rereading the book aloud. Verity, you're my best friend.

To my beloved wife, Amanda. No amount of "thank you" could ever be enough. I owe you everything, always.

Trent Reedy

I t is difficult for me to adequately express my gratitude to everyone who was ever involved in my work and in my studies that made this work possible.

I would like to thank all the English teachers who directly or indirectly influenced my learning. Mr. Ahmadi, Mr. Aref Khan, and Mr. Mirwais Bedil Akbari are a few who taught me during my school years. Later, during my time at Herat University, I had the honor of learning under the guidance of Mr. Sarwarzada, Mr. Shams, and Ms. Muzghan Azizi, who really helped and supported me as I worked on my English. I can never forget Mr. Ramin Shorish, who pushed me to work harder and read as much as possible. Finally, I wholeheartedly thank Dr. Komali Prakash, my PhD research supervisor, for her patience and support for this book while I worked on my PhD dissertation. There are many other teachers, too many to name here, who shaped my abilities in language and my character in general. I thank every one of them.

I know I cannot thank enough those who worked so hard in providing the education system in Farah and in Afghanistan as a whole. They are all real heroes and great leaders. What they have achieved will provide the young Afghan generation an opportunity to work to bring the change Afghanistan so desperately needs. These education pioneers have done their part, and now the duty falls to a new generation to stand up and build a new and better Afghanistan. For all your work and sacrifice, thank you.

In Afghanistan family is everything, and our families are very large. Individually thanking every member of my family here would require too many pages, so I thank them all, with particular thanks to my parents, who always supported me, and my uncle Mohammad Basir, who supported me financially and morally throughout the journey of my education, from the beginning of school through my PhD.

I wish I could have thanked my uncle Kabir, who answered many questions for this book, my aunt Ayesha, who raised me from childhood, and my grandfather Haji Mohammad Munir Khan while they were alive. But I wish to say to them, "I was very blessed to have been born into a family of such wonderful people. You have made me a better person, someone who can share with the world your stories as well as the story of the struggle of all the people of Afghanistan. Thank you so much. Thank Allah for you."

Thank you, Trent Reedy. If not for you, I wouldn't be able to write this book. Your patience and continued support made this book possible.

I'm grateful to our editor, Krestyna Lypen, for her editorial wisdom and patience working across time zones, as well as for understanding my need for a pen name due to security concerns. Thank you very much, Ms. Lypen. I must also thank our agent, Ammi-Joan Paquette, who believed in the idea of this book only minutes after Trent and I first discussed it. I am a first-time novelist from a different country and English is not my first language, but Joan always knew I could do it and that our book would work.

Thanks to my son, Jawad, and my daughter, Ayesha, for being the best children a father could ever hope for. I write this book and work for a better Afghanistan for you.

Last, but certainly not least, I must thank Nadiya, my wife and soul mate, a brilliant woman and spectacular mother. I cannot thank you enough for all the support you have provided. Thank you for your sacrifice during my time in the United States as I earned my master's degree. Thank you for all your help during the tough times in India as I worked on my PhD. Thank you most of all for being the perfect life companion. I will never be able to repay your kindness and love in my lifetime, but I will never stop trying.

Jawad Arash